BITTERNESS

SEVEN STORIES

BITTERNESS
SEVEN STORIES

David Orsini

Quaternity™

BITTERNESS / SEVEN STORIES

Copyright © 2009 David Orsini

Fifth Edition: Quaternity™ Books 2020

ISBN: 978-1-943691-34-0

Cover Design by James Buchanan

Other Books by David Orsini

The Woman Who Loved Too Well

The Ghost Lovers

Schemes, Disguises, and Traps

The Weaver of Plots

Vanishing by Degrees

The Subtleties of Seduction

CONTENTS

MEMORIALS

In September, exactly a year after Neal had died during the Meuse-Argonne offensive within the forests east of Verdun, Deirdre agreed to join her sister Moira and her husband as well as their parents on an afternoon's sail across Newport waters. They were (she saw because of their carefully modulated smiles) very pleased that she was for the first time in more than a week consenting to enter a day's colorful progress. That she had on more than one occasion excused herself from their amiable excursions seemed almost a natural thing. For she was adjusting slowly to her husband's having died in the war and to this vacant afterward which was unmitigated by those flickering moments when she believed him to be in the sun-touched shadows of the parlor or the library or her bedroom, here in her parents' summer home on Ocean Drive.

After the early months of Neal's being dead, she had discouraged any conversation that would too prosaically define her feelings about him or about the long, sleepless nights she had taught herself to endure or about the loneliness that frightened her and would not leave her. Nor would she express to these four relatives whom she respected and loved—or, for that matter, to the friends who had been very close to her and her husband—her uneasy memory of the two years when she and Neal were alive together and happily married.

So often in this year of her grieving, she had seen Neal standing ruggedly before her or heard his husky voice in a room nearby. She remembered accurately, as if they were speaking to each other right now, the private dialogues that had made their union both idiosyncratic and enjoyable. She remembered, too, all the specific places and occasions that had been the colorful excuses for their being together. On those days, they had appeared (her mother used to tell her) both compatible and ideal. With her titian-hair and light-skinned willowy frame and his tall, sun-bronzed muscularity, they belonged to no one but each other. Was it any wonder that her memory of the happiness she had shared with Neal had at first drawn from her both solacing and grateful tears? So, too, had his having consented to her and not only having consented to, but also having needed her supremely and vigorously and absolutely. Nothing (she told herself in the first months after his death) could steal those years from her. Their reality became insistent and vivid whenever her memory gave her husband back to her. But gradually, even against her will, her days with Neal began to seem dreamlike and mysterious. Into death he had vanished and vanished too was the palpable reality of their being together.

Grown weary at last of looking back at all that was finished and fearful that she might soon run mad because of her constant grieving, she began to accompany her mother and her sister on the frequent Samaritan visits they paid to the sick or poor as well as to the aged or injured in the working class suburbs which stood, unobtrusive and ordinary, beyond the visible rims of Newport. That her mother's father had been a minister who had devoted his life to the needy encouraged her to believe that she, too, could be more than the impulsive and self-absorbed young woman her privileged background had sometimes influenced her to be. In this second half of the first year of Neal's death, she discovered within herself a profound sympathy for the anguished and afflicted and abandoned. There grew in her a genuine desire to do all that she could to help them.

During this period, she encouraged new hope and optimism in a young, alcoholic widower who lost his wife shortly after she gave birth to their stillborn son. After winning his trust, she persuaded him to join a counseling group for alcoholics. Having freed themselves from their own addictions, the men in that group were now guiding him toward a similar recovery. In a later month she was moved by the plight of a rugged middle-aged carpenter who had fallen from the second-floor scaffolding of a house he was repairing. A team of conservative doctors thought it unlikely that he would regain the use of his fractured legs.

Resisting their pessimism, she turned to a renowned surgeon from Johns Hopkins. Because of his pioneer work, the carpenter was going to walk again. Once more, after months of rehabilitation, he would be for his wife and his three children both self-reliant and enterprising. While he progressed through his convalescence, she secured for him, from among her family's friends, important commissions that promised him a substantial future. To him and to others like him, she offered with her mother and her sister the sustenance of food and clothing and accelerated the efforts of state agencies to send money for fuel and rent.

Charitable work, church-centered meetings, and quiet afternoon teas with friends of long standing had provided her with the social interaction toward which her family had urged her. But it was not their counseling alone which had drawn her away from brooding days and solitary rooms. More than any other influence upon her, a realistic awareness that she must get on with things had slowly brought her away from her months of isolated grieving into the world again. But rarely would she enter any occasion that carried with it a light-hearted scenario and that, even in well-intentioned ways, subverted her loyalty to Neal's memory.

Today, though, when her parents as well as Moira and Derek had invited her to a sail on the first anniversary of Neal's having been killed in the war, she accepted without hesitation. For she wanted to commemorate his passing by making a journey they two had often made together. When she asked Derek if they might sail in the yawl that had belonged to Neal, he readily agreed, even if (she felt) he would have preferred to captain his own formidable boat. They would be traveling across Narragansett Bay to the Rose Island lighthouse. There, they would visit the venerable keeper Henrik Terbork and bring to that accurate workman a picnic luncheon which they planned to share with him. They were also bringing all manner of cured hams and cheeses, preserves and other provisions that would supply him with healthy meals throughout the winter.

Now, while riding over September waters with her parents and with Derek and Moira, she knew the dappled textures of the warm, evolving day. Configurations of inlet and bay were hurrying past her now, and hurrying too in the flicker of receding distance were serried groves and burnished greenscapes. On the crest of sun-glanced fertile hills, at the margins of enshadowed woods, a gray-blue immensity of larches swayed in alliance with the pastel sky. Theirs was a gentle wavering of contours left as if floating in the lift and flare of her turning glance toward zinc-white cliffs and glint of farm field and boats like shimmering amber glass vanishing within the rippled light upon Newport waters. Much nearer than that, in the spume-fed wake of their own kinetic vessel, she noticed the plash of a larger mackerel, its silver-viridian body a mottled gleam upon her fleet apprehension. She knew as well the rankled caw of a herring gull that was curving the dark glare of its wings while alighting upon the uneasy lip of a wave.

"How wonderful to be a part of all of this," her mother said. As patrician as she was direct (and meticulous in the simplicity of her fashion and her upright carriage), she was offering her words as a strategy for affirming the day and affirming too that each of them was uniquely in it.

"The summer is still here," Derek (busy at the tiller) said. With affable ease he directed his gaze upon her. For in league with her parents and with her sister, he meant (she knew) to bring her back to a comfortable belief in the future. "There will be days and days like this."

(A murmur of the heart had kept him out of the war. Neal alone had left their successful law practice to join the American Expeditionary Force. For a year now, she kept noticing in Derek a kind of awe before the fact of Neal's sacrifice, and for that she liked him immensely.)

"We are going to enjoy every one of these days," her father promised. Tall, silver-haired and portly, he brought to his remark his well-honed, lawyerly assurance. Like the three others there, he was determined—without even once mentioning Neal—to rescue her from her prolonged and muted sorrow.

"It will be good to see Henrik again," Moira told her.

Her sister remembered that, even before they were married, she and Neal had enjoyed visiting the aged mariner who was the keeper of the lighthouse.

"Yes," she found herself saying. "I always learn something new when I see him."

The four of them smiled, and she was pleased that she had made the moment appear lighthearted and casual. Now, while the imagery of Indian summer wheeled around them, they spoke of many things, including her parents' travel to British Columbia the following month and, a few days before that departure, Moira and Derek's return to their New York brownstone.

Then it was that she and the four others saw in the loom of sun-threaded distance, on an island requiring no more than sixteen acres, the gleaming white emphasis of the lighthouse. Its wood-frame solidity dominated both rock and soil. Rising thirty foot and more through the mansard roof of the keeper's dwelling, its square tower stood, resolute and precise, over Narragansett waters. When, a quarter of an hour afterward, they'd arrived to see that imposing structure as an even larger reality, its redoubtable presence evoked—in her eyes, at least—the artful rigor of Second French Empire and Victorian influences. Perhaps at the same time, all of them sighted the weathered virility of Henrik Terbork. He was waving to them from the slate-gray dock where they intended to anchor their vessel.

"That is a man whom God has sorely tested," her father said.

With compassion as genuine as his, she and the others also observed the mariner and waved back to him. Shortly thereafter, Derek smoothly navigated their craft into the anchoring place.

Her own struggle with loss and disappointment roused her special notice of the old fisher. Two or three years earlier, Neal had told her about the sorrows that afflicted Henrik's life. It was that, perhaps, or her empathy with all human beings strong enough to withstand even the bleakest experiences which drew her pensive attention to Henrik. In this year just passed, she had developed a careful respect for the sterner capacities that enable people to endure so many little deaths and larger ones, too. But she had no time to ponder at this moment what Neal had told her about this man or about its implications for her own life. Derek, with his dark-haired and muscular bearing, was offering his hand to guide her—as he had guided the others—safely onto the dock. After that, with her parents and with Moira and Derek, she hurried to greet face-to-face the venerable mariner.

"You have come at a good time," Henrik said. His sturdy Dutch inflections defined the warm greeting he was exchanging with them. "I have some free hours to make your visit an enjoyable one."

They appreciated his straightforward manner and his earnest regard of them as well, unconstrained as that manner and regard were by the rough slurring of his words and by the urbane ambiance which, despite their unpretentious composure, they may have represented to his steady blue eyes. With his tonsured mien and aquiline nose and with his long white beard and gaunt, ascetic lineaments, he existed (she mused) as nobody except himself. He was the honest ruin of the brave and humble workman he had for so many years been and now, nearing seventy, continued to be.

"You are a most effective sentry," her father remarked as he grasped the old man's hand in a solid gesture of friendship. "Only an alert keeper would have noticed our boat at so far a distance."

"Why are we here, if not to see?" Henrik asked.

"Ah, but to see well, as you do," her father said. "That is a gift."

Old Terbork (so the strong friends who with him had survived a sea-bruising life now called him) bent his wrinkled head slightly as if to salute a kind advocate. Or, perhaps (she guessed), he wanted to modify an inherent reserve or an ingrained tendency toward a merely frugal show of emotion. Whatever the case, he smiled adequately. The rightness of his intuition persuaded him to guide his guests without any other words into the waiting lighthouse.

It was at this time, as they were walking toward the lighthouse, that Neal's words about what this man had lost came swiftly back to her.

That her father regarded Henrik Terbork as an exemplary man did not surprise her, for she knew the kind of human being whom he found admirable. Aware of Henrik's story, as they all were, she recognized the judiciousness of this favorable appraisal.

Long ago, when he was not yet twenty, Henrik had with his bride made the arduous voyage to Newport from the Spartan environment of Scheveningen. It was a fishing village near the Hague which, in the years when he was growing into a vigorous youth, he had learned to love well, as had his parents before him and his three older brothers. Each of them accepted it as the place of their ancestors, who had rendered it meaningful by the boldness of their skill on the sea and by their ability to find amidst its austere obligations lives that were useful and bracing. After he and his equally strong-willed Ingrid had followed their desire to be Americans, he would speak with heartfelt recollection of this early part of himself, formed as he had been by a judicious upbringing and by experiences that had taught him the merit of hard work and self-sustaining honesty.

To her father and to Neal and Derek, as well as to those close friends who belonged to his daily life, he would from time to time recall a moment or an episode deriving from his years in Holland. He might have, only an hour before meeting them, looked upon the spectral gleam of a pond frozen in winter behind the white clapboard symmetry of his Newport house. Or he might be put in mind of his homeland while on a solacing April afternoon he observed the grace of a fragile tree. One time, he remembered Scheveningen after noticing Neal and her mooring their summer boat to a convenient buoy. Neal had turned the sturdy craft into the wind while Derek and her father brought down the mainsail and with limber skill hurried the mooring line aboard to loop it 'round the bow cleat effectively.

It was then that he would tell them of seeing, as a rugged yet taciturn boy from a fishing village where there was no harbor, incoming boats roped to teams of docile and efficient horses from the Belgian Ardennais. Their red-roan bodies were as startling as their large, expressive eyes and pricked ears and wide-open nostrils. Their strong shoulders and deep chest and muscular limbs represented so much massive power pulling the reluctant vessels onto the beach at Scheveningen.

He would also tell them of his older brother, Hans, skate-sailing with him in the west Netherlands. They moved as if they were their own ships gliding magically across a frozen river. Both of them had built masts made of hickory rods whose bottoms rested in straps fastened to their left legs. By placing one arm around the mast and with the other hand holding onto the top spar, each brother supported a sail of the strongest cotton sheeting.

More recently, just before Neal had gone into the war, he would also tell them of one time not like any other time except the moment it supremely inhabited. Years earlier, on a morning in early spring during the very week that they had married, he and his fair, raven-haired Ingrid awoke to see, from the window of a cottage in the countryside just outside Amsterdam where they were staying, the pink shimmer of almond trees blossoming above an unexpected blanket of snow. The day itself was rising easily, incandescent and natural, and the welling sheen of its sun was like sulfur touching everything.

Yes, he remembered favorably his days in the Netherlands. That imagery remained for him comforting and pure, untouched by the sorrows that came into his life years afterward. But when he was young and blissfully married, the geography of his destiny located itself elsewhere, or so he believed. Therefore, with his agreeable bride he left behind all the places that had known him and all the good people.

Then, finding his way to a compatible life with Ingrid in Newport, he knew again the fervor of life on the sea. In the early years of his arriving on Atlantic shores, he worked in unison with a team of mariners to fish effectively in New England waters. Later, honed by earned confidence and aspiration, he led a savvy crew of fishers in a prosperous business of his own making. By this time he had secured contracts with the best markets in Massachusetts, Connecticut, and New York, as well as in Rhode Island. But, though as a mariner he thrived and as a loving husband he enjoyed nearly all the rewards that a man may build through his bond with a faithful wife, he also knew the unspoken sorrow which, even while held silently taut within the most secret recesses of the heart, afflicts a man when he and the woman he passionately loves cannot have children.

True, his beloved Ingrid had, in the first five years of their marriage, twice conceived a child and successfully carried it through several months of what appeared to be a healthy pregnancy. But she lost the son she had been nurturing inside her body and, two years later, the daughter. Their little hearts (the physician explained) suddenly stopped because of a blood deficiency that assailed their mother's otherwise splendid frame. Because her very life during this second miscarriage had been grievously threatened and because she and Henrik regarded their losses as brooding signs that Heaven was not favorably disposed toward their desire to be parents, they taught themselves gradually to accept this sparser life without children. Even in their young time they were wise enough to acknowledge, ardent and grateful still, the tremendous blessing of their having found perfect love with each other.

Now, while Henrik brought an even greater enterprise to his seafaring business, Ingrid—in league with a guiding minister and his wife and a group of equally altruistic women—devoted her energies to maintaining a retirement home for old and often indigent men of the sea. There, in a refurbished Victorian house owned by their church, she and the others, without salary or fanfare, cooked and sewed and washed for these tough-hearted men who, though loyal and hardworking during their useful time, had entered their final cycle without wives or families or friendly cohorts even. Remembering how well they'd always acquitted themselves during the harsh disciplines of their maritime years, the sympathetic inhabitants of Newport privately called them orphaned men. Most of them had never married, and the few who had done so had outlived both wives and offspring. With rigid calm, they had acceded at the last to their Spartan aloneness.

It was through her unobtrusive charity toward them that Ingrid discovered how necessary she was to her community. Her being a woman who could not give her husband a child suddenly became an incidental note in the public's affirming definition of her. Thus it was that she and Henrik, though childless, continued to bring joy to one another. All the hours that made them separate and individual—he through his rugged vocation on the sea and she by her service to others—enhanced and deepened the meaning of who they, as husband and wife, were together.

But in the eighteenth year of her marriage, when she was nearly forty, Ingrid—with Henrik—once again conceived a child. After meticulous attention from a midwife and a prudent confinement to her bed during the latter months of her pregnancy, she presented to her husband a bright and healthy son. They named him Vincent, and he lived—athletic and insightful and proficient—for sixteen years. By that time, he was a husky youth of medium build and brown-eyed intelligence and hair a handsome tawny red. Always, he embraced the splendid adventure that is the world. For he had learned from his warmhearted mother a congenial manner and from his strong-willed father and other manly tutors the disciplines of mind and body that enabled him to excel in sailing and swimming and fishing...in baseball and soccer...in chemistry, botany, and physics...and in geometry and calculus, too.

"He will serve the world well," his teachers as with one mind agreed. They never imagined that he would soon die on the soccer field from sudden heart failure. The secret malady betrayed the natural rhythms of his breathing and pulse and honed-sharp awareness and with unexpected swiftness killed him.

When he died, the bright colors of the earth, to Henrik's and Ingrid's eyes, instantly faded. Then, a mere six months later, Ingrid—racked by debilitating grief and the onset of severe arthritis—also died. A massive stroke overwhelmed her uneasy frailty.

Condemned to live after these two essential beings without whom there could for him no longer be joy or hope or heartening sustenance, Henrik confronted his bleak life with quiet, ingrained patience. Alone as he was and reluctant at first even in his early sixties to leave his life as a mariner, he consented finally to be the keeper of the Rose Island lighthouse. The careful members of a committee appointed him to that post because they respected his knowledge of the sea and his unfailing diligence and because they were aware that he had recently lost his wife and his son. Compassionate and realistic, these men and women well understood that the solitary nature of the lighthouse keeper's position might invite a forlorn man's brooding. Yet they believed nonetheless that a new and demanding assignment would very likely prevent Henrik from dwelling bitterly upon his hard sorrow. Besides (they said), it seemed appropriate that he should be the keeper of a lighthouse that stood as a memorial honoring all those Coast Guardsmen and other brave seafarers who had died in the line of duty.

And so, a decade later, austere and methodical in his guardian capacity, the strong-minded mariner continued to endure.

Now, at the margin of this September afternoon when she intended to commemorate the death of her husband, Deirdre and the four others followed Henrik into the lighthouse. At first she found within the lower floors a vaporous gloom or inwoven darkness that surprised her senses as it drew her into its strangeness. Even Derek and Moira appeared to enter the rooms as if they had never before been here. Yet, with her muted nostalgia and his rugged benevolence, they also had often called upon the aged mariner whenever Derek could be away from lawyerly obligations to her father's New York office and, in search of a new scene, they had hurried away from the amenities of their Manhattan brownstone to join her parents at their summer residence here in Newport. Their eyes never ceased to be held surprised by the mystery within the sudden and glowering dimness. It was as if the interior of the lighthouse, the shrouded and intriguing fact of it, was translatable only through oblique suggestion and increment. Within coils of muted light, its implicated reality disclosed gradually each ordinary object of their apprehension as something unusual and possibly exotic.

She had come primarily to see Henrik and to observe merely as an ancillary presence the witnessing lighthouse. With her mother and her sister, she was bringing to him a picnic lunch held cool and crisp in a hamper. Not only that lunch which they personally had prepared were they bringing. In respectful friendship, they were offering the kind, old mariner other gifts of food. These were made decorative and pleasing with circles of colorful fabric that clothed the lids of tightly sealed jars and with festive ribbons and bows or strings or yarns that anchored themselves to stenciled labels. For several Wednesdays they had worked with her parents' main chef, Marcel Rousselot, and his equally inspired wife, Françoise, to preserve within immaculate jars a splendid assortment of fruits and vegetables.

There were wide-mouthed jars and small-mouthed jars in the hampers and lighter baskets that Moira, their mother, and she—as well as their father and Derek—were now carrying to a cool storeroom within the spotless cellar of the keeper's residence. There were jars pint size and quart size secured with new metal vacuum lids and new metal screw rings, and all of them appropriate for canning. There were jars and jars filled with apricots and currants and blueberries, figs and blackberries and peaches--a dozen of them at least. An equal number of jars teemed with chicken à la King and vegetable beef stew, with peppers and eggplant (in garlic oil) and split pea soup. There was as well an excellent sampling of homemade jams and jellies: strawberry rhubarb, coriander and honey, blackberry, and apple ginger marmalade.

Besides these gifts from her own efforts and those of her sister and her mother, as well as from the Rousselots, their father and Derek were bringing the burgundy heft of Jabugo hams imported from Spain. Each ham was precisely cured and sweet with scent of molasses and chestnuts. From Holland, there came thick wheels of aged Gouda cheese.

The amber color and a butterscotch aroma promised soothing lunches and satisfying dinners.

It was this brief journey to the cellar that drew them first into the lighthouse, rather than to the cedar table outdoors where later they would enjoy a delicious picnic and pleasant conversation with Henrik. Once they were inside the house and had placed their hampers and smaller baskets on the cool shelves of the cellar's storeroom, they—at Henrik's invitation—returned to the main floors. There, with studious interest, they passed through the various rooms. Their intention (as spontaneous as it seemed inevitable, now that they were making inquiry of the place) was to see the powerful Fresnel lens in the uppermost level of the lighthouse.

Today sunlight, though reticent or tentative or perhaps merely frugal with its gifts here in the principal living space of the keeper's residence, did nevertheless impart a fleet glow upon and through the array of long, narrow windows that peered from every room and hallway in the place. Carefully, she and the others followed in unison Henrik's firm and consistent gait. As their journey advanced gradually toward the upper rooms, she acquainted herself once more with the homespun imagery that in her elliptical sighting became a montage.

When entering the lighthouse, they were—she knew—visiting the home that Henrik had brought with him from his life with Ingrid and Vincent. The committee that had appointed him to this service-duty station (one built to house a keeper and his family) understood that, even while his new assignment might urge him forward into the present, Henrik would carry his past with him. As we all do (she reflected). We all carry our past—our body of death—into the present. The memories that stir our minds and souls, as well as the familiar objects that invoke benevolent household spirits and the spirits of loved ones taken by death from us, define us to ourselves and sometimes to others.

Now, as it appeared on this specific afternoon in the middle of September, she knew again the entry hall with its curious, illumined shadows and built-in cabinet clock made in the Shaker style. A natural luster enhanced its smooth cherry wood. She knew as well the polished floors made of steadfast hemlock and walls of mint green and azure blue and equally solacing beige, all of them extraordinary with hand-painted scrolling. Extraordinary too were the carved moldings and wood trim describing harpoon and oar motifs.

For her cursory appraisal (a nimble glance or passing regard), the parlor with concise subtlety in an easterly direction expressed itself through handsome ceiling fans which Henrik's oldest brother had, decades earlier, brought from Tangier as a gift when he and his wife and three children were visiting young Ingrid and Henrik during the second summer of their married life in America. With comfortable assurance, the parlor also expressed itself through four upright Victorian chairs, each of them meticulously upholstered, and through a richly textured Oriental rug.

As she moved always with circumspect awareness, the faint glow of early afternoon light and Henrik's deliberate gait influenced her passage and that of the others. Now she made her way out of the parlor and arrived inside the spacious living room. There, in fleet summary and with respectful appreciation, she scanned the Queen Anne highboy that Henrik and his son had themselves crafted in cherry, maple and birch during their free time over the course of two years. They had modeled their fine work upon that of a superb artisan from Providence in the 1740s. She noticed too, and so did the others still in scanning motion and just as appreciative, the Hepplewhite-Chippendale transition chairs flanking the highboy, which this mentoring father and his versatile son had, nearly fifteen years gone, also made.

While with the others she threaded her way through the light wavering before and above and around them, she moved out of the living room. With clarifying glimpses toward her left, she saw the immaculate appointments of the dining room. Its tall cabinet stood stalwart and orderly near the north wall, all the while displaying an impressive union of mahogany and maple. It also displayed hand-blown glass from Delft and Wedgwood china. Substantial nearby were a table melding mahogany with ebony and reliable sideboards glittery with pistol-handled service. All about the room comfortable English Windsor chairs beckoned the visitor to sit and stay for a few hours.

When she reached the end of the fluent if intricate space which all the while was bringing her and the others to the iron staircase hurrying upward to other levels, she (still moving studiously) glanced toward her right at the efficient and tidy kitchen and in the ellipses of this ongoing montage saw in the cool-shaded side of the room facing east the old-fashioned coal stove and ice box. Shaded as well, though in a southerly corner, was the breakfast nook with its drop-leaf table (which was made of yellow poplar wood) and well-built matching chairs. Not far from the table, on a gleaming counter by a peering window, an imposing group of pewter plates and drinking mugs waited and--resting next to them--a quaint, black walnut coffee grinder.

After Henrik had guided the group to the second level, she paused long enough to observe the symmetry of four bedrooms. In each of them stood early American canopied four-posters, colorful with antique quilts and down comforters and pillows. Just as distinctive were the burnished oak bureaus and a sturdy armoire that blended ash, oak, and cherry.

Had he been here, she was certain, Neal would have been made uneasy to see in nearly every room the photographs of Vincent Terbork. (But, because he was a

Conroy, he would have held his sorrow in check by whatever powers within himself helped him to reconcile the brighter past to existence as he was now experiencing it.) Using what she guessed was an Elmer 55 millimeter lens for their Leica, Ingrid or Henrik or one of their artist friends had recorded Vincent's handsomeness and rugged muscularity. Photographed with Neal and a fellowship of athletic peers during swift and pleasing summers, he appeared to exult in early boyhood adventures and later in the tremendous thriving of his young manhood.

She too was made uneasy as she noticed in these same photographs the transitory appearances of the mariner and his family. Henrik himself, when long ago he was a rough-hewn groom of twenty, was standing elated on his wedding day by the side of his bride, the fair-skinned Ingrid. Her flowing raven hair and flawless oval features enhanced a demure and natural stillness. In a later photograph, taken perhaps on the deck of his commercial vessel, Henrik now become the brawny, weather-toughened fisher who with matter-of-fact authority and large, proficient hands was displaying his prize catch of the day for the consideration of those persons outside the picture observing him. It was a glistening blue-fin tuna, about three foot long and nearly fifty pounds. From that same era a photograph of Ingrid, as apt as it was remarkable, showed her in the crisp-gray uniform of a dutiful nurse's assistant. She was tending her withered charges, three worn-out fishers seated, neat and comfortable, within white wicker chairs on the summer lawn of a community retirement house.

Photographed years later, no longer young, Henrik and Ingrid met the spectator's glance with keen enthusiasm. They were sitting on a sun-glanced hill beneath the billowy poise of an apple blossom tree. In her capable arms was an infant sleeping swaddled and contented.

The child himself was translated by time—and identified through succeeding photographs—as a confident boy of nine or ten roughhousing with other boys including Neal. All of them looked sturdy in tank-top swimsuits on a private beach to which the Conroys had invited him.

The Leica also presented Vincent as a carpenter who had smoothly acquired his father's skill. In a series of photographs, father and son appeared in their workshop at home crafting an ox-bow chest of drawers made of curly maple and linden and Japanese pagoda.

The youth's sanguine handsomeness informed at least one other picture. By this time he was sixteen or so and in his muscularity suggested a carefully honed prowess. At the edge of a soccer field, he was standing with the teammates he captained. With a commanding assurance, he held a large trophy so that the other players could also touch it as a sign that the cup belonged to all of them.

It was this last photograph that, in spite of the affirming occasion it signified, disquieted her. All the other photographs referred to evolving contexts that Vincent inhabited in succeeding photographs. But this last image of him summarized all previous contexts yet evolved no further. Its serial implications had been interrupted and left unfinished. For the vigorous youth (his father in terse understatement explained as she and the four others in passing review beheld the athlete's smiling countenance) died unexpectedly only a week after the picture had been taken.

Unnoticed, she studied now with reticent compassion Henrik's ruined physiognomy. She wondered how he could endure his grave existence, his prolonged death-in-life, when only his beating pulse informed him that he was, after all, alive. How, while suffering without complaining, could he go on after losing the two persons most essential to his happiness? To lose everything—to lose the person or the persons one perceived as everything—that was also death.

From her recent experience, she had learned what this other death was. Neal had died, and her life with him had died, too. During this death that she shared with him, she had grieved for him on every day of this year just passed. But now, though with a cautious uncertainty, she found herself wanting to go forward with the life she must accept without him and to whatever possibilities it held for her. This going forward after a grievous loss was, her reason told her, a proper response to loss both natural and healthy.

Neal's parents and his newly married brother (she perceived whenever she spent time with them in their summer residences in Martha's Vineyard or in their homes in Virginia) were striving to go forward. Her own parents, who had loved and respected Neal as though he were their own son, also understood the necessity of going on to whatever new cycle was awaiting her.

"There is so much that you can accomplish," her father had counseled her. "Stop looking back. Make something special from the life you have now."

She had listened silently to his words and to those of the Conroys. But for many months she had resented their suggesting how she should feel or how she should proceed toward a future that deprived her of Neal. Only in early May had she agreed to return, come late September, to her teaching post at Pembroke College within Brown University. There, as an assistant professor in the comparative literature department, she would guide young women, most of whom came from a background not unlike her own, through the novels of Balzac, Tolstoy, and Cervantes. She was planning, as well, to continue her work on behalf of the elderly, the handicapped, and the unemployed. She needed to fill all her time, so that she could dispel the shadowy presence of Neal that would otherwise linger at the rim of her consciousness.

Just for today, because she believed that her commemorating Neal would be as appropriate as it was authentic, she had willed herself to accept the gravel sound of his voice that was available now only to her ears and to imagine that here in the lighthouse, within the shadowy corners of each room or by the long, wide windows that showed her the mottled blueness of the bay and smooth, green hills in the distance, the tall and rugged imagery of her husband silently observed her. That she and Neal had visited the lighthouse four or five times two summers earlier, shortly before he left for the war, gave special meaning to her visit today.

She had to admit, though, that she had come for still another reason. She wanted to see Henrik again and, seeing, discover whatever capacities had helped him to go forward to the years that remained for him. But now, as she moved through the rooms of his home, here in the lighthouse, she saw that he had not left anything behind. Instead, he had carried the burden of his loss with him. He had not let go of it, perhaps out of devotion to the wife whom death had taken from him or out of a dismaying guilt that she, not he, had been the one to die. Or, possibly, he had tried to let go of it in that first year he was alone after she and their son had died. Perhaps, he found that it could not be done, this releasing ourselves from our dead--from the person or persons whom, when they were alive, we have loved most of all and who, even after they have died, still mean the whole of existence to us.

Suddenly, because of these ghostly photographs before her or because of the mute lostness of this ghostly old man or because of her understanding that her own life without Neal condemned her to a similar lostness, she felt that death was all around her. Quickly, though, she strove to resist the thought. She cared for life, and life was all about her, not here in these glimmering rooms of the lighthouse that were as an altar to Henrik's dead, but out there, beneath the blue sheen of the sky and in all the circumferences of space that to her eyes were vibrant and inviting.

Once more they paused, just before making their journey up the iron stairs to the highest level that would reveal for their contemplation the tremendous powers of the Fresnel lens. It was the formidable beacon guiding vessels through the east passage of Narragansett Bay or into Newport Harbor. As they paused, the four of them there who had a more favorable impression of the place than she did began to praise the good fisher. Her mother, who had noticed the accurate care with which Henrik had made the building an exemplary presence, offered first her gentle and approving words.

"You bring so much to this place," she told the weathered mariner, "...so much attention and love. I can feel them in every one of the rooms—all your care and patience and your contentment being here."

Henrik smiled appreciatively. "That is the way with lighthouses," he said. "Whatever good you bring them, they will give you back a hundredfold."

"Your knowing the sea and being a good mechanic come in handy here," Derek mused aloud while his rapid glance went on surveying the more shadowy area they had just entered.

She, too, remembered from previous visits how deftly Henrik had operated this station's light-and-fog signal and with what precision he had polished its lens, oiled its machinery, and repaired its gears when they were failing. He had repaired them as effortlessly as he had repaired the hand-pump that provided water for him and for any visitors. On another afternoon, while Neal assisted him during one of their visits, she had watched Henrik repair the wind generator, with its intricate electric circuitry.

As a boatman, Henrik was not only skillful (Neal had told her), but also wise. He knew when to fear the sea and when to confront it bravely. More than once, because of his extraordinary abilities, he had by hurrying forth in his fisher's vessel rescued men and women and children trapped in malfunctioning sloops or yachts or yawls on the turbulent ambivalence of storm-raveling waters. In so many remarkable ways, this aged workman with modesty and determination had validated the self-willed union of technical acumen and reliable courage.

This thought of his courage influenced her now to stand near him, so that she could quietly ask him how he was able to get on with things so effectively, even though he'd lost the two persons who meant most to him. But, while they continued to pause at the bottom of the stairway that would lead them to the great lens empowering the lighthouse, her father spoke up instead. With his special affinity for those tough-minded individuals waylaid unfairly by chance or fate or some other untoward circumstance, he respected Henrik for struggling to find some authentic meaning in this late cycle of his life and, in so doing, extend his covenant with the powerful sea which had always influenced his well-being.

"The nice thing about all of this," her father told him with matter-of-fact discernment, "is that you're keeping your friendship with the sea."

"Ah, yes, the sea," Henrik said. His thick Dutch inflections granted his voice a sober authority. Clearly, he was pleased to echo what was for him a favorable word. "The sea has been a demanding and unpredictable friend."

Her father (she knew) admired the still-robust fisher for the steadfast disciplines which he'd brought to and maintained in the lighthouse: his maritime skills and sense of order, his Spartan cleanliness, and his monastic simplicity.

How good of him, her father had a few years earlier remarked, to rent for a modest sum to a young fisher with a wife and four children the home which he and Ingrid had built in a middle-class section of Newport. With his inherent awareness of the needs of others, Henrik believed that a young and healthy family should enjoy the large home that for many years had brought him, with Ingrid and Vincent, so much happiness.

He was a man, her mother had readily agreed, who was both resilient and altruistic. How clever he was, she had added, to make his new home here on the sea in the very space where his duties were inspiring new applications of his knowledge.

"This is first-rate," her father now remarked, mindful as he was of all that the mariner was accomplishing in this guardian station. "A navy commander couldn't ask for a more effective attention to details."

"That is the sailor's training my father gave me, I suppose," Henrik said, with the polite reserve which in him appeared natural and agreeable. "Everything has to be in its proper place and in proper working order, clean and usable."

"Well, everything here is as it should be," Moira concurred. She, who very often shared their father's sympathies, admired the balance and symmetry of the rooms and, even more so, the ingrained work ethic which Henrik, with a humble man's clarity, embodied.

(Her sister appeared healthy and happy. Never before had her auburn hair, blue eyes and smooth skin made her genteel manner so attractive. She was a good sister who had quietly suffered with her all during this hard year. But by the middle of the summer she had wanted her to be finished with that suffering. With their friendly tact, she and Derek had in late July brought Jeffrey Latimer into her life again. He had, they told her, recently been appointed chief of surgery at New York Hospital. A few years ago, her parents had happily anticipated their marriage. A Latimer married to a Harcourt would make, they'd remarked, an ideal partnership. But when she accepted Neal instead, they had not been displeased. That Jeff still loved her brought her a reticent pleasure. Still, in their summer meetings that always took place in the company of her family and their friends, she could not summon words which would tell him that they might eventually share a future together. She could not yet summon those words, because with a strange finality they would declare Neal dead to that same future.)

Now, as they all entered the dark of the stairs together, she felt herself alone until, as if she were being lifted from herself, she rose toward the dazzle of sheerest light. All around her its shimmering candescence seemed to lift her even higher. The stairs to her eyes became hazy and nearly invisible, so that each step by which she was advancing became a mysterious ascension. Her every movement seemed, just for that instant, an illusion...a levitation...a floating through tremendous phosphorescence. No longer did she seem pinioned by ordinary gravity.

Then, after climbing several stories above brisk, Indian summer waters and once more sighting the others, she with them entered a large and circular room that was the building's tower opening onto a panorama of the city. Newport unfurled in the plummeting surround, and Narragansett Bay hurried toward boundaries beyond her seeing. Here, she saw the true sources of the light, for dominant before her in the center of the room stood the station's grand Fresnel lens. Its light was empowered not only by the glare of the day outside the eight-foot high windows, but even more so from within itself by hundreds of polished glass prisms, an impressive matrix arrayed in a glittering brass frame. Rotated as it was by heavy machinery, the lens gathered and focused into a beam every flicker of light from the burning wick of an oil lamp and threw that flashing beam a dozen miles out to sea to warn boats and ships away from unforgiving rocks and shoals and dangerous currents.

It was this sight of the building generating light from within itself and thereby defining its influences upon the world that instantly thrilled her. The phenomenon of a lonely and isolated building becoming a beacon unto itself as well as to others answered her need of some sign or message promising her rescue from her unhappiness. Even in the midst of her private grieving, she was learning to do the right things. Without Neal, she was making a path for herself that kept testing her self-reliance and her resilience. How good it was to be reminded in this moment of the guardian beacon within herself which could light her way past the obstacles confronting her. Surely, through her own powers—through the light that was herself active in mind, body, and spirit—she would gradually secure her rescue. Suddenly hopeful and refreshed, she persuaded herself to accept her visit to the lighthouse as a harbinger of better days.

Yet all too soon her realistic appraisal of things dissuaded her from this easy optimism, which she leagued with her girlhood. As an imaginative child, she had often found in random occasion or imagery a meaning that her assailed will imposed upon it. In those years, when she was weary or wary or panic-struck after the earliest hours of disappointment or grief, she had composed wish-fulfilling scenarios that often came to naught. Her self-deception anticipated spring when brooding winter had barely begun. Her willful desire saw snow-white flowers where there was only snow. But today, as a twenty-five year old woman, she saw more clearly. Her self-rescue, she was well aware, required the building of a new plan for her life. It would take more than a year or two for her to learn the formidable strategies that would bring that plan to fruition. Still, the quick analogy she found between the power of the lens and the effectiveness of her own capacities held some part of the truth. She and no other must be her guide to freedom.

Once again, with her parents and with Derek and Moira, she gave her attention to the wise old fisher. In clear and unpretentious language, he was explaining the intricate workings of the lens that gave to the lighthouse a reliable vigilance.

"It's beautiful," her mother said. "And it's here for every one of us."

The good mariner, having completed his concise anecdotes about the engineering feat which the Fresnel lens represented, regarded her mother agreeably, as did she and the others who were there listening to him.

"Yes, it's very beautiful," Henrik agreed after a moment's stillness. With the others he smiled, obviously pleased by praise that was as genuine as it was extemporaneous.

Now they turned from this room of light. With the aged fisher effectively leading them, they made their way in single file back down through the darkness of the long stairway and through the keeper's residence. As they made their descent, she felt for a lingering instant that Neal had come again to watch her. Even in the dark she saw him, alive and rugged and smiling. Then he was gone, lost once more to her seeing. Today, because some ambivalent part of her willed him to be gone, he'd disappeared into the gray shadows that kept rising about them.

She was glad to be released from the uncertain darkness of the stairs and to leave the keeper's lonely residence behind her. In the full sunglow of day, she walked briskly with the others to the picnic table and the chairs on the verdant grounds of the lighthouse. Their Eastern-red cedar wood was gleaming in handsome alliance with the delicious lunch that she, her mother, and her sister, as well as the Rousselots, had prepared. Now she helped the two women to bring from a crisp hamper cold slices of chicken, Jabugo ham and Gouda cheese, as well as freshly-baked French bread. There was also a ginger-ale salad, with its medley of pears and peaches and pineapples, its lemon and cranberry juice and chopped toasted walnuts, and its signature ginger ale--all chilled into a gelatin mold and something extraordinary. As a memorable dessert, there was a vanilla-scented Lady Baltimore cake, with white layers filled with pecans and chopped figs and raisins, and on its top and sides fluffy white frosting sprinkled with more raisins, nuts, and cherries. Accompanying it was a fine punch, plum- and raspberry-flavored.

Even now while she sat at the table—more than when she had begun the day's excursion—she was determined that this hour with Henrik should remain uncomplicated and cheerful. Though she had little appetite, she compelled herself to share the meal with the others. Small portions of the food were enough to restore her spirit, and the various conversations she shared with this sociable company left her feeling much easier. She enjoyed exchanging with her father, Derek, and Henrik some memorable experiences of fishing, canoeing and skiing. Because Neal had guided her through her experiences, she often mentioned his name and always casually. Later, she heard herself make a tentative promise to travel with her parents and with Moira and Derek to Palm Beach during her winter break from teaching.

So also did she find herself eased when, from her place at the convivial table looking out at the viridian waters of the bay, she noticed the wind-tossed alacrity of the waves rising into quicksilver hills. As if it were claiming for itself the circumference of the azure sky it inhabited, a small and solitary cloud stretched its form, as firm and rugged as a man's hand. She also noticed, within the day-bright hues of the west corner of the lighthouse, not far from the wind-touched greenery on which it stood, a tall Scots pine attending all of them who were there at the table. Its leaves clustered goldenly and its orange-red bark glowed like fire. Late-blooming white geraniums, bright pink dianthus, red and blue phlox, and yellow and orange helianthus filled the circular flowerbed as a southerly presence beside them. The wind rose softly and touched her skin, and the air breathed a clean, sea-borne fragrance. A glaucous-winged gull soared above the bay and past the white angular rocks that rose out of deeper and mysterious waters. Just as smoothly, it flew past blue-white clouds that poised themselves above the sails of a faraway yawl. It also flew past wavering sunspots on resonant waters and all too quickly past her accurate seeing.

While a mild contentment visited her in this hour, she found her way once more to a spontaneous smile that pleased all the others at the colorful table, none more than her father.

"How good it is to see you smile," he said, understated and careful.

"Oh, Father, the day is so beautiful," she said. "I would be very foolish not to smile."

No sooner had she spoken, than Neal waved to her—there, in the sun-touched shadows of the Scots pine. Seeing him, she started to rise from her place at the table. But some wise instinct held her back. He could not be there. Although the army had not recovered his body, Neal was never going to come back to her. Even now after a year, she had to summon the strongest powers of her will to keep herself from hurrying to the tree where his shadowy form still waited.

"He is not here," she kept telling herself silently.

At the same time, she found words that praised Derek's captaining of her husband's boat and that drew Moira into a conversation about the couple's recent victory, along with a crew of sea-worthy friends, in the Newport regatta. But the instant that Neal disappeared from her seeing, loneliness came swiftly—hovering—back to her.

Only when their visit with Henrik had come to an end and they were walking to the dock did she place herself beside him. Almost at once she spoke the words meant for him alone. For, without confessing the specifics of her case, she looked to the aged fisher for some wise counsel that she would keep in mind as she made her way without Neal. She recognized in the aged fisher a deep-seated unhappiness not unlike her own, mute though his was and harnessed by the taut strictures of his will. It was this belief that he could help her which moved her to speak.

"It must be very lonely for you here," she said. Her voice in this moment sounded strained and tremulous and, in spite of herself, melancholic.

"You can get used to loneliness," he said.

With pensive interest he studied her shadowed radiance for a fleet instant before offering his arm so that he could guide her down the wide stairs that led them to the dock. Her parents, as well as Moira and Derek, had already hurried ahead of them.

His deep voice was a husky energy upon the suddenly buoyant air as he continued to answer her.

"You get used to loneliness the way you get used to a lot of things when you don't have much say in the matter."

Now, because they had arrived at the dock and because he had no need to speak further words, he drew her into the company of the others and helped all of them to enter their boat smoothly.

For weeks afterward, as she heard in the echo of his words a stoic acceptance of the way things were for him, she wondered how much of his heart he had learned to close off from feeling. She wondered, too, how many months and entire years, even, his anguish had needed to live before teaching him that hard lesson.

AFTERMATH

When he arrived in Paris ten days after the car accident, Ted Lorrison, visiting Paul within his room in the convalescent wing of the hospital, noticed at once the worn-down look of his son. A loss of weight and of spirited self-assurance made Paul's muscularity a more vulnerable power. How ruined he appeared. His weary demeanor subverted the bronzed hue that gently touched his face. The subdued tan gave evidence of those afternoon hours when he'd sat on the terrace of this, his temporary home, within the modulated radiance of days in early August that occasionally breathed with an autumn crispness. But no longer did he glow from within. Whatever coherent and singular attributes once lent vigor to his identity had left him. So Ted observed and, observing, determine to throw out to him some belay or rescuing rope or Prusik-loop for the long, precarious climb up the mountain which loomed before him.

"What's done is over and finished," he said. He had allowed his son to tell him in detail about the day of the accident and, in the telling, to pause more than once and keep at bay the bitter remorse defeating his best rallying capacities. "You must turn away from the accident. This guilt and recrimination won't change things. Get on with your life. Make it something important...something of value."

Gone gray-haired and a bit heavier, he anchored his rugged masculinity nonetheless to a no-nonsense approach to the world—to its unpredictable people and its wily circumstances. The senior Lorrison meant to ease his valued son, even as he prodded him toward a tough-minded dismissal of his past. At least, he must dismiss its betrayals and disappointments and whatever failures he could neither refute nor repeal.

"You need a place that will push your life into a new direction. You really should come to New York."

Understanding the effort his father was making on his behalf, his brusque-seeming words a way to deflect this show of fatherly love, Paul tried to smile. Yet, his heart was not in it. There was in him a grief too harrowing for a smile, especially now when he'd called forth blunt, honest words that told how his carelessness had hurried his life, and Claude Durand's, into the fatal accident. Those words revealed how, in his recollection, the scene existed still—constant and visible and changeless.

"I can't turn away from it and pretend his death doesn't matter," he said. His voice was a taut, constraining whisper. "Claude was like a brother...a brother. I loved him. He should be the one here and alive. He was so much better than I."

He rose from his chair and from his father's attentive eyes to stand before a sun-misted window. So overwhelmed was he by this confession of his fault before the predominant figure of his father, to whom—emulous and respectful—he'd always carefully related, that he needed this moment to be as if alone and draw from his adamant, masculine resources the deep breath that would keep secure his tenacious hold upon an acceptable stoicism. His face hidden from his father now, he lifted his hands toward his brow, as though he were blocking the sunlight from his eyes. At first, Ted wondered whether he was crying. But his broad shoulders and sturdy back gave no evidence of his trembling with raw sobs flung out of himself or of his groaning with suppressed cries, guttural and raspy, that wrenched his entire body. Rather, by this simple gesture of brushing his hands across his brow, he appeared to summon even sterner aptitudes and then stare, belligerent and willful, toward the perfectly quiet azure sky and the feathery clouds poised casually in the faraway distance. When he turned back to his father, he wore a deeper frown. Grim-faced and tight-jawed, he murmured the words revealing his harnessed grief, because they held the embittered thought that he could not elude.

"He was like a brother," he said once more. His inflections were so taut that he was barely audible. "He was like a brother."

How battered he looked, as though he'd been whipped and sternly punished. Yet, even under the tremendous weight of his guilt, there was in him a harsh courage and an angry strength that refused to bend before the convoluted workings of the sorrow he had brought upon himself. Had he been a sentimental man, his father decided when witnessing this stifled anguish, his son would probably have broken down, exposed and insufficient. But, though he conveyed in his writing a sentiment both poetic and adventurous, he was in almost every phase of his life a matter-of-fact realist. So being, he had developed a fierce pride in his manly engagement with the world. Like most vigorous men, he would not, under duress or in the path of waylaying circumstance, permit himself to cry out his pain, tearful and panic-struck. Whatever grief in this period had overtaken his equanimity, the better to bring him low, he was determined to go on fighting it with his own austere wiliness until, through sheer grit or sorrow-proof stamina, he brought grief low. Gradually, his unhappiness might fall away from him, forgotten—if not utterly defeated.

Aware of how emotionally bruised he was and of the lacerating battle he was waging, Ted became, at the dismaying sight of him, more moved than he'd ever wanted to be before anyone. Obeying the impulse of his earnest feelings for his son, he stood before him now and gently patted his shoulder. This fatherly gesture he quickly reinforced by grabbing Paul's large, athletic hand and clasping it, comradely and familial. Only then, and after his son accepted the clasp, did he take up again a blunt counsel.

"Come to New York," he said. "There's so much going on there now and so many opportunities to do something worthwhile. You can't help being energized in positive ways. Besides, I can teach you all about being a creative force in the business world."

Pensive and interested as well as touched by his father's show of love for him, Paul needed only an instant to clarify his feelings about his immediate future.

"I don't want to run away from my life," he said. "I've got to stay in Paris for a while and sort out things right here, where so much has gone wrong. I have to turn things around before I go back to America. I want to prove that I haven't absolutely jinxed my life here."

Ted frowned. Clearly, he was uncertain about whether Paul, without his fatherly association during what was for him a difficult time, could make things work for himself.

Noting his unease, Paul hurried to reassure him.

"You needn't worry," he said. "Catherine will be here to see that I stay on the right track."

"So be it, then," Ted answered him, raising the palms of his hands to indicate that he would not challenge his son's decision. "Do whatever you think is right for yourself and for her."

That Paul was preparing himself to take charge of his life once more was, Ted believed, a good sign. Although, as a concerned father, he planned to be far more involved in that life, he did not intend to steal away his son's autonomy. His having witnessed him, spirit-spent and self-condemned, did not disturb his admiration of a young man he had always deemed exceptional. On this day he'd found new reasons to respect Paul after listening to his thoughtful point of view about remaining in Paris until he'd won back his effective capacities. At the same time, he thought it advisable to reiterate to him the offer that, he hoped, this strong-willed man might one day accept.

"Maybe, today you don't want New York," he said. "Maybe, not even tomorrow or next week. But keep it in mind. Some day you may see how much good it can do for you and for Catherine. At any rate, you may feel better knowing that the offer is always open to the both of you."

Too pleased to withhold a quiet smile and pleased as well by his father's generosity, Paul readily concurred.

"I'll remember it," he said. "I can easily promise you that."

It was now, when Catherine came to them, that Paul held himself thankful that she had not been there to witness his latest battle against grief. For, upon his father's arrival a half-hour earlier, she had excused herself. She'd preferred to saunter in the garden, located within the southwest corner of the hospital grounds, so that father and son could have a private and more probing conversation. Their initial greeting, hers and Ted's, had been a most amiable one, in which the elder, courtly Lorrison, appreciative of her patrician and cosmopolitan manner, imparted toward her a genuine regard. He had, in fact, already decided, through previous meetings at the beginning of her marriage to his son, that Catherine was not only a beautiful young woman, but also an authentic individual. She was a worthy addition to the Lorrisons' ongoing story.

She'd returned from her brief sauntering in the garden to accompany Paul to his afternoon hour of physical therapy. As it had become her practice, she would join him in the careful exercises, while a physician's assistant monitored their adeptness. Before they went forward to this session, they bade Ted a fond goodbye and arranged a time during the next day when he might once again visit. The three of them approaching the threshold of the room and the door from which he, first of all, would leave, Ted directed toward Catherine and Paul a keen-eyed, studious gaze. It eased his heart to see how promising they still looked together. So cheered was he in the instant of this scrutiny, that he hurried to express to Catherine the auspicious words he meant his son to hear and, in union with her, to act upon.

"You must bring him into life again," he said. "You're the one who can do it."

Grateful for his trust, Catherine smiled.

"I'll do my best," she said. As she moved closer to her husband, she allowed him a freedom of space to walk, independent and self-determining, though with a cane by which he maintained a proper balance. Only recently had he shed his leg-cast.

Ted noticed, respecting anew her unfailing intuition.

Walking side by side with him, nonetheless, she drew Paul into the promise she'd just made to his father.

"It will be not only my best, but Paul's as well."

Now Ted offered his own smile to her and to his son. He'd recognized in the remark a favorable capstone to their visit.

Moments later, while he walked briskly through the long, gleaming corridor where a harboring quietude attended him and after he entered his chauffeured limousine waiting in the parking area nearby, he reflected upon his best hopes for his son.

Even before Paul was released from this hospital care, he must will himself to go past his sorrow and past this assailed version of himself. The death of his friend would, of course, remain a scar upon his soul. But he must learn to live with it. So he believed. He saw that the necessary journey that his son must make would not be an easy one. Hard task it is to discover that one does not, after all, possess the mythic qualities or invincible powers one had taken to be the essence of one's identity. To be a proper Lorrison, though, he would—when all was said and done—

have to stand alone and accept his pain, brutal and searing as it was. He must accept the lashings of conscience and the punishing hours. Then, one especially austere day, he would declare himself finished with that part of his life. Many Lorrison men, including himself, had gone through similar hells. Each of them had learned to live with the liability that was himself, sin-blemished and disillusioned— the mind gradually adjusting its self-regard to this more fallible imagery.

Early in September, a few weeks after Ted's visit, the still-promising married couple left the convalescent wing of the hospital. Paul had been restored, or seemed so, by intricate surgeries and months of care and by the nurturing of his passionate nature which mischance had recently subdued. With Catherine, he returned to their apartment in Paris and to the work that gave to their lives a semblance of forward-moving engagement. Now it was that he summoned a discipline and determination to complete the closing chapters of his second novel. In this same period, she embraced a rigorous schedule of classes and papers and examinations to fulfill the requirements for the second year of her undergraduate studies at the University of Paris, within the Sorbonne.

All appeared to be going well, save for the occasional nightmare disturbing Paul's sleep or the random image or voice reminding him of Claude. As if their good Fate meant to offer further proof of her returning friendship, Scribner's commissioned both of them, as Americans and Francophiles, to write and to provide photography for an ambitious book of essays about the many cultures which make of France a luminous diversity and about the many peoples who bring their own light to that country's unceasing surprise. To complete this assignment (their aim the creation of a beautiful coffee table text), Paul and Catherine would travel, during the next year and more, to every corner of France—across its land and waterways, through its valleys and mountains, and into its villages and cities. In each of these locations they would explore and identify through word and picture the country's vivid physicality and, by way of its multi-national inhabitants, its pulsing heart.

They believed that they had gone past their bleak time after all. They had paid with anguished hours and weeks and months whatever debt Paul's error had incurred upon him and, because of her bond with him, upon Catherine, too. They found themselves happy, as well, to know again that they loved one another completely. Once more, each of them became the other's predominant reality.

Nearly buoyant now and believing that favorable Time had, in this new cycle, made herself his ally, Paul decided to drive to Sancerre. He wanted to offer Marguerite Durand not only his genuine apology for the accident which had killed Claude, but also a large financial settlement which would give her security and would provide, in addition, a trust fund for Claude's and her two sons.

Catherine, at first, agreed with his lawyers that he should, during this period when the loss of her husband was still a raw wound, refrain from personal contact with Marguerite. Much later, perhaps, if his heart still told him to do so, he could speak with her privately. For now, though, only his astute lawyers should communicate with Mrs. Durand about the generous settlement he would like to provide her and her children.

Before this good counsel, Catherine's and his lawyers', Paul found himself hesitating. All the while, he was weighing the merit of going before his friend's widow to ask for her forgiveness. His humble entreaty was a way, possibly, to ease his guilt and to declare himself openly as the catalyst in Claude's undoing. But no sooner did he assess the cost to his conscience of not making this visit to Marguerite, than in spite of his newfound hope he fell into brooding anew. He retreated alone to the study where, at his desk, he sat in stern-faced silence.

A half-hour later, Catherine approached him and, standing there at his desk, caressed with her lovely fingers the frowning handsomeness of his face. Now she urged him to listen to his own heart's need and follow through with his plan to visit Marguerite. Only then did his smile return. In this moment, he drew her to himself and, still seated, with his strong arms enfolding her, kissed her stomach and her breasts and, afterwards, rested his blond head at her firm, ample bosom. His love for her and for her quiet empathy validated and revived his hope. It was her sensitive awareness of how important this visit to Marguerite would be for him which convinced him that Catherine must accompany him to so crucial an occasion. In fact, it was Catherine who telephoned Marguerite to say that they wanted to pay her a visit. Constrained yet courteous, Claude's widow agreed to see them on Thursday of that week. She invited them to the noon meal which her parents and her two brothers and their wives, all of whom worked in their vineyards, would be sharing.

So it was that, a day or two later, Catherine and Paul drove to Sancerre. His rugged will subdued all hesitation and permitted him a muted tension—that familiar stranger come now to watch him in his journey. When, two hours later, they arrived at the main house which stood, picturesque and immaculate, in the northwest corner of the spacious land, Marguerite's mother received them politely. At once, perhaps because she'd been expecting them, she recognized them as friends of Claude and Marguerite. Several times previously, they had spent enjoyable afternoons amidst the teeming farmlands and vineyards. In this way did Yolande Bonnaire surprise Paul, if not Catherine, by being very pleased that dear friends of her daughter and of her lost son-in-law had come to express their sympathy to the still-grieving widow and to share reminiscences of the strong bond they'd created with the Durands.

"I'm glad that you've come," the good woman said. "We are always pleased to see our friends from the city."

Her soft, white hair was pulled into a sensible coil at the nape of her neck. Her dark, sympathetic eyes and aquiline nose, her gleaming smile and caramel skin, and the plumpness that sat so neatly upon her big-boned girth—these emblems of who she was externally defined as accurately her maternal disposition.

"We would have visited right after the accident," Catherine explained, "but Paul was in the hospital for several months."

Good-naturedly, Mrs. Bonnaire smiled at them. Her worn face carried forth the imprints of long, arduous years of nurturing vine-stocks and farm-fields.

"Well, you are here now, and that is a very good thing," she declared. The West Indies timbre of her words, Gallic-flavored and idiosyncratic, accompanied the rhythms of her motherly gestures. "Marguerite and my husband will want you to see our splendid harvest."

Mrs. Bonnaire had completed all preparations for luncheon with the assistance of Mrs. Dusseault, an amiable, middle-aged woman from the village who often helped her with cleaning chores and cooking. Now she sent pretty Amélie, one of their foreman's daughters, to the vineyards in the southerly portion of the property. At thirteen, the girl was strong-bodied and quick, yet possessed none the less a supple grace. She rode into that expansive territory on a Portuguese Lusitano, bay-colored and agile, to tell Mr. Bonnaire and Marguerite and all the others that their guests had arrived and that they should come now to greet them and share the noon meal.

Within minutes, Catherine and Paul relaxed themselves into a free-flowing conversation with the two personable women. The four of them exchanged anecdotes about horses and farming and high-quality vineyards. Paul also spoke about the excitement of flying a plane, and Catherine mentioned her current studies at the Sorbonne. Together, the young couple remarked as well upon their plan to travel as journalists and photographers through all of France and eventually through other countries. No sooner had they described their plan, but just before they saw a tincture of sorrow lightly crease each other's demeanor, Marguerite appeared at the opened door. October's luminous rays were infusing that entrance with a halcyon glow and bringing into its folds the tall, limber woman standing on the threshold. Profuse and italic, the light of the sun gave to her lean athleticism a stoical presence. She was poised as if to hurry forward, perhaps, after this momentary arrival or to hurry away.

"So you have come, after all," she said. Still at the doorway, she observed them carefully. Her thin smile was an intimation rather than an emphasis of remembered fellowship. "I wasn't certain that you would, even after your call."

She was addressing her words to Catherine. Her attention to Paul was merely oblique, but never less than courteous.

"We've been wanting to see you for a long time," Catherine assured her, as she rose from her chair to meet her extended arms.

So, too, did Paul rise. Grateful that this gallant woman allowed him to do so, he embraced her with the taut stillness come upon him that only she recognized, having refused to be broken by furious anguish. He struggled with an anguish that was different than hers, but just as furious and relentless.

She had recognized in him this tensile masking of deep-seated grief the moment he'd noticed her, as she stood in the sun-fall radiance that filled the doorway. He kept his guarded wretchedness at bay (she imagined) by living through a too-busy regimen. It was this awareness that helped her to harness the anger and hatred and contemptuous pity she bore him.

For a moment, she'd thought he would, right then at least, say nothing to her. So careful did he need to be, lest his sorrow break through the barriers he had, in these months after Claude's death, built up against it. Her father's entering the room—with her sons and with her brothers and their wives and Amélie only a minute or so after her own arrival—reinforced her impression that she could elude any exchange of words meant for him alone.

Her father (tough-skinned Olivier), her able sons (Balthasar and Mathieu), her two invaluable brothers (Gérard and Anatole—younger than she and hardy-handsome), their reliable and pretty wives, and pert Amélie drew the attention of the room to themselves. At the same time, Catherine hurried to them, meeting their hand-waves of affability to Paul and to herself with her own warm greeting. Then they took their places at a long, sturdy table where they would enjoy the mid-day meal. Already, they had washed their hands and faces at an outdoor pump next to the stable. Each of them was dressed, as was Marguerite, in farm-workers' flannel shirts (light-blue or beige or russet), loose-fitting corduroy jackets (deep green or navy), dark-brown riding trousers and long black leather boots. With Catherine, this pleasant company filled the room with exuberance, as Mrs. Bonnaire and Mrs. Dusseault brought the meal to the table. Paul, on his way to the table with her, detained Marguerite long enough to speak the private words he'd needed to say.

"I've come to tell you that I'm so sorry," he whispered. His fear that his grief would unman him compelled him to say no more. But he made his remark when others, unable to hear him, were nonetheless present.

While his face grimaced with the pain of his guilt, he waited—uncertain—for her reply.

"I'm sorry, too," she said. She distanced herself as much as she could from whatever pity his pain inspired in her. "I'm very sorry, indeed."

What did she mean? He wondered instantly upon hearing her. Was she sorry only because Claude was dead or because Claude, not he, had died?

He wanted her to say more and waited inside the well-honed manliness that was as a sentry guarding his Spartan self-governance. But she would not speak the sympathetic words that might grant him a reprieve from his grief and his guilt.

So, before she could draw away from him, he—determined and controlled—pushed himself to say more.

"I need to talk with you," he said. "There's another important reason why I've come here."

Shrouding her feelings in silence and in a cold courtesy, she at first made no reply. Her face, burnished by her hours of labor under a sun-blanched sky and under the warm touch of early October winds, wore its own mask of modulated despair. She was wondering (he could tell) why she'd allowed him to come, now that her seeing him, alive and intact, had answered her curiosity. No, she did not want to go on with any of this.

Still, upon noticing his nearly insistent manner, she flung from her soul the few words that might pre-empt all other words with him.

"There's nothing more to say." There was a rapid curtness at the edge of her inflections. "It's done...finished...final."

Now she turned quickly from him, leaving him standing alone to ponder her ambivalence. Only when she'd passed beyond him did she permit herself to speak. She spoke without glancing back, as though she might be addressing some disembodied guest or simply the vibrant October air that carried with it the delicious fragrances of the meal wafting from the kitchen.

"Everything's ready. We mustn't keep them waiting."

Clearly, with him she did not want to share any other words. Instead, she chose a hurrying gait that would bring her to the gathering at the table.

Casual-seeming, he followed her into the dining area of the large room which easily accommodated the thirteen persons who were there. Now he summoned the stoical practices by which he'd so often subverted, or at least kept at bay, the tension welling inside himself. Quickly, he brought a studious gaze to the physical space about him and to the distinctive objects defining the room's warm spirit. It was the prodigious size of the room which once more impressed him, as it had so many times before, when he and Catherine had shared halcyon afternoons here with Claude and Marguerite. How wise the Bonnaires had been to build so capacious a room. Its twenty-five by forty-foot dimensions allowed the family to arrange its space as both a living room and, to the right of that, a dining area. Two stories high and flowing with the pitched roofline, which was supported by big, strong beams, the room smoothly drew the visitor into its elegant informality. In this manner, a frieze of antique French tapestries accented the walls and, in east and west corners, limestone fireplaces suggested a pictorial comfort. Placed above the mantels, richly textured engravings of agrarian scenes complemented the ambiance of this home.

It was, he found, easy to admire the plank-top farm table at which he and all the others sat, because it had been crafted so skillfully. Long and wide and altogether flawless, its light cherry-stained hardwood structure possessed an authentic simplicity. Above it, an elliptical chandelier, with its eight steel arms and Fruchie shades, evoked a justly renowned Provençal scrollwork.

Exemplary, also, were the country farm chairs in which they sat. Their ladderback solidity, both rustic and formal, had been composed with superior acumen. Crafted of fine hardwood with a fruitwood finish, the chairs were fitted with natural rush seats. Mrs. Bonnaire had enhanced them with thickly padded foam cushions that wore a red-check pattern matching the lampshades.

He noticed, too, as a way of holding his tension still, the first-rate reproduction of a Louis XV French *vaisselier*. The two-piece hutch offered a three-shelf plate rack atop a service and storage buffet that held a cutlery drawer and one-shelf cabinet. So many hours the diligent artisan must have given to the solid mahogany wood with natural cherry veneers and to the hand-carved details: the elaborate molding, the scalloped apron with rosette, the snail legs and antiqued solid brass hardware, and the mortised lock and key.

Never before while he was dining had he given his attention to such objects, though as a student learning to make, from excellent wood, objects both functional and aesthetic, he had devoted many hours to so challenging a craft. But today his apprehension of the order and balance and purity of the hand-wrought objects about him calmed his unease. Calming it was, as well, to perceive in the scalloped dinnerware the same order and balance and purity. It was as if the maker of all these things—tables and chairs and more—had worked in alliance with spirit-driven, albeit earth-bound, impulses. With their Louis XV design and their mix of blue, ochre, and green, the plates and bowls...cups, saucers, and mugs fairly glowed in union with the Maianenco Blue placemats and the green medallion glassware and with the silver service which, many years earlier, Mrs. Bonnaire had received as a wedding gift from her parents.

On this special afternoon, autumn light, as a fuse to their sociability and to their spontaneous appreciation of each other, came drifting through the panoramic window.

Its brightness amplified—or seemed to—the room's inherent capaciousness. Hurrying past his unease now and while partaking of the meal, Paul spoke to Claude's and Marguerite's sons, who were seated nearest him. They were on a week's recess from their village school to help with harvest chores. Eleven-year-old Balthasar, a dark-skinned wiry lad, was already honing a gift for confident openness. Ten-year-old Mathieu, by means of his light, Creole skin and a careful reserve that busied itself with tacit calculations and acute judgments, leagued himself with his mother's coloring and her realism. During their conversation, Paul discovered that each of these levelheaded boys flanking him shared his interest in sports. As active participants, they three had experienced the joy and challenge of soccer, lacrosse, and tennis, as well as sailing and skiing.

Paul ably drew forth from them anecdotes that told of their current involvement in these activities. Just as ably, he provided brief comments about his own involvement, from the time of his boyhood until the preceding winter. As he called forth spirited anecdotes with them, he eluded the unease that, for a few minutes, had begun pressing upon his senses. Shortly afterward, he exchanged with Olivier, who was sitting close by at the head of the table, remarks both affable and instructive about crop rotation and about the proper care of a horse that had injured its foot. As if it were a harmony feminine and contrapuntal to his conversations with still-muscular Olivier and with the two sturdy boys, he heard the two older women at the opposite end of the table describing to Catherine and to Amélie their special recipes for cooking *foie gras.*

From time to time, he spoke with Gérard and Anatole and their wives, Camille and Mylène. They were as young as he and Catherine and, like them, caught up in the surprise and elation of being to each other married and essential. Forthright and congenial, they told him about the village of Sauliac-sur-Célé in the exquisite Célé Valley, within the south of France. There, the wives of the Bonnaire brothers had been born and reared. They, in fact, had been sisterly friends since early schooldays. Before the war, the Bonnaire men they were to marry spent with them exuberant seasons amidst massive hills, rugged woodlands, and shaded river banks; limestone cliffs, hidden gullies, and prehistoric caverns; and ample meadows of wild flowers.

All during this meal, Paul listened for Marguerite's words. Her smoky timbres maintained a cool authority whenever, as a generous influence or a clarifying presence, she joined the ladies or her sons in their respective conversations. Peripheral and semi-detached, she sometimes annotated, with a precise explanation or a fleet description, her father's discussion of horses and of crop rotation. But never did she address him directly. Her engagement in the many conversations that included him merely scanned his presence, as if so opaque and efficient an admission of his being there fulfilled the requirements of a measured courtesy.

Maintaining, nonetheless, the order and balance and rigor of his own discipline, he gratefully partook of the meal. In this way, he saluted—and rightly so—Mrs. Bonnaire and Mrs. Dusseault, the excellent cooks. At the same time, he acknowledged his pleasure at being there with so many good people. Nor did he have to simulate an appreciation of the meal. The ladies had, as always, made of their cooking an extraordinary art.

A glass of delicate Rosé from the Bonnaires' vineyard preceded the meal with a fruity lightness satisfying to the palate. Then, with the assistance of Amélie, the two cooks brought the meal to the table. On each plate, three diamonds of red *gernet* (the fish skin up and melded with a colorful tomato and basil sauce) were arranged around a neat, creamy scoopful of potatoes. These were topped with a mini-palm tree of chives. Slices of duck *filet* followed, served with stuffed zucchini and tomatoes and a red-wine sauce. For dessert, a *tarte* arrived. It was decorated with a single, fanned strawberry and enhanced by chocolate powder, icing sugar, and a honey and cinnamon cream.

A second glass of the Rosé concluded a repast Paul thought perfect and solacing.

Shortly after Catherine and Paul bid a fond adieu to everyone else there, Mr. Bonnaire invited these two guests from the city to come see his harvesting vineyards. As they emerged from the interior, Paul looked with approval upon the twenty thousand square feet of the tile-roofed farmhouse that impressed itself upon the two voluminous courtyards surrounding it. How apt it was, he thought, that Olivier and Yolande had selected for the exterior of the house a wheat hue that matched the summery hills and, within this hilltop town of Sancerre, looked upon a neighboring lake of the Loire River.

Here, the Bonnaires' one hundred eighty acres followed a tule-lined shore and gave life to a biodynamic farming. On this land and from these courtyards, vegetable gardens and vineyards and orchards kept fanning outward to the hills beyond. Here, the family raised sheep for wool and chickens for their eggs and, consonant with the nearby lake, grew the tule or necessary aquatic plants. Then, with the tule and with the manure from the sheep and from the chickens, they made a compost which they used in the vineyards to grow the vines and to make the wine. Each year, sheep grazed and ate cover crops of geraniums, lavender, strawberry clover, dandelions, yarrow, and chamomile. Each year, gardens of melons, tomatoes, eggplant, and basil provided good food for the Bonnaires, as well as future compost material for their vineyards. Each year, egg whites from their forty chickens helped the Bonnaires to clarify their red wines.

So it was that Olivier explained to Paul and Catherine how the land cooperated with and reflected the order and balance and purity of nature. Was there any wonder, Paul mused, that Olivier and all the other good people contributing to the farm and to the vineyards worked with an enthusiasm which created a spiritual alliance with the earth?

"To make good wine," Olivier told them, "you must maintain the French tradition of *terroire*. You must draw upon the things of the earth to help the vines and the grapes. Wines are meant to taste akin to the soil from which they grew."

They—this silver-haired and bearded man, still vigorous and hearty in his senior years; beautiful, demure Catherine; and tall, athletic Paul—were at that moment riding in Olivier's truck. They observed the plenteous orchards of olive and walnut trees in the far distance and, much nearer than that, the teeming vineyards. There, Gérard and Anatole and their wives with an accurate poise were picking by hand the large bunches of grapes from the vines.

"You have given your best to the earth," Catherine said. Her sensitive face as well as her words expressed an admiration of all that he represented.

"And you have made her your friend," Paul added, keen-minded and respectful.

"Yes, the earth has been my friend," Olivier said. "She can be very harsh, though, and very careless. Sometimes, she disappoints and fails me. But I remain her friend, nonetheless. I choose to remember all the good times we've shared. I keep on being loyal. I do not desert her because she has sometimes failed me. I forgive the earth her occasional errors, which she makes without malice, and she tolerates my own blunders. That is all that we can do. We learn how to be friends and to forgive one another."

To this idea and without any words of their own, Paul and Catherine quietly assented. From each of them a slight nod of the head and a thoughtful smile intimated their fellowship with this upright man.

How wonderful before Paul's and Catherine's eyes the land appeared. So smoothly did all the human activity upon these acres merge with nature's monumental design. Here, there was an interplay of the manmade and the natural. Here, the vital energies not of opposites, but of living elements ably entwined themselves. Their traces were the very imprints of the expansive mosaic of fields and orchards, of trees and vineyards and flowers, of livestock and sun and rain, and of the intelligent heart of each laboring human being.

How wonderful, too (Paul reflected), that Claude, with his wife and his sons, had experienced the pristine reality of this land—its beauty and order and balance. And how sad that he would no longer be here to enjoy it.

It was this thought which stirred within him newer tensions, as Olivier brought them back to the home field and to the immaculate, red-brick building which housed the cool, vaulted cellars that were so important for making an excellent wine. Now, he showed them the intricate machinery which pressed the grapes into a promising liquid that would be allowed to ferment within giant casks and, later, within vats, before being bottled. Though this visit to the cellars intrigued Paul, as it did Catherine, the thought of Claude would not leave him. By the time they three had left the cellars and Olivier had driven Catherine and him back to their car, Paul realized that he had told Marguerite almost none of the things he'd come here to say. He felt a need to speak once more to her before returning to the city. In this way, he might appease (at least temporarily) his rueful conscience.

It was not only the thought of all the things which Claude had lost that goaded anew his remorse and self-hatred. It was not only that. His friend *had* experienced many beautiful seasons—every part of their fervent and colorful emphases. No, it was not only what Claude had once had for several years, while he visited his wife's family and, assisting them as a knowledgeable volunteer, helped to harvest the replenishing land. It was not only his having, by his death, lost all of that. He'd lost, as well, the memorable times when he was teaching his sons to ride affable Caspian ponies or to plant the seeds which would bring forth melons and tomatoes or to swim in the nearby lake. But it was also, and even more so, his having been deprived of all the experiences that he would never have of these vineyards and farmlands and of his wife and sons. The mind and heart and body that were himself unique and irreplaceable had been, by death, dissolved.

When Olivier brought him, with Catherine, to their Bentley, the aged man looked steadily at the two of them. He noticed in her an ingrained devotion to the tall, introspective man standing beside her. In him, he perceived a chipped self-mastery. Paul was a rugged selfhood consciously navigating, and for the first time since his adolescence, his raw vulnerability. In him, the wise vintner recognized as well a repressed suffering and a private combat with the grief that would not leave him. But, not wishing to unsettle him further, he did not tell Paul that he must learn to forgive himself.

Instead, in these moments before they parted, he spoke other words. They were just as genuine and, he hoped, helpful.

"Go with God," he said, addressing the two of them.

Then, after extending a heartening invitation to come back soon and, paternal and well-wishing, embracing them, he drove back to his work in the vineyards.

Now, a mindful recipient of his benevolence, Paul felt newly encouraged. He considered leaving for the city on this positive note and without stopping to say any other words to Marguerite. This visit, in spite of her ambivalence toward him, had gone well. Better to leave things as they were, he might have told himself. Better not to jostle the temporizing solace which Marguerite had, after all, granted him.

His canny instinct had almost persuaded him to start the car. Though he was grateful that he'd been allowed to show his respect for Claude's widow by this simple visit, he was disappointed that he'd not found a way to tell Marguerite of the financial settlement that would make secure her life and the lives of her sons. He did not care to rely alone upon whatever diplomatic overtures his lawyers were devising to convince Mrs. Durand of the wisdom in accepting his generous gift. So, he did not start the car.

Instead, while assuring Catherine that he would quickly return, he left his place behind the wheel and hurried along the path that would bring him to the stables. There, Marguerite was standing beside a dun-colored Sorraia that, when she was firmly astride its cantering energies, would bring her back to her work in the vineyards.

Seeing him there, as sudden as he was unexpected, she greeted him with a cool detachment that hovered on the rim of disdain.

"Well?" she asked, elliptical and self-contained and without pausing in the task of adjusting correctly the horse's stirrup irons. While pulling them downward, she kept them away from the horse's sides so that they would not bump him.

Now it was that he told her of his rescuing plan for her. Not that she was lost and had asked to be saved, he quietly added (even while guessing at how lost she really was) or even needy. But his plan meant, nevertheless, to keep her from worry or hard labor or from a narrow existence that offered few amenities. It would make even more secure whatever security, on her own or in association with her parents and her brothers, she might build for her sons and for herself.

At once, dismay took firmer hold of her. Her furrowed brow and gleam of angry eyes, as well as her tightened lips and rigid posture, conveyed without any new word spoken darker influences upon her contempt for him. Then, in a spate of words hastening out of her, she found the thought that revealed clearly how much she loathed him.

"You Americans are so arrogant," she said. "You think that money will solve everything. Well, it won't bring Claude back. It won't solve anything."

The Sorraia whinnied and, while she re-checked the bridle and nose band, moved nervously. Her roused voice, growing harsher with each word flung out at him, made the horse suddenly tense.

"Can your money save him? Will it bring him back to life?"

Stalwart as always and in command of a stillness within himself that to his assailed senses felt so nearly like breathlessness, Paul met her fiery glance directly. In his mute sorrow and gentle manner, he was making his oblique appeal.

But his stillness, rather than appeasing her, roused her anger even more.

"Will it save him? Tell me! Tell me!"

Now, with her gloved hand, she struck him repeatedly and, for one wilder instant, raised her stirrup as if to beat him. Perhaps it was her awareness that, stolid and unflinching, he was willing to accept her beating of him which held her back from whipping him. Or possibly it was her knowledge—intuitive and abrasive—that he also was suffering. His was a man's grief, held prisoner of whatever codes required him not to show its powers over him. Perhaps it was that. Or, more probably, it was her memory of the strong bond he and Claude had created between them. Their friendship had been a solidarity of trust and respect and love.

Or, most likely of all, she'd perceived that, when all was said and done, Claude had by his own will participated in the dangerous game which cost him his life. It had not been the first time that the two of them, in search of adventure during a break from their assignments as journalists, had tested the speed of Paul's newest Maserati across long, winding roads thirty miles or so outside Paris. They would take turns behind the wheel, each of them fearless and proficient as they competed with each other to bring the car to a greater speed. She had learned of this game on an evening when she and Claude were having dinner with Paul and Catherine. At once, she had tried to dissuade her husband from taking such risks. He, in turn, had smiled without granting her the promise that she sought.

"We're just having a good time," he'd said. "That's the best reason for a man's making his way through this planet."

Then his dark eyes had taken in her feminine regard of him with unspoken appreciation.

Whether it was the memory of any of these things that held her back from whipping him, Paul—recalling this moment for years afterward—could never fathom. By then, he'd come to understand how conflicted the human heart can be in its loves and in its hatreds.

Something it was that made Marguerite stop hitting him. Perhaps it was, after all, his consenting to be punished. He himself was a formidable strength made oddly vulnerable by the surprise of a beloved friend's death and by the surprise of himself as a wayward champion.

Turning away from him abruptly (her hand, holding the whip, no longer raised), she meant to mount her stallion and ride away. But his quiet, parched words this time held her still.

"I want to help you," he said. His voice was a manly petition and a heartfelt entreaty.

She, keeping her back to him, answered him as if murmuring words that belonged to an irrevocable nightmare.

"You can't help. You wouldn't even know how to begin."

Now it was that she mounted her horse, prepared to ride away from him.

But he couldn't let her go, without saying more. So much did he want her to accept his plan to bring financial security to her and to her sons.

"You and your boys will be the better, if you accept my gift. I want you to have it, because of my friendship and respect for Claude and for all of you."

No longer disdainful, but heartbroken and bitter yet, she eyed him with a cold weariness.

"Did I forget to tell you that I come from a proud people?"

Now she signaled her horse, already walking forward, to ride past him. She squeezed both legs against the Sorraia's sides and softened her hands forward, so that her horse would feel free to increase its pace into a trot. Only then did Paul understand that she was not going to accept his money. That she did not wish to grant him absolution by accepting such a gift, her hostility toward him made very clear. More than that, even, she did not want to diminish the value of her husband's life by setting upon it so finite a sum as a wealthy man's currency.

When he returned to the car, Catherine noticed at once the gray pallor that had overtaken his sun-tanned demeanor. Without any words from him to clarify her impression, she knew that his brief meeting with Marguerite had not gone well. So, anchored as her spirit was to all that an auspicious future promised them, she spoke of their journeying through France to discover at close range its various identities. During the long drive home, she directed their conversation to the itinerary which they two, with Scribner's executive editors and with government officials, were creating. Their careful preparation was a prudent strategy for ensuring the effective unfolding of their exciting project.

All through this drive her voice maintained its affirmation and exuberance. Gradually, she coaxed Paul to respond in kind, at least on the surface and with inflections far more understated. By the time they returned to their apartment, she'd convinced herself that their going forward would save them. The complicated assignments by which, together, they would compose an impressive book would leave Paul no time for self-defeating recrimination or for that cruelest of all guilt that renders insufficient the penitence toward which one has struggled.

They might have run free of the terrible blame that weighed so heavily upon Paul. But his injured leg, having only recently healed from several surgeries, still caused him pain. Within the next few months, he would need an additional surgery. Afterward, with Catherine, he could trek across various and difficult locations in France to gather material for their ambitious book. It was now that Scribner's persuaded them to put aside temporarily their plan for the book. Fortunately, his editors had designed for them an itinerary of a far less taxing kind. They—Paul and Catherine—would travel by train and ship and plane through every major European city to herald the publication of Paul's second novel, *A Brave Exploration*. There were few better ways, Catherine told him, to experience days and weeks of exhilarated fellowship and to invigorate one's hope and self-assurance.

So, for several weeks Paul did rally. His tattered belief in his possibilities gradually, albeit tenuously, mended. Embraced by so many persons who found pleasure and encouragement in reading him, he began to think that he was not such a bad fellow, after all. But all too soon the additional surgery to his left leg, though far less grievous than the preceding surgeries, impeded him for three long weeks. Each new hospital day was now given up to cautiously monitored physiotherapy and to the tensions of his reluctant confinement. Not even the success of his new book or the still-vivid memory of his favorable encounters with many readers during his book tour could allay his wary discontent. Only Catherine eased his anguish, through her lighthearted way of drawing him into an intricate game of chess or through her reading to him from

Plato and Montaigne, Balzac, Walt Whitman, and Rilke. Sometimes, she played Frédéric Chopin or Cécile Chaminade on the piano in the hospital's common room. There, he listened appreciatively with other patients and with their visiting relatives, while he was confined to his wheel chair. Only Catherine it was who could ease his spirit through all these wonderful things she kept offering him and, most of all, through her loyal presence.

Once he'd recovered, Catherine busied herself with her university studies and with Samaritan organizations bringing needed sustenance to city ghettos and impoverished, forgotten villages. Apart from the sporadic occasions when he, too, gave his time to these Samaritan projects, Paul found sufficient occupation while at his desk creating a pair of novellas. Two or three times a week, at his private club with a lively company of athletic comrades, he honed his sinewy capacities by careful exercise and by swimming as vigorously as his slowly reviving mastery allowed. And always there was the solace to his soul of Catherine's love for him and his for her—their authentic passion made new and vital in the privacies of night-time sensuality.

But in early April, exactly a year after the accident, the imagery of Claude came back to haunt him. Now it was that he began drinking heavily, consuming while he was alone or with one or two of his freewheeling comrades at local bars or in the private club where they shared membership large quantities of vodka and whiskey and scotch. Only gradually did he show the terrible effects of his addiction. Only then, because his excessive use of alcohol left him pale or sick or foul-tempered, did Catherine become aware that, with a willfulness insidious and immolating, he was throwing his life away.

All through those earlier weeks he'd appeared—resilient and versatile—to rebound from the disappointment of having to postpone the Scribner assignment that would draw them into the wider reaches of France. His quick-wittedness had discovered a new literary project, and leisure hours had rekindled his athletic prowess. While these ambivalent weeks kept translating their incremental values into fleet-seeming months, Catherine—busy with school and with altruistic missions—believed that Paul was revitalizing his powers by means of commendable activities. Once in a while, though, she detected, as if exuded from deep within his hard-bodied frame, the fumes of alcoholic beverages and a smoky tartness upon his breath. It was at those times that she gently advised him to go easy with his intake of liquor and cigarettes. But she accepted the tangy scent of him as part of his rugged masculinity.

Then, he started to be very ill. His intake of liquor became so heavy that it sapped him of the brawny health that, always before the day of the accident, his perfect physicality had easily possessed. No sooner had his addiction revealed itself to her, than she quickly devised ways to secure his rescue. For a time, she persuaded him to return to Dr. Girardot for more counseling, and with effectual urgency she alerted the bars and clubs he frequented not to serve him liquor. With equal efficiency, she took to discarding or hiding whatever bottles of vodka or scotch or whiskey she'd plundered from the cache he'd made of their apartment. He'd secured these bottles from the bars and clubs unknown to her and from seamy ghettos or alleys. So eager was she to save him and so disheartened by the effects his need for alcohol wrought against him, that she would not allow herself to flinch before the grueling pain which his body, without the alcohol, would have to endure. She hoped that, with no access to the liquor, he would consent to enter a clinic. There, he could reclaim his health and his accurate independence.

But it wasn't long before she became alarmed, even panicky, whenever, frenzied because of his need for vodka or whiskey or scotch and in search of the bottle that would stave his craving and that he would not find in the city or alleys which had closed themselves down at three or four in the morning, he tossed their rooms asunder. Because his initial search almost never yielded the longed-for bottle, he would begin his hunt again, hoping he would find in the rooms he'd already thrown awry a flask or half-full bottle he might have overlooked. Then it was, while kneeling upon the rich textures of their carpets to peer beneath a bed or behind a desk, that he, noticing her as if for the first time and as a possible quarry, would rise before her. His bronzed handsomeness, faded now and wretched, wore the pallor of the sick. It was as if the accursed soul that he felt himself to be was traveling through hell to re-live his transgressions. Once more, he would heave before him all their clothes and shoes—their mattress, even, and fresh bed linen.

Sometimes, during these bursts of violence, he would do frantic things like riffling through her wardrobe and ripping out the insides of their luggage. Still unsatisfied, he would tear away from her willowy blonde frame the dress and slip she was wearing. It was in these moments, especially, that the wave of anguish she'd been racing ahead of broke over her, leaving her bereft and abandoned. She was certain now that there was no hope for their lives and that she was utterly alone.

Yet, even in these moments, she would hold her voice low, as if she thought her pretended calm could soothe him back to his better self. Perhaps she pitied him for his vulnerability and for the anger that reflected her own, though she'd never expressed it so fiercely. Or, perhaps, she held her voice calm because she refused to find herself so afraid that she'd need to leave him. Whatever her reasons, she'd always try to talk Paul out of his fury, promising him that she would make things better for him. Occasionally, this promise was enough to bring him around. She would apply the ice packs about his forehead and upon his stomach, because that familiar remedy seemed to ease him.

On their carpeted floor, she would sit beside their bed and hold him in her arms until his agony temporarily faded.

One time, though, more terrifying to her than any other time, he cornered her while she was hurrying out of his study with a flask of scotch which, she guessed, a careless friend had given him or a cynical bartender had, for an inflated price, sold to him. His ghostly face—wild now and suddenly vicious—was transfixed by this imaginary enemy he held before him. With all the weight of his muscular frame, he slapped her and she fell out of consciousness.

When she found the room once more, she discovered, too, that he'd carried her to their bedroom. Carefully, he had placed her upon the bed. Now, he was the one administering a cool compress to her face and, seated by her, holding her hands tenderly. With a low, guttural moan and the raspy, awkward sobbing of a man not used to weeping, he whispered the fractured sounds of his compunction.

"I'm sorry," he strained to say. "I'm sorry for putting you through this mess."

She, aware of how destroyed he was, squeezed—as a sign of her forgiveness—the hands that held hers.

"We'll make everything better," she said.

Then, taking up this promise she held out to him, he kissed her hands fervently and went on crying.

"I'll try," he said. His voice was still fragmented with the sobbing he'd wanted to keep buried. "I'll try my best."

And so, for a time, as a proof of his love for her, he did make an effort to return to his writing and to their more sedate friends and to a healthy regimen of exercise at his club. But, though he willed himself to reduce his intake of liquor, he could not stop drinking completely. Nevertheless, through new habits and a revitalized will, he—for the most part—drank in socially permissible ways.

Yet, even in this temporary return to acceptable days, she found that something essential in him was missing. Something had died. Whatever marvelous spirit had worked as a fuse to his heroic-seeming energies had left him. Vulnerable now rather than charismatic, he appeared to her eyes a battered manliness struggling to find his way to new, fortifying possibilities.

On some brooding days, in thrall to the haunted stillness come hovering upon him, he appeared to be utterly lost and lost, as well, to her. Only then, fearful of what might lie ahead for them, would she discover her own bitter thoughts assailing her. They left her to solitary battles and restless nights. Now, fitfully in the beginning and then more insistently, she wondered whether she would, after all, not be able to save him.

BITTERNESS

After their daughters were killed in the bombing that summer, André and Denise Rouart thought of them every day for all the long years that remained to themselves. They remembered the happy times when they shared with Dominique and Arielle days that flashed with quick life and spontaneous laughter. As good parents, they took care always to guide them to the wholesome peers they allowed them to befriend. In every season their daughters belonged to a circle of agile, keen-minded boys and good-natured, confident girls who were their own age and shared mutual interests. When summer came, André and Denise sailed with the two of them across a wind-swept burnished sea. They swam with them in sun-raveled waters and rode, lithe and merry, upon waves that were spume-flecked and barreling. With a group of life-loving friends (their daughters' trustworthy school-mates, along with their own proven-loyal circle of parents), they entered the quicksilver motion of a village fair. Agreeable mentors in those summers of surprise, they sometimes guided their girls through exhilarating climbs to higher hills. Once, as the four of them ascended proficiently to a ledge as smooth as it was wide, Arielle and Dominique saw and heard, as for the first time because so near and kinetic, the rapid wing-beat of a glaucous gull. There, on that same ledge, they also observed sun-washed cumulous clouds hovering by a cliff above them and for one remarkable instant understood as well the equilibrium of the azure sky.

André and Denise most often remembered how they had taught their daughters to ride a horse. That year and in all the visits afterward, they lived in his parents' large house in the midst of their Provençal farmland and vineyards. Only nine and eight years old, respectively, Dominique and Arielle soon became supple and alert and proficient. As they themselves were, so their girls were dressed protectively in hardhat and chin harness, in long-sleeved sweatshirt and comfortable breeches, and in boots and gloves. Their daughters learned well, for instance, that one sits with the weight of one's body in the center of the saddle, thereby allowing one's hip joint to be open and one's legs correctly positioned as close as possible around the horse's sides. What a lift to the spirit it was to watch wiry Dominique mounted on a sleek-brown Dartmoor pony. She properly relaxed her arms at the shoulder and elbow, so that they could move with the movement of the horse's head. On that day, and on all the other days when she was attuned to André's effective supervision, she held her hands correctly, with palms facing each other and thumbs uppermost. Without using her arms, she clasped the reins by wrapping her fingers around them and almost closing her hands to make a fist. It was as though arms and reins belonged to the horse, the better to follow its motion.

"When I grow up," she told her father on an afternoon when she worked with him and her grandmother in the stables grooming three rugged Camargue stallions, "I want to take care of horses."

"You are a true Rouart," André said. In that moment, while he beamed with happiness at Dominique, he looked almost as young as when he had met her mother during their student days in the Sorbonne. Only the flecks of gray in his dark, curly hair and beard suggested that, in spite of his trim girth and healthy muscularity, he had already entered his thirties.

Mathilde Rouart also smiled broadly at her granddaughter. In an earlier hour she had watched her riding spiritedly along the wide road on the north side of their property that was flanked by strawberry trees and lavender fields and the greenness of undulating hills. She was pleased now to observe the firm yet gentle strokes the older of her granddaughters was applying with a currycomb to the gray coat of one of these stallions. With perfect circular motions, the girl was removing dried mud and loose hairs from the horse's coat, even as she was massaging its skin. Mathilde was also pleased to hear her granddaughter choose a future life that would keep her on farmland rather than in the city.

"You will take care of horses wisely," the big-boned woman said, "because you love them."

In that same week, Denise was favorably impressed when she saw her ethereal Arielle poised erect and responsive upon a beautiful Welsh Mountain pony. The pony itself was a blend of palomino spirit and docility. Bright girl that she was, Arielle walked the agreeable horse by using her leg nearest Denise, the good-natured instructor around whom in a circle she was riding, to create a superior forward gait. She used her other leg to hold the muscular hindquarters in place. The horse nodded its head to balance itself, and the girl sat attentive and companionable in the saddle, so that her body in synchronous rhythm absorbed the horse's impulsion.

"I love this pony more than any other horse that has carried me," Arielle told her mother on a radiant July afternoon as they watched the Welsh horse grazing in the paddock nearest to the home field on the Rouarts' land.

"Why do you love this particular horse?" Denise asked her. "There are many horses that move as swiftly and some even faster."

Arielle paused, at first a little shy to explain her preference. With her blonde hair and light skin and her sensitive analysis of things, she was a young version of her mother and of Emmanuelle Thériault, her maternal grandmother.

"I love him for his beauty," she said, finding now the words that explained her affinity for the horse. "I love all things that are beautiful."

Other mornings in succeeding years were also sumptuous with the bright colors of vineyards and orchards and the tangy scent of clean barns and stables, of ample paddock and granary, and of burnished leather saddlery. While continuing to offer his parental skills as an instructor, André (who, like Denise, was an excellent horse-rider) found an immense pleasure in coaching plucky Dominique to bring her horse, a chestnut Caspian, to trot. A clever rider, she squeezed both of her legs actively against the horse's sides and softened her hands forward so that the horse felt free to increase the pace and go forward as well into the trot.

There were also afternoons when the murmuring chant of the wind and the sun-glow greenness of undulating fields and distant hills and the fleecy nature of the azure sky influenced Arielle's elation. Sometimes, within these afternoons, she discovered the heart of her pleasure in asking her horse, a bay-colored Morgan, to go forward into a canter on the left rein. She sat deep and pressed her inside leg (the leg nearest Denise, who on that day was her instructor) on an Atherstone girth, the fine leather band contoured about the belly of the horse to keep the saddle in place. In the next instant, she asked more actively with a squeeze or a nudge of her outside leg back behind the girth.

On still other days both fleet and summery, it was wonderful to glance at their daughters riding together. Dominque's almond-shaped eyes and smooth-olive skin resembled those of her father. Translated to her girlhood, they granted her an exotic comeliness. At that same time, fair Arielle was a contrasting radiance. Lithe and diligent in that kinetic moment, their well-trained daughters were mounted on roan-colored Saddlebreds. Gamely, they raced each other around a turf-laden practice track. Their horses lengthened out their body and neck and fully extended each leg as it powered forward over the ground. Riding with commendable ease and with the seat taken out of the saddle, they tucked their upper body in behind their horse's neck and extended their arms forward as with each stride the horse stretched his neck forward. That day, they were riding with shorter stirrups, the better for their weight to be lifted out of the saddle. Through the reins they were always keeping a contact with the horse's mouth in order to help balance him.

Many decades later, when they had entered their nineties, André and Denise reminded each other that those years with their daughters had brought them their best happiness.

But in 1915, during the second year of the Great War in Europe when they were a successfully married couple in their thirties, André and Denise lost their daughters—sweet-natured Dominique, just turned thirteen years old, and the younger Arielle, who was a dainty twelve. Having lost them, they lost all of the happiness their earlier lives as emerging artists had granted them.

On that morning, they had hurried away from their studio apartment in Paris, because rumor had warned them that the Germans would soon begin bombing the city. While they were on their way to the safe retreat they believed they would find at the home of André's parents in Sault-en-Provence, aerial bombings overtook their well-organized group. They and their daughters were sharing with three fellow artists, their wives, and their five children their own Mercedes and the two Bentleys which their agent had lent them. For these friends and their children, André's parents would also be providing refuge.

Hours later, when the group reached the village of St-Auban-sur-Ouvèze, even Denise—with her cautious realism—began to feel safe. Because André was driving their Mercedes at a fast clip, he influenced their friends who were riding behind them in the two Bentleys to hasten with steady momentum along the undulating road that descended into the wide valley. All around them bronze wheat fields glowed, and the mellow scent of lavender caressed the air. Cobalt green hills kept rising in the distance, and orange-tinted apricot orchards peered occasionally through the summer haze. It was then, while they noticed this dazzle of colors, that the exploding bombs tossed their cars asunder. The aerial barrage killed everyone in their traveling group except the two of them. Before they lost consciousness, their eyes searched frantically beneath the smoke that reeked of gasoline and other explosives. Then their gaze paused upon the chrome pieces of their group's automobiles that were strewn along the road and the blood that kept spilling from the crumpled bodies of their friends. Now they saw their daughters. They looked as though they were sleeping peacefully, because their bodies were still intact. Weeks later, after André had prodded him for an answer, a medical officer explained that the shrapnel that killed Arielle had left a tiny, bloodstained hole just above her right ear. The bullets that killed Dominique had blown out the walls of her heart, though the riddled jacket covering her concealed the gaping wound to her body.

Left critically wounded, André and Denise endured many surgeries and four months in two hospitals. At this time they learned that, because of her injuries, Denise would not be able to have another child. Eventually, their physicians assured them that they had recovered from their wounds. On that day they left their hospital quarters dismayed. Even after all that had happened to them, they would have to go on living.

"We are obliged to go on living," André told her as gently as he could, in that first hard week when the hospital was no longer their refuge. "If we can stay alive, then we can build again after the war."

He was guiding her to what he believed was a reasonable path. But, as she listened in polite silence, she told herself that—behind his strong-minded effort to rouse her hope—he thought as she did. A future without their daughters could never bring back happiness.

So began their long descent into hell. Only intermittently, while they were caught up in bringing succor to others or in exploring the mysteries of painting, sculpting and photography, did they forget their despair.

Yet, paradoxically, it was the war that also saved them. As soon as their wounds had healed at the end of that autumn of 1915, they joined the fight against the Germans. As an infantryman serving in the French Tenth Army, André helped to re-take the town of Souchez and miles of German trenches in the Arras sector. Afterward, with an equally brute willfulness, he survived the onslaughts of Messines, Cambrai, and Verdun.

In the spring of 1916 he learned of the brave death of his older brother, Martin. A first lieutenant with the French Fifth Army, Martin had fallen at Ypres in Belgium. His brother had been so hopeful on that August morning nearly two years earlier when he left the ample vineyards and magnificent farm fields within picturesque Sault-en-Provence. Ever since his boyhood, he had loved and nurtured those fields.

Vigorous and patriotic he now appeared as he laughed away his parents' trepidation and casually accepted the humble awe and affection of the old and loyal field hands who stood with the senior Rouarts at the familiar west gate of the expansive property. They watched him maintaining carefully his show of courage, poised as he was on the front seat of a horse-drawn carriage which was already hurrying down the road that would bring him to the embarkation point in nearby Valréas, where conscriptees were required to report. Brawny, tough-spirited and self-reliant, he believed he would do everything that needed to be done. After acquitting himself capably in the grim, necessary business, he would return-- probably within a matter of a few months. Already, in the five years before the war, he had earned a substantial share of the farm fields and vineyards he had diligently cultivated with his parents.

So André, still holding himself free of the war and its battlefields, was told by those same patient and hard-working field hands in that October of 1914, when he and Denise and their daughters were visiting his affectionate parents in the midst of a harvest splendor. Then, while waves of brotherly regard swept over him, he remembered with pensive nostalgia the quiet, advisory meetings at which Martin and he had privately shared each other's counseling perceptions. He remembered, too, their springtime fishing excursions and the partying quartet their strong friendship inspired—he with Denise and Martin with Lisette. She was the neighboring farm girl whom he'd intended, upon his homeward return, to marry. Would they ever again savor such self-affirming days? He had wondered, sometimes at night waking in distracted apprehension beside his fair Denise, who remained sleeping in the peaceful clasp of solace and with no premonition of their imminent losses.

Years later it cheered him, perhaps because the news so clearly illustrated the reliable skills and leaderly prowess he associated with his brother, to learn how well Martin wielded a breach-loading magazine rifle and more often a flintlock musket, which he could load in merely a minute. (This, he heard not from the field hands, but from a rugged lieutenant—Martin's best friend—who had survived the war.) For nearly two years his brother advanced with soldierly expertise and dauntless grit across all the battlefields to which his singular fate had assigned him. But, no matter how grave the dangers pursuing him, he found himself, in those quiet moments after a perilous skirmish or a savage offensive or decimating trench warfare, secretly rejoicing in the life that still throbbed within him. In these moments he allowed himself to think about the familiar road that would lead him to Sault on the far-flung day he expected to return home. It was a wonderful road that climbed and climbed so high that, arriving upon its crescent, he could see once more the tidy lavender fields.

Stirred by a softer wind, they appeared as an array of purple stipples swaying as if floating at the foot of lush mountains. This essential dream he mentioned in all his letters home-- even in the last one, which he wrote only hours before he was to reach Ypres with his brave unit.

Not until after the war did André learn of the deaths of his fearless parents and of their wild courage. A hatred of the enemy and a desire for vengeance drove them at the last to shoot two lieutenants and three corporals who had overtaken their farmstead with a cadre of other soldiers. All of them were using it as their temporary barracks. While they were awaiting new orders from their commandant, these Germans treated his parents and field hands as prisoners. With a weary insolence they intended on the day they were called back to the battlefield to kill their docile captives. Compelled to act as servants and sometimes as medical assistants to the Germans, his mother and his father as well as their loyal staff of ten had at first complied with even their smallest demands. They made themselves as agreeable as they could not only because their lives were imperiled and because they would be instantly shot for the smallest infraction. They also complied with their enemy because they were secretly harboring a wounded French aviator. They were hiding him within the upper floor of the large granary that stood at the southern rim of their abundant wheat fields a tenth of a mile from the home buildings.

Flying a Sopwith Dolphin, this pilot—Laurent Audran—had shot down two German planes during a fierce aerial combat over Paris. In that encounter, his plane sustained some damage to its cockpit and its motor, and he was seriously injured. German ammunition had ripped holes through his left shoulder and his left leg. His left arm dangling and raw pain invading all of his body, he nonetheless managed to bring his craft away from the fiery scene of battle and into Provençal farmlands. There, years earlier during his boyhood and with his parents who were prosperous clothiers, he had often spent a few weeks of each summer. Now, unable to return to his air base and unwilling to bring harm to city dwellings should his plane crash or explode, he felt reasonably assured that he would receive from the good people of those villages first-aid and food and shelter. Wracked by searing disablement and sensing himself drifting in and out of consciousness even as he noticed his plane losing altitude, he willed himself through well-honed tough-mindedness and superb skill as a flyer to land his malfunctioning craft many miles from the city. He found himself at the foot of autumn's dark green hills and crimson-and-gold trees and not far from abundant farm fields waiting to be harvested.

The crash of the plane, all of its acrid, smoky flare and rising flames a half-mile or so from the Rouarts' property, drew to it several of the men and women who were then tending the vineyards and the wheat fields. They hurried to the scene on horseback or in carts drawn by stallions. There, two hundred feet from the burning Dolphin lay strong-hearted Laurent. With lacerating pain, he had crawled out of the cockpit and away to safer ground. Through the sheer force of his will, he remained conscious thereafter. Lifting him gently into one of the carts and swaddling him in blankets, the field hands—led by old Melvil and his wife Annie—brought him directly to the upper floor of the large granary. This building stood tall and appropriate at the boundary of the wheat fields that these men and women were in the midst of harvesting. They believed that there, inside the granary, Laurent would have a better chance to remain undetected. If the Germans sent their soldiers to reconnoiter the area for deserters or for wounded enemies, as they occasionally did, even such heartless adversaries might accept a granary for the thing it was made to be: a storehouse brimming with the earth's plenty.

After reaching the second floor of the granary, Melvil and his brother François had placed Laurent in a clean, comforting bed. Then, with matronly adeptness, Annie and Honorée (François's wife) began to bathe the pilot's grimy face and fevered body and to give him cool water to solace his parched lips. At this time two other field hands hurried to tell the news of the pilot to André's parents, large-souled Eugène and Mathilde Rouart, the employers to whom they were so devoted. Once safely hidden, the lieutenant began a well-monitored recovery. For the senior Rouarts immediately sent for an aged doctor who served their village well. With simple yet effective skill, he set in its initial stages the repair of the young man's bullet-torn shoulder and his fractured leg.

For three weeks and more, the Rouarts nursed the tall and stalwart lieutenant. His dark-skinned handsomeness gave him the look of a Spaniard and reminded them so much of their first-born son, whom the war had stolen from them. Within the artfulness of their homely skills and a well-managed secrecy from outsiders, they and the men and women who for years had shared with them the duties of the farm land and vineyards provided for Laurent days and days of spotless refuge and reviving baths, nutritious meals and a restful bed. All the while they harbored with quiet diligence his rugged presence—there, on the upper floor of the ample granary, within the living quarters under the eaves of the double-sloped roof. That nineteenth-century brick structure overlooked the abundant southerly fields and, staid and methodical, observed the far-distant home buildings.

During this time, they took the precaution of concealing the burnt remnants of the plane. They covered it and the seared foliage around it with thick brush and the fallen branches of pine trees. Should a patrol of Germans discover the wrecked plane in spite of their camouflaging efforts, the Rouarts were prepared to show them a fresh grave and convince them that the shrouded body, respectfully buried within grounds deemed sacred by the local church, belonged to the downed pilot. (In truth, the grave was home to a frail young hobo whom the Rouarts had, because of their compassion for a good human being blighted by want and disappointment, offered food and clothing and shelter. He worked light jobs on their property whenever his health permitted, and they accepted him without reservation as one of their extended family. Their kindness gave him two years that he might not otherwise have enjoyed. But not even their care of him or the prudent attention of the village physician could cure his heart's terminal malady.)

Only a month or two since this frail, unfortunate man had passed away, sturdy but wounded Laurent Audran had come into their lives. For two weeks and more, the senior Rouarts felt blessed with this gift of a son who was, they told themselves, as a twin to their equally brave Martin. Laurent, even more than their introverted André, embodied the husky inflections and matter-of-fact assurance and casual openness of their beloved and first-born heir.

One especially memorable afternoon, they shared a furtive half-hour with him. They had entered the granary quite naturally while carrying, in a horse-drawn wagon, baskets of apples picked from the trees in their orchard. On this day the young lieutenant, who had come to regard them as his second parents, made them an extraordinary promise.

"When I am well again and after the war is over, I shall teach both of you to fly," he said. "Then, you will be my co-pilots, and we shall know the adventure of the sky together."

The elder Rouarts beamed, happy in their anticipation of such an episode.

"I'll be your mechanic, as well," Eugène said. "I can take apart any engine or motor and put it back together."

Laurent smiled heartily, sharing to the full the clipped inflections of this momentary happiness.

"You'll be the best," he said.

Mathilde, usually taciturn, on this day permitted herself a modulated exuberance, chary though she was of having the Germans discover them there.

"We'll have wonderful times," she said. Her motherly eyes once more perceived Laurent as a God-sent third son. His remarkable biography, entwined as it was with courage and daring, would now and hereafter include her husband and herself. "You'll show us a new road to heaven, surely."

The two men, hearing her elation, laughed in low, husky tones which were moored to their need to be unobtrusive while Laurent hid in the granary.

For many days they were unobtrusive.

But on the fifteenth day of Laurent's convalescence, a German squad of seventeen men, exhausted and bitter in what would be the final year of the war, overtook the Rouarts' farmstead. They compelled its inhabitants to house them and feed them and ease their more visible wounds. All their demands they expressed in the curt undercurrents of menace.

For several days, harnessed as they were to the constant danger of Laurent's being discovered, the Rouarts acceded to their enemies' demands with an efficient courtesy that pleased the tattered unit's commanding officer, Major Helmut von Trotta. With a tense secrecy, they continued to care for the brave and convalescing pilot. Well did they also tend the seventeen enemies who held them as prisoners. They provided for them spotless housing and reviving baths, nutritious meals and comfortable beds. With quiet diligence, they tended their wounds or other ailments. Nor did they neglect to open their wine cellar to these hardened men, whose casual and youthful handsomeness the war had brusquely marred, replacing it with a gaunt brutality or eerie grimness or a mute self-loathing. Invoking still the rigid disciplines which their training had taught them to master, these Germans never allowed themselves to drink so heavily that they would become carelessly raucous or recklessly sadistic or, in any other way, take leave of their militant codes. Sharp-witted and keen-eyed always, they had decided, after these first days when all was going well, that they would not kill these assiduous French farmers who were so competently serving them.

For nine days they dwelled there, arbitrary and predominant. They were awaiting new orders and, in the last year of the war, more aware than ever before that victory had turned her face away from them. But on the morning of the tenth day, two from their group came upon the French pilot, who was still incapacitated by his grievous wounds. Yet always he kept his pistol nearby, should he need it to thwart an enemy intruder. While they were here on the Rouarts' farmland, these Germans had often reconnoitered the area around the granary and more than once had entered the vast storehouse. But they had never discovered the concealed man. What they saw were huge bins of golden grain and tightly bound bales of wheat and rye waiting their turn to be threshed.

On the morning that they confronted at last the intrepid Laurent, his left shoulder in a sling and his right, slightly elevated leg in a cast, the two German sentries were returning on horseback from their posts by the south entrance to the property. There, the road hastened toward the buildings that housed their squadron. By chance, they noticed Eugène, François, and Honorée, who were (with gait efficient and natural) entering the granary. Having emerged from a horse-drawn carriage, each of them carried what appeared from a distance to be large baskets of apples gathered in that early hour from the pendulous branches of autumn trees, which stood protuberant and teeming in the orchard nearby. However, the apples occupied only the circumference of an upper lid placed near the top of each basket. Hidden adeptly below the lid, within a wide and deep interior, were fresh linen and blankets and steaming food.

Their horses with cantering energy bringing them swiftly to that location, the sentries hurried into the granary, where they expected to find the three French persons whom they had minutes earlier sighted from the distance. But Monsieur Rouart and his relatives were nowhere to be found. So the Germans waited until François and Honorée cautiously descended from the living quarters that were nearly invisible beneath the eaves of the roof. Only then did the sentries notice how smoothly the door opening to an ascending stairway and to the sequestered loft blended with the surrounding wall.

Then it was that the sentries confronted them. Pointing their Lugers at their heads, they signaled the startled couple to stay silent and, re-entering the passage, lead them to the source of the mystery. Once they had returned to the stairs, though, François and Honorée cried out, thinking to alert Eugène and Laurent. Immediately, the Germans shot them and hurried into the secret chamber while rapidly firing their weapons. They killed both Monsieur Rouart and Laurent, but not before they themselves were felled by Rouart's rifle and by the aviator's accurate pistol.

Not until a half-hour later did the Germans discover what had happened. At that time, five or six of their soldiers were patrolling the area while they rode the Rouarts' stallions and palominos with superior ease. No sooner had they reached the granary, than they noticed the sentries' waiting mounts as well as the idle wagon and draught horse. For the granary stood too far from the home buildings to reveal at that location whatever activities ignited its presence. Now discovering all, the sentries rode swiftly back to the main buildings they had been using as their barracks.

From her bedroom window on the second floor of her home, Mrs. Rouart saw them coming, brooding and grim-faced and murderous. With Cécile (Honorée's and François's nine-year-old granddaughter), she had been giving the room its daily cleaning while recounting to the sober, good-natured girl her latest visit with Laurent.

Minutes afterward, from beneath her window, she overheard the tallest of these horse-riding soldiers telling all with concise and understated inflections to his commanding officer, Major Helmut von Trotta. From this tall soldier's blunt and hurried words, she learned that these enemies had killed her husband and killed Laurent, who had become to them in these few weeks as their own son. They had also killed strong-minded François and Honorée.

Even though her husband had told her about the Germans' efficiency as murderers, she found herself vaguely surprised by their dispatch in rounding up three of the loyal men who for years had worked with her husband and herself in the wheat fields and vineyards, as well as in the orchards and other farm fields. How quickly these Germans shot them. Right after that, and beneath her very window, they shot Melvil, Fernand, Yvan and Émile.

Now the soldiers ran into the house. At once and with blunt finality she pushed petite Cécile under the bed and took from a secret place in her dresser a loaded Beretta handgun. Hearing the soldiers clamber up the stairs to overtake all those French who had harbored one of Germany's most formidable enemies, she hurried forward to meet them. At the moment they reached the threshold of her room with pistols readied to fire, she shot the three soldiers again and again, two lieutenants and a corporal. Only vaguely did she feel the jagged harshness of a wound to her right arm. But the impact of the bullet threw her against her bedpost.

Standing massive and formidable yet, she noticed Major von Trotta entering the room. He was aiming his Luger toward her head, which was covered by a white turban to protect the cleanliness of her gray-brown hair. She noticed, too, his battered face, which had been made sinister a year earlier by the discoloration of burnt flesh and caustic scars. His calculating eyes (dark brown and imperious) studied her with a mixture of hatred and interest and grudging respect. For this middle-aged, overweight farm wife had, without flinching and with flawless ability, killed three of his best men. It was, no doubt, his Prussian temperament and razor-sharp training which allowed him to pause in ambivalent admiration before the cold-heartedness of her fury. Perhaps he would have spared her life, not because she was a woman—he and his men had casually killed women belonging to the enemy. But never had he observed in any of them such deadly and effective instincts. In this instance of her killing big-boned and lethal adversaries, Madame Rouart represented characteristics that his militant life had taught him to emulate.

Still he aimed his handgun at her. With blunt appraisal he spoke the plain words which for him gave to the moment a passing significance.

"You are a good soldier, Madam," he said. "You have killed three of our best men."

She answered him as plainly.

"I would have killed more, if I'd had the bullets I needed."

Perceiving in her manner and in her words a steely disrespect of her danger, he was not displeased.

"Spoken like a true soldier," he said, "...a well-trained killer."

As if testing her mettle further and moving directly before her to observe her responses with cold accuracy, he now told her bleak news. While peering from her window minutes earlier, she had overheard only a portion of it.

"But we have killed even more of yours—all that we could find, including your husband and your relatives and friends. They had enjoyed this heaven you call your Provençal farm lands long enough."

Still she did not flinch.

"You are mistaken, Major," she answered him. "Heaven watches from a distance. It is not here. You are here. And wherever your kind is, there can be only hell."

Saying so, she spat directly into his face.

Stunned even against his will for a second, he watched her watching him. Her bitter face revealed her contempt and her hatred. Then, while her spittle dripped down his left cheek onto his beribboned jacket, he shot her through her forehead. Her body buckled and dropped upon the immaculately brocaded carpet that she and the women who always assisted her had woven many seasons before.

So Honorée's granddaughter lived to tell. Petite and agile, she escaped an hour later from her hiding place beneath the large bed and from the unattended house. By then, the Germans were scouring the distant area for any field hand or neighboring farmer whom they instantly shot.

For two days afterward, while the bodies of the dead lay strewn across all the places where they had fallen, the squad of soldiers went on enjoying the food and liquor and housing which their years of war had, for the most part, denied them. On the third day the new orders that the Germans had awaited from their command post arrived. Each man found himself assigned to distant and unforgiving battlefields. Before leaving, though, and in reprisal of their loss of five patriotic comrades, they destroyed the Rouarts' property. They grenade-bombed the farm fields, the orchards and the vineyards, as well as the houses and the granary, the stables and barns and winepress. Always, until the Germans killed them, the Rouarts and their assistants had carefully nurtured their property.

In those war years, there were other kinds of losses, though not so grievous or in any way irrevocable. Sorrowful it was for Denise, nonetheless, even as she found herself grateful for their safety, that her father, a wealthy Thériault and renowned gemologist, and her dutiful mother had left their beloved Paris and relocated to Québec with their son (her keen, spirited brother, Alain, at that time only thirteen and too young for soldiering). They had wanted her to accompany them, since André was away at war. But in a hurried note she'd written from the dangerous boundaries of the front lines where she served tirelessly as a nurse, she had refused their invitation. Instead, she had chosen to remain near the battlefields to help the wounded and to ease the agony of the dying. With quiet tenacity, she continued to struggle against her still-muted death wish.

After the war ended, André and Denise made their way to Québec and spent some convalescing months with her parents and her brother. Now, in extemporaneous moments which subverted hard-won detachment, the unalterable truth of having lost forever their two beautiful daughters came with grim cruelty to watch their eerie stillness before the sight of elementary school children singing with dulcet simplicity in a churchly choir or romping airily in September on an Indian-summer beach, negotiating the trajectories of a large, multi-colored ball. Its wheeling sphere and the frolicking children became an after-glow for the dazzled eye. On other days they watched the raucous merriment of boys and girls pushing yellow leaves along the meandering gutters of an October road. During winter's snowy briskness, they observed a long-limbed nine-year-old boy and his two dainty sisters, probably five and seven years old, standing with a quiet glee outside a department store window which displayed a tinseled Christmas tree and a medley of beribboned packages. Before the sight of these life-loving children, André and Denise understood all over again that no beneficent Spirit would bring back their daughters. Nor would there be a miracle to bring back André's parents and his brother and the relatives and friends whom they had also loved and respected.

Because they believed that they were destroyed, they accepted with numb acquiescence the hospitality of Denise's parents in Québec. But as the months passed and while new energies sparked their days, they found themselves gradually returning to their art. Then, in the spring of 1919, they made their way to New York. Living in a Greenwich Village loft, they gave private art lessons to the matrons and daughters of eminent families. Without charging a fee, they sometimes offered encouraging counsel to young, struggling artists who requested their watchful guidance. It was in this period that they created nurturing friendships with the Marsdens and the Courtneys and with other favorable persons drawn from the teeming life of New York. Through them, they secured many commissions for landscape paintings that explored the ambiguities of city streets and country retreats and for portraits which discovered understated accuracies. Now each day reinforced their decision to go on with their lives.

In this period Joseph Courtney, who was a junior partner in his father's international corporation of lawyers, and his wife Nancy—whose father (Everett Marsden) had carried forward the Marsdens' long-established success with global businesses in iron, oil, and steel—invited André and Denise to bring their teacherly presence to summer programs which taught disadvantaged orphans and public school boys and girls. The school was located in that portion of Everett's property in Newport, Rhode Island, which was given over to granary and barns, stables and paddock and fields. There were three fine cottages there, as well, where lived the astute foreman, his able crew, and their equally adept families. With mentorly aptitudes, volunteers devoted several days from their own vacations to teach to boys and girls athletic games as well as classes in the fine arts, in woodworking and industrial technology, and in science and mathematics. Several volunteers taught the children to ride a horse with limberly assurance. Sometimes these students were nine or ten years old and sometimes thirteen or fourteen. All of them came from impoverished backgrounds.

That in this Samaritan effort André and Denise were joining a generous cadre of professionals was, Joseph and Nancy believed, all to the good. There was something life affirming in this effort to help needy children. Surely, by helping these boys and girls, the Rouarts would find a reason to believe in the future.

"You have so many talents that you can share with these children," Nancy said. Her erect poise, genteel manner, and auburn-haired femininity never failed to please the Rouarts. She put them in mind of their own special time when the world had promised them a share of its happiness.

"We'll teach them how to swim and sail and how to build fine things with wood," Joseph said. A tall, dark-haired ruggedness, he had fought bravely in the war. But he did not care to speak of that experience. For this, the Rouarts liked him especially, understanding that he too carried ghosts with him. They saw his casual affability as his own stay against confusion.

The youngsters, though at first shy or anxious or uncertain, gradually became comfortable with the wise and patient coaching of André and Denise. Theirs was the healthy experience of enjoying days and weeks away from the crowded drabness of an orphanage or a Providence ghetto or from the working class paucities of obscure Middletown streets or from Boston's volatile Bay area. These children often came to their summer experience disheartened or sullen, angry or suspicious, so battered had they been by poverty's lacerating deprivations. Yet after a week or two, they permitted themselves to be eager and cooperative, good-hearted and hopeful.

During these restorative days and weeks, they stayed a mile away at an exemplary youth center, with its precise arrangement of Romanesque buildings. Once, those buildings had served as a seminary where young men, pious and studious, prepared to become Jesuits, even as they labored in the expansive farm fields there that supplied them and the city's poor with nourishing food. This center, which was as pristine as it was Spartan, stood in sight of the sea. It was amply endowed by corporate sponsors and by private benefactors such as the Courtneys and Marsdens. All of them were affiliated with an ecumenical group of churches, including Newport's Saint John the Evangelist. Instructors from local private and public schools and volunteer physicians and nurses ably administered the fine programs which guided these needy youngsters through lessons in swimming and sailing, fishing and canoeing and biking. Twice a week these vibrant, quick-witted children and adolescents came to Everett's splendid horse farm. There, in groups of fifteen, they attended each day's morning or afternoon riding session. It was an activity both communal and leaderly which fostered their self-discipline and confidence.

Though they were accomplished riders, André and Denise chose not to join those volunteers who were teaching their pupils how to ride a horse. They were chary of calling back to themselves an activity they had enjoyed with their daughters. Instead, they offered to train a group of students in the art of photography. On Wednesdays and Saturdays, they would saunter along the crisply mowed path that guided them to the tawny sands of the Marsdens' private beach or through a green-gold, southerly meadow behind Everett Marsden's house. Sometimes the Rouarts brought them to Middletown or to Nantucket. Early in the morning, as judicious instructors, they guided their students to express through the searching lens of a Leica their unique impressions of the world—its ambiguities and fluxions and revelations. This art of photography both complemented and intrigued the willingness of these boys and girls to explore and record within the always surprising earth an instant's teasing information. Coaxed by André and Denise, they sought out its variable implications and its bruising factuality, as well as its sorrow, joy and accusation. They also sought its bold ellipses and its momentary flash of truth.

Two girls in the group brought to their view of things a genuine originality. They were sisters whose parents had died when the factory in which they worked burned down. From time to time during these summer weeks Denise and André advised these enterprising young individuals while accompanying them through many productive photo sessions. Claudette and Julie Serrault discovered a measure of truth in their awareness of other people. Their understanding (tentative and evolving) of human ambiguity was often anchored to a moment's spontaneous revelation or to a complicated subtext or to an unobtrusive recognition of the fallible or vulnerable. Sometimes, Claudette—the elder of the sisters who was lithe and titian-haired and twelve years old—was drawn to the carefree human gaze tinctured with tenuous defiance or to the rugged muscularity validating its integrity in arduous labor or to the sweet-faced contentment of a child. Her camera's eye— which reflected her own tough spirit—also recorded the strong arms of a middle-aged nurse guiding to a wheelchair a scar-faced young man. This veteran of the recent war was brown-haired and big-boned and gauntly pale, as he leaned on a cane. His frailty was unable by itself or even with a cane to negotiate an effective mobility. How adeptly

Claudette's lens caught the afternoon sunlight streaming upon that pathway in a public Middletown park, so that its flow appeared to rise from the wounded soldier. The scarred face and maimed body revealed an italic and formidable reality.

Just as remarkable was her photograph of a plump, motherly woman frolicking within that same Middletown park with her three children, the oldest no more than seven. With her, they sat on a large blanket amidst summer-crisp grass beneath a shady elm, while with her fruitful abundance she went on feeding peaches and plums and watermelon to her delighted offspring. She was lighthearted because at recess from chores and in this hour lolling with her two sons and her daughter within the comforts of August greenery.

Compelling, too, was ten-year-old Julie's photograph of hardworking, brawny fishers unloading their splendid haul of bluefish in a Nantucket harbor. At the same time, a one-armed, grizzled fellow with seaman's cap and haunted face looked on from an isolated corner of the wharf. As persons outside windows look on, so did he peer warily at the fellowship that had abandoned him. Possibly, he was at the same time imagining a scene from the happier past come back as ghostly apparition to haunt him.

On a day in mid-August, when Denise decided that she would in the evening suggest to André that they adopt Claudette and Julie, they had observed the girls once again compose through photography articulate impressions of the various images inhabiting the Marsden property.

On this afternoon Julie photographed a decisive moment that involved an aged farmwoman assisting a young veterinarian as he tended a sick pony in the Marsdens' ample stables. An hour later, with camera held poised at the edge of a viridian bluff, Claudette recorded in the distance below her, along the silver sands of the beach, a ten-year-old girl with saffron hair and balletic arms and legs. She proceeded to record her from a panoramic, tilting angle. While this girl's long, slim back concealed her identity from the camera's eye, she was chasing a large, multi-colored kite whose drawstring had escaped her too-delicate grasp and was flying now, the opulent kite, with the seaward wind. Always, the girl kept chasing the kite, as she watched it hasten toward a colony of gulls soaring, white and imperious, above the rankled waves of the ocean.

In that same hour, at the close of their photography session, Julie asked Denise the question that had been on her mind for many weeks.

"Are you somebody's mother?"

They were moving briskly along the path that would bring them to the south lawn of the Marsden property and to the large canopied tents where they would enjoy a catered lunch with other students and teachers.

Denise did not answer her. Instead, she gave her attention to a flock of white herring gulls flying down from the brightness of the sky toward the sea that stirred restlessly in the distance not far beyond the south lawn.

Imagining that Denise had not heard her words, Julie spoke them once more.

"Are you somebody's mother?"

Understanding now that she could not elude the question, Denise offered her a brief reply, even as they continued to make their way briskly toward the tents.

"No," she said.

The dark-skinned girl permitted herself a careful smile. Her jet-black hair, cool brown eyes, and willowy form suggested that in three or four years, when she became a young woman, she was going to be a confident beauty. Today, though, she held in check whatever assurance she had earned from her hard experience of life. So she summoned new words even more carefully. She wanted Denise and André to be her parents and the parents of her sister.

"Do you want to be somebody's mother?"

"No," Denise said. Suddenly she had grown tense, and her answer sounded harsher than she meant it to be.

Julie studied her quietly. Then, because Denise's reply did not satisfy her, she asked still another question.

"Well, who do you want to be?"

"I am already the person I want to be," Denise said. "I am a wife and a painter. And I am your teacher."

They had arrived at the place where they would take lunch with Claudette and André and with ten other students and their instructors. Quickly, Denise brought Julie to a group of her friendly peers who proceeded to draw her into their excited conversation. Only when she joined André and Nancy Courtney did Denise breathe more easily. Only then could she dispel the image of Julie's muted disappointment.

But after the lunch hour, the memory of Julie's polite reticence and the girl's awkward affection came back to disarrange her certainty about the way she and André planned to live out the rest of their lives. Possibly, they could learn how to be happy again if they adopted Julie and Claudette.

"They are so like the daughters we lost," Denise told André when they were taking their early evening walk.

They had just left the Marsdens' main house, which was located not at the water's edge, but farther back into the land where it gained elevation, foreground, and prospect. Now they were making their way down the long series of steps that were surrounded by the banked expanse of lawn that addressed without challenging the sea's monumentality. From there they sauntered along the path that would lead them to the cool sands of the beach.

"Let us make them our family."

Hearing her words, André grew still. Only the roar of distant waves challenged his silence.

"I don't know," he said after she touched his rugged left hand, as if she were allaying his doubts or perhaps imploring his consent to her words. "We might lose them."

"There isn't any war now-—not in this country. We wouldn't lose them."

"We might lose them in some other way," he said. "It could happen."

His remark was a weary understatement.

"No," she heard herself whisper in feeble protest. "It will never happen."

"Would you want to go through all of that again?"

"They love us. With them, we can be happy again."

"It won't work, I tell you."

"But they need us," she said. "We can make *them* happy."

"They need someone else," he said. "They need parents who are not damaged."

"We need them."

"They are not Dominique or Arielle."

"No, they are not. These girls are alive. They need us as much as we need them."

"No," he said. "There's too much risk in it."

"What risk could there possibly be?"

"The world," he said. "Everything."

AFFINITIES

"I am what my family calls a belated Mackenzie," Adam remarked one summer day in 1921. He felt light-hearted and complacent after a vigorous swim with Ellen and with Joseph and Nancy in Newport waters. They, each as a couple, were lolling across multi-colored blankets that stretched comforting and proprietary upon the tawny sands of the beach.

He was, he said, referring to the accident of his birth. He had not been anticipated. His parents-to-be, Iain and Sara, once they turned thirty-eight, had forsaken any further hope that they would be blessed with a son who might one day join the three sturdy sons of Iain's brother as architects in the long-established Mackenzie firm. Years earlier, Iain and Sara had received a two-fold blessing, to which they responded with easy gratitude. Their adept and lovely daughters enhanced their marriage. But, conservative and overly protective, they endorsed no plans that might invite them into the too-public and sometimes abrasive world of business. Mackenzie daughters must, instead, cultivate a quiet allegiance to their spouses and to their offspring.

So, when in her middle years Sara gave birth to a son, Iain—overjoyed—wept softly while embracing her in the hospital's delivery room. Peering upon the new-born scion of his success and needing to recover his masculine reserve, he spoke the words which he would for years afterward call forth from time to time whenever he was especially pleased with this child, whom he and his wife proudly named Adam.

"This is my belated son—my strong-minded and reliable and only son. I need no other."

How fine it was, especially when the child through earliest experience had begun to hone his awareness, linking at seven or eight remembered forms—still loved—with the imagery unfolding new before him. In that bygone era Iain and Sara were pleased to share with their emerging son days and days of solacing leisure that informed his spirit and theirs as well. Even as Adam expanded and deepened his consciousness of the natural world's plentiful gifts, they—as nurturing parents—were themselves not only nurtured, but also reinvented. They felt baptized because re-born and implicated once more. Their gaze as in childhood knowing became once more original before nature's processes. Now they looked with new, curious eyes and fresher intelligence upon the magnificent things of the earth that, because of busy adulthood, they had only obliquely and sometimes too casually attended. Yet it was Adam, their solid and disciplined son, who understood best of all and with an intuitive boy's awakened clarity, the raw powers and unbridled energies of nature. He felt within himself correspondent powers that, gently stirred at first by quickening apprehension, gave him an intense awareness and revelations that sometimes vexed their perceiver.

In these elementary years, so essential to his becoming, they would within various New England seasons but most often in summer guide him through the islands of Narragansett Bay—Conanicut, Aquidneck, and Prudence...Dutch, Patience, Rose, and Gould. On those islands, he came to know—while observing the fertile life of tremulous tide pools—the red-brownness of Irish moss seaweed which had washed ashore a day or two and was bleaching already to white. Its flattened blades leaned still away from its short stalk to form firm-grasping fingers with round, blunt tips. Adam knew as well, upon sighting it offshore in shallow waters, the yellow bay scallop. The mantle of its shell gleamed with thirty or more blue eyes and its wily alertness propelled it with clapping motion at the Bay's meandering edge, away from an adversarial sea-star or an inquiring boy's nimble hand.

One time he saw a cobalt blue mussel anchored to the sea's white, glittering rock by hardy byssal threads of its own evolving. Later that same season, he watched a black-fingered mud-crab hurrying stout and dark into brackish waters, just before the tooth of its larger claw (a jagged, sun-reflected gleam) crushed the shell of a delicate oyster.

Shortly thereafter, while he was still young in his seeing and earning now at nine or ten a reliable independence tethered yet to safe authority, they as his mentoring parents taught him to swim in the coiling July waters of Eastern Beach in Newport. They also taught him to sail across the brisk waves of Conanicut Island, between the Bay's east and west passages. More easterly, they sculled with him on the temperate sheen of the Sakonnet River in Little Compton in a boat which Iain and a Scandinavian friend (a fellow architect) had built together five years earlier. On that sculling day, Adam had shared with his parents a nice precision working in smooth unison the pairs of oars jutting from each side of their vessel. For his part (so his father seated behind him noticed), he co-piloted with the boldness of a midshipman or boatswain or quicksilver mariner. Upon arriving with them on the shaded bank of their destination and excited beyond ordinary measure, he was moved to declare an athletic boy's husky enthusiasm.

"This *has* to be my best day of all."

With the familial wit to revel privately in his moment and yet assure him an auspicious future, they smiled in agreement, even while Sara—speaking for Iain as well as for herself—promised more.

"Yes, I think it must be your best," she said. Her motherly composure quietly approved his merit and, with brown-eyed gentleness, urged him forward to new occasions for a boy's self-mastery. "But there will be other days just as good, you'll see, and some even better."

A year later at Gould Island, once more in the east passage of the Bay, he (guided still by his matter-of-fact parents) found himself startled—and quite happily—by the purple iridescence of the glossy ibis. A supreme tenaciousness, the ibis waded through the shallows of salt-water marshes and with keener instinct probed the mud with long, insistent bill. Its downward curve smoothly grasped crayfish or crab or moon snail.

It was in this period, too, that he recognized, from a recollected sighting of a previous year that provided him his first acquaintance, the imperious majesty of the osprey. He sighted it this time at Sachuest Point on Aquidneck Island. Its white head and dark eye-stripe were a different flare upon space and altitude and water. Its three-foot wingspan, deep brown back, and mottled underbody became an enormous power while hovering momentarily over submissive waters just before plunging feet-first—a razor-sharp swiftness—to pierce a rotund bluefish.

Afterward, when he was eleven, he explored alone with his father a comradeship fostering manly aptitudes. At this time his mother withdrew to housewifely occupations, satisfied that they—father and son together—were crafting a lasting solidarity. In that specific time, as he advanced by way of his boyhood, he—in a sturdy pinnace that they two had, in their spare hours over the course of two years, built in hardworking partnership—learned to improve his fishing technique. Then it was that Iain taught him how, when casting his line overhead, to allow the wrist and forearm to do all the work, married as they must be to smooth-flowing motion. The wise fisher, his father told him, used the top section of the rod for unhesitant thrust.

He taught him also, diligent and generous father that he was, how to execute a proper side cast, desirable or even necessary when the fisher is constrained by windy conditions or by a jutting boulder or rugged bushes or a pendulous tree overhead. On that day Adam learned how to begin his cast with the rod low and pointed slightly outward. Using his wrist and forearm to flex the top section of the rod back and forward, he released the line just before aiming the rod tip at its target. Concise and agile, he followed through with the forward motion to bring the line in front of himself.

During that same summer, he enjoyed a camping trip with his father in the Weetamoo Woods in Tiverton. There, they were in the presence of the East Bay's superior fishing waters, yet at the edge nonetheless of a towering forest of deciduous trees—beech and ash and honey locust. It was within this summery experience that he heard the strong, slurring notes of the tawny ovenbird even before his glance had met in fleet acknowledgement the small bird's incisive eyes-with-bold-white-rings pausing to study his loping gait upon the sinuous path of the woods where with accurate confidence he tread. Sensing no enemy, the wily bird resumed his task of turning over fallen leaves—the better to find a crisp beetle or fat, wriggling worm. It was then, in this specific July—while they were preparing to launch their skiff on the crystal-bright river which held beneath its waters a multiplicity of fish—that he and his father saw a white-tailed deer leaping with athletic ease into shaded, receding space that was the forest path behind them. Days earlier, he had witnessed the sprint of the snowshoe hare and the scurrying motion of the red squirrel.

It was in this period, though on a warm, sweet-scented night, that he stole away from his sleeping father to experience an adventure all alone.

Launching his skiff with stealthy competence and an already troubled pleasure onto moonlit waters, he—with a rower's accurate agility—pushed his oars against the plash of ripples. He pushed again, propelling his craft with stately evenness away from the rocky cove where, for a night's respite from fishing, he and his father had decided to camp. Rowing all the while into the luminous space before him, he saw beneath the moon's spectral glow many of the familiar shapes that rendered location a plausible reality: the ferny bank which he now was leaving, the smooth river on which he briskly rode, and vaporous mist rising and wafting a gentle veil or net around him.

Far away in the accurate-seeming distance, on the opposite bank, the still constant light of the moon revealed silver-tipped bushes and a promising trail. The light offered as well the burnished flicker of the trees that on that very day he had walked by or touched or leaned against. He saw now the gnarled sureties of copper beech, which at noontime had been a fully received imagery of giant, aged trunks and burgundy leaves. In a cool alcove, there rose the beech called by some "weeping," with branches pendulous and greenness cascading. That tree made a superior canopy that provided a hiking boy and his father a comfortable refuge from languorous heat and from a surfeit of exploring. He saw also the white ascensions of ash trees, stalwart along the secluded path that meandered far away into the woods and invited a young traveler's further reconnoitering. Golden rain trees displayed delicate foliage like bright filigree and fruits lantern-shaped and wafer-like. He could not see them entirely. The kinetic flashes of their forms as well as the expanding linearity of the river and the solidity of the fern-crested banks rose before his seeing as if to maintain his acquaintance with them. But the evening light showed them as swift and merely partial impressions. His apprehension for that instant was a sleight-of-eyes seeing in full what was disembodied. His having with palpable satisfaction sighted them completely only hours earlier permitted him now to imagine that the integrity of each of them was there unimpaired in the very place where he'd earlier located them. By that means, he felt confidently tethered to the alacrity of his craft and to the reassurance of the space about him and of the sky above.

For the first ten minutes of his secret flight from the camp, all went well. His sleek pinnace like a stately swan carried him agilely across the river. But then a band of floating clouds began to overtake the stars and the moon. Gradually the natural forms that to his eyes had, even in the moonlit night, remained familiar were suddenly become alien things, betraying their original imprint upon his perceiving. It was then, while he searched out the opposite bank and sighted at the threshold of the horizon's boundary the summit of the craggy ridge, that his confidence faltered. For there, behind the summit of that once-familiar ridge, a dark ambivalence suddenly upreared its head. It was a towering peak with measured motion striding as if in unison with the swift rhythm of his oars toward him. That time, alone on the water, he knew the ghostly hooting of the barred owl and the fearful rustling of the trees in the uncertain distance toward which he was advancing. Or was it they who were advancing toward him? Some far-off dying creature shrieked—a red squirrel perhaps or a hermit thrush being torn into edible pieces by the swift-cutting talons of an owl. Still the looming, ambiguous ridge upreared its head, camouflaged fitfully by the too-casual light of the moon and by the auxiliary glow of temporary stars.

But soon, as if to test his boyhood mettle or trap him inside a cavernous darkness or deliver itself unto the sky's eerie mysteries, the moon disappeared. So too did the stars, leaving him a solitary voyager untethered from the light that joined him to the known. He was without even the fisher's lantern that would have glimmered its definitions of the immediate space before him. In his haste while leaving the camp, he had neglected to bring it into his skiff. Yet, with whatever steel fibers in his heart had not forsaken him, he with consistent oars journeyed onward. All the while he was resisting the thought that the whole of space behind and around and before him—the craggy ridge and towering hills and innumerable trees—were pursuing or closing upon or hurrying toward him.

Only when he'd reached the opposite bank did the moon and the stars return, displacing the convoluted gloom of clouds that had, for a time, concealed all luminescence. Then mooring his boat and stepping onto the dew-laden, ferny bank, he stood with cadet stance before the forest of trees observing him. Gathered unto their own darkness, they allowed the glow of new light to touch them with merely oblique appraisal. After turning about to observe in the far-away distance the cragged ridge that watched him with brooding stare and the formidable hills that with imperious calm stood silent, he paused. He felt leagued with them in capable, though somewhat uneasy, fraternity. And that was all of it—this journeying there not as a preface to a night-time exploring of the forest, but as a sign to himself and a notice to the secretive earth that he had consented even in the dark to venture toward whatever mystery was there to meet him.

But a half-hour later, after—in his familiar skiff once more—he had made his way back to the camp, he was grateful nonetheless to find the known reality of his father sleeping peacefully by the fire's steady light which all the while had stayed with him. Still, he did not—on the following morning or until four years afterward—tell his father of his eerie adventure or of his new distrust, just a little, of pleasant-seeming trees and the solidity of hills and mountains, and the certainty of stars and clouds and moon. Only then, a vigorous youth of fifteen, would he allow himself to reveal so much of his soul to the matter-of-fact and no-nonsense father whose good opinion he found indispensable to his well-being.

"Your experience on that night wasn't so different from anyone else's," his father told him. He surprised him with a forthright empathy for what he himself had deemed too sensitive a response to his night on the Weetamoo River—too hesitant or poetic or self-conflicted. (He, after all, was his father's son, disdaining any emotion that could unman him.)

This day, as on other days, his father with wise understatement offered a quiet remark.

"Most everyone finds out at one time or another, though not necessarily in a boat traveling through the dark, that the world's an uncertain place. But you have the grit to like it no less and to go on doing your part to make it something better."

It was in these vivid and influential years that he and his father met Joseph Courtney, a dark-haired athletic boy just as tall and as leaderly as he, and *his* father. Fishing together, they caught black sea basses in rocky bottoms at Sachuest Point. Their bulbous eyes were set high in flat, smooth heads. Their blue-black, robust bodies and large, arrogant mouths were superior emphases within deeper waters.

He caught as skillfully the aggressive bluefish, a long, torpedo-like swiftness fierce to behold when attacking its prey. With forked tail and snapping jaws upon the Bay, it churned a kinetic power that heaved hills over hills of waters until they seemed frenzied and boiling.

Still later, when he was eighteen and secure in adult fellowship that paternal instruction and his own attention had over the years inspired, he and his father journeyed together across a wider sea. They were still in Atlantic waters, but this time in a spacious walk-around boat, with ample cabin surrounded by a broad sunken passage and high top side and rails ideal for fishing on large inland waters and along open coasts. They trolled precisely for white marlins that were leaping, acrobatic and solitary, in roiling locations. They trolled, too, for flounders and halibuts—their flat, platter-like bodies milky white on one side, even translucent, and on the other a mottled glimmer of reds and greens…whites and browns.

Sometimes, though never in consecutive years, Adam and Iain journeyed to Florida to find yellow-fin tuna. Searching for its pointed head and tapered tail and resourceful swimming, they sometimes sighted its two-hundred pound body cruising, accurate and determined, at thirty miles an hour.

In this period, Adam completed his secondary education at Moses Brown, an exemplary private school on the east side of Providence where he excelled in all fields, especially mathematics and art and mechanical drawing. Then he began his undergraduate studies at Brown University in a program that amplified his knowledge of architecture by allowing him to study as well at the equally distinguished Rhode Island School of Design. Now comfortable with his evolving assurance and talent, he translated with ever-burgeoning enthusiasm his affinity for architecture.

Since boyhood, he had been as an earnest or gifted apprentice collaborating with his own remarkable gifts and with his father's careful mentoring. During free summer days and sometimes during a spring or late autumn recess from school, he visited the sites where his father and other architects were building new landscapes and where, adept and imaginative, they constructed or restored pristine homes. With a keen appraisal of things, he perceived, because of his father's tutelage, how the implicated reality of the environment—particularly its geology and vegetation and climate and the construction techniques and local materials transforming it—can inspire an architect as well as the builders and landscape architects with whom he creates.

He learned to observe carefully, as immense variations of the earth, the spatial mosaic of fields and hills and plains defining the circumference of an ample farm. When he found himself in coastal locations, he noticed the contours of the land hurrying toward the sea. He also noticed in a waterfront setting, elevated and proprietary as it peered upon the ocean, the amplitude of a year-round, three-story home with decorous gables and wrap-around porches. So perceiving, he remembered that his father had advised the builder to install with a crane twenty steel I-beams and countless special connectors—the better to brace and protect the house from high winds or uplift. When he was in East Falmouth and was surveying a splendid Tudor estate, he understood why his father, in structuring the large home, had designed many curved rooms and spacious archways and detailed millwork. They were control points that established centerlines, curves, and intersections for the entire house—from basement to rooflines. While he was in the midst of venerable city offices on prestigious streets, he recognized the stateliness of an elegant building joining its modernist breeding to the handsome formalities of tradition.

Iain and Sara were pleased to see him in this young period testing himself as a surveyor and as a designer of houses and sometimes as a builder. They saw him, four years later, being graduated with honors and continuing to prepare himself for his mission as an architect in his father's firm. By then, he had become engaged to lovely Ellen Templeton, who—while with him at Brown (she being a student at Pembroke College in that University) and later with him at the School of Design and at the Graduate School of Harvard University—found her proper niche as an interior designer and a landscape architect, as well. Through their love for each other, she became a steadying influence upon—and partner to—his indefatigable passions. After their marriage took place in the summer following their Harvard experience, they joined his father's firm as more-than-ordinary creators.

It was in these swift and active years that they brought their gifts to a formidable commission, the redevelopment in Middletown of thirty blocks of rubble-strewn lots into townhouses and rental and cooperative apartments which would offer to working-class families, many of them immigrants, attractive housing in a healthy environment. Now they worked with the Rhode Island Urban Development Association and collaborated with political leaders and neighborhood residents to devise and implement a plan for the restoration of a whole community. They discovered in a new way, made emphatic and startling through its immediacy, the injustice directed against impoverished citizens and hapless, though legal, aliens. As enterprising as social activists as they were as architect and designer, they joined democratic groups who strove by means of disciplined protests and urgent petitions to rouse the consciousness of the wellborn and of congressmen and senators. They worked to secure legislation that safeguarded immigrants from exploitation by the owners of small businesses and large corporations.

"I want to go on helping needy people," he told Ellen after that. "There's so much I want to do for them."

"We'll help them together," she said.

Because they brought to their activism a tough-minded determination, they also influenced the passage of laws that protected women and children from excessive hours of labor. These laws invoked as well a factory inspection system ensuring industrial safety for all workers. They mandated schooling for children and a reputable juvenile justice system that could rehabilitate young offenders. On weekends or on afternoons when they took leave of their busy careers, they joined resilient cohorts to urge government leaders and corporate executives to recognize the egalitarian auspices of labor unions and to respect, through pragmatic deeds instead of empty rhetoric, the ethnic plurality of our country.

During the early summer of 1921, to celebrate the fifth anniversary of their marriage, they journeyed to

Scotland, so that Adam could introduce Ellen to his ancestral home, a large country residence on the Isle of Arran. American Mackenzies had owned the estate for nearly a century. All through these years they maintained and sometimes revised its immaculate appointments and visited it regularly. Now, still feeling young in their marriage, Adam and Ellen made their visit to well-tended gardens and a crystal lake, rooms comforting and expansive, a private family chapel, and a gated lodge. To their eyes, nature seemed more animated here. There were fleet symmetries of deer and pheasant and eagle, colonies of seals near coastal caves, trails to Bronze-Age stone circles, and a multiplicity of fishing locations encompassing local streams and the wider sea.

That June they swam in the fresh waters of Loch Morar, and they knew the warmth of the beach's sun-glistening sands. They explored the whitewashed fishing villages of Crail, Pittenweem, and Saint Monans, and they experienced together the greenness of Tweed Valley, with its panorama of fields and woodland and river.

It was in Lochalsh that Joseph and Nancy joined them. Adam and Joseph had been friends for nearly twenty years. In early adolescent days they swam and kayaked and sailed during Newport summer days with cadres of other dexterous youths and later with them and with adept girls. On winter jaunts in the company of still other young and adroit youths (most of them militant alter-egos), they skied and hockeyed and ice-fished. With their athletic prowess and assured negotiations with the world, Adam and Joseph had recognized in each other a firm, brotherly cohort. It was their friendship that eventually brought Adam to Ellen. Meeting him, she saw a brown-haired self-possession, an altogether rugged stability. He, in turn, saw that her titian flair and matter-of-fact directness granted her an easy authority and sometimes a tinge of saucy banter.

Months earlier Joseph and Nancy had agreed that, during their wedding travel in Europe that summer, they would meet Adam and Ellen, whom they considered among their best friends. There, at the Deeside Railway, they four boarded a train that carried them, with intermittent stops at other picturesque stations, all the way through the Highlands almost to the other end of the line by the Cromarty Firth. At Dingwall, they visited a convivial pub and later enjoyed a bowl of soup at the Station's tearoom. Afterward they spent an hour in a cedar-scented shop with its locally made, quirky chopping boards and wood-handled knives, its knitwear and pottery, and its cards and paintings. It felt good to enjoy the ordinary and find it special and different.

Later that week, having returned to the Mackenzie compound in Arran, where Joseph and Nancy would stay another three or four days, Adam and Ellen hosted a festive party celebrating the twenty-ninth anniversary of Joseph's birth. After all the guests had retired to their own homes, the two couples found themselves speaking about various subjects, including music and art, science and poetry.

It was Ellen who mentioned that, just before the month of her own marriage to Adam, she had been reading once again Plato's *Symposium*, a lively and probing dialogue in which—at a gathering of philosophers—Aristophanes tells a fable. By means of its witty narrative, he suggests that each one of us seeks a beloved with whom we might find the completion of our soul.

The three who sat with her there at the table listened, receptive and convivial. They were surrounded by colorful party favors and half-eaten cake, by decorous china, and by the delicate wine glasses with which the twenty guests and more had raised a champagne toast to Joseph and which the keepers of the house, Mr. and Mrs. MacDonough, would clear away in the morning.

Now, drawing upon her own witty resources, Nancy (fair-skinned and brown-haired and comely) asked Ellen a playful question.

"Well, have you found your completion? Is Adam the one?"

"He is," she said, "and for always." Her warm voice embraced each word as she glanced serenely at her husband.

"And you, sir?" Nancy, light and airy still in her teasing inquiry, asked of Adam. "How does your search fare?"

Adam, like the others, had raised his champagne glass many times that evening. He felt lightheaded and buoyant and yet fully attuned to his heart's desire.

"I cannot say I know very much of the spiritual," he began, meeting quietly his young wife's favorable gaze. "But I do believe that Ellen's soul and mine knew one another long before we met."

"Isn't it lucky?" Joseph mused aloud, supremely contented as he sat beside Nancy within the comfort of an upholstered chair. "I mean that each of us has met the only person we could ever really want to love."

Those had been altogether joyful years, made sumptuous with hope and possibility and love. Shortly after this special time with Nancy and Joseph, Adam and Ellen returned to New England, where they celebrated the second anniversary of their having built their first home together. It was a three-story flowing property (allied and consonant with swimming pool, cabana and dock, a three-car garage, and separate living quarters for guests) in painterly Wellfleet, a nautical town in Massachusetts where in the midst of its seaside amenities and occasional, storm-tossed perils their architectural and design commissions placed them.

While he and Ellen were experiencing together the beauty of the earth rising resplendent all around them, Adam fell ill. A series of dizzying spells deprived him temporarily of his equilibrium and of the acuity that had always been his clear-eyed vision.

At first, and reasonably so, he attributed his malady to a rigorous work schedule and to a sea-battering episode during a midsummer squall when he and a fellow yachtsman rescued four children and their parents who were trapped in a malfunctioning boat on turbulent waters. After a few days, the symptoms that had quietly given him pause began to wane appreciably and then altogether. So he was able with plausible conviction to tell himself that his interpretation of his own ailing signs had been correct. His rugged manliness had rightly disdained the inquiry of a physician for what might have been no illness at all, but merely the consequences of a sometimes- punishing schedule.

But when, a few weeks later, his headaches and dizziness returned, this time becoming more intense and frequent, he permitted himself to consult a respected physician in the town. After that, directed by this general practitioner with the terse counsel that makes urgency a stark necessity, he learned from a team of specialists in a Boston clinic that a large and pernicious growth had enfolded his brain. Already, it had begun to impair the keenness of his senses and to overtake the unique consciousness and living pulse that made him Adam Mackenzie and no other.

That his illness did exist, unalterable and grievous, he knew with certainty once these doctors had completed their extensive x-rays and other pertinent examinations. After a week of deliberation, they determined in cautious unison to open his skull and cut away as much of the tumor as possible—as much, that is, which was accessible to their skill—to relieve the mounting pressure in his brain. Striving to be braver than ever in spite of an inward terror before the stringent reality of his case, he consented with admirable self-control to the tortuous journey into which his doctors were guiding him. Because of their extraordinary gifts and his own strong will to live, he—young and hardy still— survived the long and invasive surgery. In convalescence and for some time afterward, he possessed the husky build and brown-eyed intelligence that informed the person he had come to be.

"I'm not finished yet," he told Ellen. A tough-heartedness masked his awkward sorrow once he'd returned from a month's confinement in a Boston clinic. "We have days and days and whole months left to us. And they will bring me special happiness because we'll be in them together."

She, also keeping fear at bay, though with a young wife's unobtrusive resilience, took his large, proficient hands into her own. She was offering him whatever strength through arduous and private disciplines she could by herself maintain. Possibly, she also wanted to share all the powers that in him yet remained intact.

"I'll always be with you," she said. She planted a tender kiss upon the large, white bandages that like a formidable helmet encased his skull and a kiss as well upon the rough-hewn hands she firmly held. "I'll always be there."

In this last cycle of his life, when wellness returning seemed almost plausible, he with his Ellen knew once more the bright colors of the autumn earth. A harvest glow was vibrant upon his senses and vibrant, too, upon his spirit. For there, amidst the farmlands of Portsmouth, Rhode Island, they spent a warm October day picking apples from abundant orchards whose proprietor allowed visitors to stroll through the ruby incandescence of Spartans and Courtlands, Galas and Empires and Delicious and pluck the fruit directly from the trees. They had driven north from home in early morning to arrive in time to find their place on a trailer that was hauled by a farm tractor and that would bring them into the harvest splendor.

How moving it was for him to notice, as though it were a scene unfolding from his own boyhood, an agile lad of seven—guided by his father—reaching for an apple from one of the generous dwarf trees whose laden branches were swaying close to the ground. The man might have been *his* attentive father, translated from an era no longer available, explaining as did this father now that the high birch fence behind which the brindled cows stood listening was there to keep out deer. He also explained that the small mesh screens placed around each tree's base guarded it against intruding mice and that the black pipes traveling in linear patterns through the orchards were connected to the waters of a nearby pond which the owners had built specially to provide the trees necessary irrigation.

"When you pick an apple, turn it and lift, just as you do when you open a peanut butter jar," he heard this same boy's mother tell him. So, too, had his mother advised him. Never to his eyes had she been as young as this one, but she had been just as teacherly. Always, she had expressed a proper respect for nature and for its abiding gifts.

On this later day, a week or so after he became twenty-nine and the whole of his life was nearly completed, he climbed a stepladder to a semi-dwarf tree's highest amplitude. There, he found for Ellen and for himself firm and aromatic fruit. Together, they savored the taste of a pair of the apples New Englanders called Freedoms, large and crisp and fine-textured.

"I don't think I ever *really* tasted an apple before," he said, pleased by the heft and value of ordinary experience. He was pleased as well by his having effectively accomplished the journey up the stepladder. It served as proof to himself that some of his healthy powers were returning.

"Nor I," she answered him. Surprise touched her voice because of this unexpected happiness.

Afterward, they emerged from the orchards with a half-bushel of Spartans and Galas and Freedoms that they intended to share with their parents and their neighbors. The trailer and its essential tractor brought them to the threshold where they'd begun and then to their car, a model T, which stood as if waiting patiently there for them. When they had stored their plenty in the trunk of their auto as inside a temporary larder, he clasped her hand to his own and led her toward three southerly autumn fields. The lady of these farmlands must have planted them for no better reason than that they would bring extraordinary beauty to her husband and children and herself. The fields would also bring their beauty to the many visitors arriving to buy their produce and pausing to admire the land and to all the good workmen who, with the family, labored diligently on the farm planting and tending bushes and trees.

Three hundred acres and more offered the more pragmatic beauties of blueberry and blackberry and raspberry...rhubarb, pumpkin, and strawberry...and peach and cherry. The family and their workmen tended as well the hundred acres on which the apple orchards prospered. The trail from these orchards now drew Adam and Ellen to the three sumptuous fields by which the farmer's wife meant to solace her family and so many others. Within these fields delicate flowers (blue and orange and magenta), shimmery silver grasses, and flaming maples, gold poplars, and yellow robinias flourished with Indian summer airs.

As Adam and Ellen moved within the soft billows of temperate winds along a trail meandering a mile or so from the orchards, they saw white and pink flox with long, tapering clusters of purple blooms rising two or three foot above a casual fellowship of lance-shaped leaves. Knotweed spikes of tiny, bell-shaped flowers were a rose-lavender sheen upon their seeing. Michaelmas daisies showed their soft hues of red and white, and bright yellow cone flowers lolled in picturesque alliance with their green-centered adornment. "Autumn Joy" stonecrop displayed its smooth viridian leaves and lithe stems with bronze-red starry flowers basking in the ease of afternoon warmth. Silvery miscanthus swayed with yellow meadow rue, and goldenrod glimmered languorously near rough-fruited orange cinquefoil.

The trail kept welcoming them, with cedar benches thoughtfully arranged in shaded locations. Not far from a wooden bridge that curved its passage across a ravine, the white purity of a gazebo also encouraged them to sit awhile and properly attend an autumn day that knew how to express a summery brilliance, without an art for keeping it.

"How tremendous the earth is," Adam said, while with Ellen he sauntered in the comforts of their promenade. "And how fine to have this day together."

Ardent and strong-willed, he paused on the path that was glowing with fervent life all about them and drew her closer to him.

"Everything is so good for us right now," he said. "It's a day to remember."

By saying so, grateful for all the joys small and large that they had been granted, he was (she knew) showing her the way they must behave in the months looming before them.

It was at this moment that he kissed her, with impassioned gentleness the press of his lips upon hers an imprint of the desire and need and potency that had not yet left him.

Roused by her own desire for him, she returned his kiss even more urgently. Then, once they'd resumed their journey toward the crest of the hill overlooking the flickering waters of a river, she offered her own affirmation.

"Yes," she said, still teaching her heart to subdue its sorrow, "today has been very good, indeed."

That they had been granted a reprieve from the end awaiting him, the several weeks succeeding their visit to the orchard effectively demonstrated. For in mid-October while in Newport, they knew once more the elation of riding spotted horses whose athletic assurance and handsome aptitudes validated what Adam called a first-rate experience. He felt alive and healthy as he mounted a smooth-black Brazilian Tobiano. The stallion's neck and chest and flanks made a pleasing white contrast. Honed-sharp and assertive, Adam rode him across the rolling greenery of a horse farm not far from the sea. Exciting, too, was his clarified awareness of lovely Ellen, who was beaming and adept beside him, mounted as she was on her own favorite Pinto. He was to cherish the imagery of that stimulating day almost to the end of his conscious hold on things.

Later that same month, he brought Ellen to the Wood River in the southwestern part of Rhode Island. Its crystal waters flowed cold and fertile for seventeen miles through various towns including West Greenwich and Exeter, Hopkinton and Richmond, and Woodville and Alton. It was in West Exeter, within a pristine and Arcadian environment, that he taught her fly-fishing, as his father had in that same location once taught him. A keen and spirited student, she learned quickly to aim her rod toward the slick waters rushing downstream from an eddy or toward the deep-river pockets behind rocks or toward unexpected spring holes. That day she brought to the surface a golden-brown trout with speckled back glistening in the afternoon slant of the sun and itself all the while jumping with a fighter's angry swiftness.

In early November, he felt completely revitalized during this apparent deliverance from his grievous malady. Now he consented to Ellen's wish that they use for a more solacing and immediate purpose the days of wellness that had returned to him. He agreed that they should honeymoon once more, this time in Miami, swimming and water-skiing and sailing. Young and easy in the swing of occasion's temporary grace, they knew again the ecstasy of love-making, awakened new by each other's quickened body, so that everything that had seemed hurt in them, everything maimed or haunted or damaged, became for that hour transformed.

So revived did he feel after their three weeks in Miami—so stable and vital and whole again—that he began to believe, even against the tough grain of his realistic judgments, that his physicians had miscalculated the aftermath of his surgery. They had, he felt, misdiagnosed the nature of his specific tumor. His youth and vigor had, against all odds and their morbid expectations, subdued the malady or, at the least, compelled it to pause, remitting its pernicious effects until some far-off, nebulous era. He did not allow himself to express these thoughts openly to Ellen, because he did not care to disquiet whatever blind chance had granted him its mercy. But she saw, in the returning crew cut and the tanned ruggedness that was himself with her and with their good parents and friends during these glad, hopeful days, a tremendous fervor of new energy. A swift, natural poise found its balance inside the purity of his masculine impulses: in the muscular arms that wielded with quick accuracy the serpentine helve of a steel-blue ax to cut wood for their evening fire, in the athletic prowess of his wiry alacrity climbing a ladder to replace a wind-torn shingle on the roof of his parents' house, and in the high-spirited precision of his dancing a festive polka at a grange supper in Middletown.

Because his secret conviction seemed to him altogether plausible and because his hardy physique enabled him at this time to venture into the world with the sinewy confidence that had, before his illness, been his custom, he decided that he and Ellen, with their friends Joseph and Nancy, should go glade-skiing in Bretton Woods, New Hampshire. They would spend a weekend at a lodge there, just west of Mount Washington. How surprised Ellen was (and pleased at the challenge, she being like the others an excellent skier) that the glades through which they would glide across space and elevation and momentum were not the familiar clearings in a forest at all. Instead, the convoluted terrain beckoned them away from the cleared areas. The woods themselves now became the trails offering them a journey of obstacles and the thrill of skiing closer to nature. They offered them as well the gift of pausing in the woods to glimpse, within the loom of sun-cold proximity, hoarfrost like a delicate caul or membrane or glass encasement covering steadfast goldenrod at the rim of their southerly path.

Just beyond that seeing, a tawny-red fox scampered across their witness into an adjacent alcove of rufous brush. Farther than that, though but a few yards from the place where they'd paused, the intense scrutiny of a barred owl (with speckled brown plumage and dark, searching eyes…orange-yellow bill, streaked belly, and short tail) was searching for rodents while perched high on the branch of a scarlet oak gone ghostly with winter's white stubble and rime and creases.

On this day it was that they perused at their will and all about them the beauty of birch trees clad in snow-touched scrolls. They also peered at the ascending tangle of corkscrew hazels, their odd handsomeness embellished by catkins clustering upon bare, muscular branches. With a quieter awe they attended the enormous columns of white spruce, splendid with whorls of needlelike leaves and pendant, ornamental cones.

How extraordinary and altogether inspiriting it was, having removed the wrist straps of their poles before the start of their run and having tightened their helmets should they in the hurl of velocity meet the veering path of a tree, to take flight from the tremendous earth while sky and sun and clouds and snow-banked hills rising behind weaving trees wheeled around and behind and below them. The world itself kept hastening away as if in upheaval or kaleidoscope or catapult.

"You've come back to us," Joseph declared, after they completed their run and after he embraced in a spontaneous bear hug this loyal friend who from their boyhood days had been to him as a special brother.

"Yes," Adam agreed, equally pleased by the fine skiing the four of them had that day achieved. He was pleased, too, that—not desiring anyone's pity—he had refrained from telling even these close friends the unfavorable prognosis of his physicians. Joseph and Nancy now assumed that his recent surgery had effectively thwarted whatever malady had been poised to overtake him. "I've come back, and I want to stay."

It was then that Ellen and Nancy began to cheer Adam and his deft maneuvering, an hour earlier, across the space that sprang unknown and thrilling all around him. That time, the hills themselves attended his swifter passage. So that they would not embarrass Adam or treat him as anyone except his reliable self, the women cheered Joseph in turn and just as exuberantly. Inspired by their intense affirmation, the men took up their own courtly part and proceeded to cheer the ladies. The four friends with spirits exalted dined afterward at a restaurant not far from the lodge. There, they enjoyed a rich vegetable soup and a fine soufflé-omelet and, while saluting once more this marvelous day, a warm and tangy apple cider.

For the rest of her life, Ellen was to remember this weekend. She regarded with a grateful heart the kindness and sensitivity of these dear friends whose camaraderie and genuine belief in Adam's show of well-being brought in a very special way the favorable world back to him.

"If wanting counts for anything, then I *will* stay," Adam told her late that night when they, alone then, were lolling in their bed at the lodge, vivid and deliciously complacent.

"You will," she found herself exclaiming in the midst of kissing over and over his full, satisfied lips. "I know you will."

And now, for the first time in all the hard months of his illness when, advised by his physicians, she was learning with rigorous abstinence to quell her hope for a miracle, she permitted her heart to believe in that very possibility. The thought quickened her solace as though solace had wings, ascending.

But a week later, after they'd returned to Wellfleet and he had resolved to resume his duties as an architect, he fell ill again. His grievous headaches returned and with them a dimming of his vision. Within two weeks, a total blindness like an iron clamp or steel vise held him, taut and stringent, in its darkness. Now, understanding at last the unrelenting nature of his malady, he quietly accepted his fate.

During this last month, his parents stayed with him and Ellen for a week in the ample home which they, still young in their marriage, had only recently and with a promising vision of their future designed and built. Iain and Sara tried at first to ease him by speaking of the good times they had shared together when he was a boy learning to swim and to fish and to sail. But invariably, and against their pledge to themselves that they would not express their sorrow openly and thereby intensify their son's heavy burden, they would suddenly pause in their telling of these episodes. Their voices would break apart from the sobs they had tried to stifle or by the wearying sadness that wound tightly about their souls. Then it was that the room with its vibrancies would fall away from him, his breathing gone hushed and apprehensive. Soon recovering his guarded equanimity, he would with calm words and soothing timbres allay the fears of his cherished parents.

"We had swell times together," he would declare. "You two taught me so much."

They, grown shy before the austerities of his courage, would find again their own tenacious wills.

"It was sheer happiness, every minute of it," his mother would say, her clarified voice reclaiming its strong-minded identity, "because you were the brightest and best son we could ever have had."

"You wanted to know everything there was to know," his father would recall proudly. "That's what made you a good architect."

Only when Ellen, alone with him in the last weeks of his consciousness, broke free from her stoicism and by his bedside wept profusely—only then did a tear escape from his brown, unlighted eyes that saw only her shadow and yet saw so much more.

"You needn't cry," he told her gently. His still-rugged hands were being guided by the soft texture of hers so that he might caress her tear-stained face, which was smooth and yielding as always to his touch. "I've lived. I've lived in the tremendous world."

With her hands guiding him yet, he felt his fingers discovering once more her full, nubile lips. Compelling himself to rise from his pillow and with her assistance, he met them with his own lips, gone pale and anointed with a physician's balm because they were parched from heavy medication.

"I've lived. I've lived with you," he said.

Inside each of these hard days, when consciousness still clarified his awareness, he began to wonder whether he and Ellen might even after death see each other once more. He remembered that years before, when he was a youth of sixteen, he had with a precise and methodical studiousness sought out ministers and priests and an eminent bishop from Boston, as well as the sacred texts which might give him hope that one day he would rise from death and live again—all the healthy form of him...all his commanding height and muscularity and keen-eyed physiognomy. How, he would ask them—these men who devoted themselves to careful interpretation of Holy Scripture—how could he or anyone else rise from death, when even during life on earth the human body does not have the same material particles in it from minute to minute? The body receives the subatomic elements informing it as so many charges of electricity evolving and changing, coming and leaving. How then are we to know which of the billions of arrangements of particles which it possessed while inhabiting its place on the earth will be resurrected?

All these religious men assured him that the resurrection of the body was an essential part of his Church's revelation, as certain and predominant as the immortality of his soul. They comforted him while referring to the wise pronouncements of David and Paul and Matthew, Aquinas and Augustine about this matter of the reconstituted person of each one of us after death. Yet he could not really believe that he would one day—an eternity away—live again exactly as he had, within the solidity of his manly frame, existed. Not even the wisest man or woman could prove from personal experience that the dead lived beyond the life that had left them.

Now, in his last days, he told himself that it was not especially important to have proof of his existence after death. What was important was that Ellen would find his Spirit alive in all the places where they had experienced the beauty of the earth together. Whenever she swam or sailed in Newport waters or glade-skied in New Hampshire or rode her beloved Tobiano across the green hills behind their home in Wellfleet, she would know that he was there. His Spirit-life would rouse her memory so that in the sun-touched space beside her or sometimes in the shadowy distance even his body would to her quiet intuition seem nearly visible.

MÉNAGE À TROIS

"My granddaughter represents, of course, a special case," Gerald Marnham said. "But I have no reservations about leaving her in your care."

It was not difficult to offer the Aubrays his unqualified approval. After spending a week with them here in his home in Newport, Rhode Island, he was certain that they would be of immense assistance to his granddaughter. But when their visit ended on Monday morning, he had not yet invited them to join the well-qualified staff who maintained the smooth workings of his household. Never precipitate in his judgments, he resumed his business schedule and waited for three days before inviting the Aubrays to return. During this period, they permitted themselves a brief vacation in nearby Nantucket. There, they had been swimming and sailing with friends from Alain's Harvard days.

They were conferring now within the burnished amenities of Gerald's study, sequestered as it was inside the southwest wing of the ample house. Every Thursday he permitted himself to be away from his New York office for a few hours. It had been his custom to arrive in Newport promptly at nine o'clock, after Sommers, his driver for three decades and more, and Robert Finley met him at the train station. He had never admitted to anyone except himself that in their different ways both Sommers and Finley were of immense value to him. His keen-sighted Amanda had known without his ever speaking of the matter. She had known much about him of which she had had the good sense not to speak. Because she had been a more-than-ordinary wife, she understood when it was not necessary to remark upon his habits or his ambition or his business travel across the globe. Nor had she ever questioned his expectation that those in his service must be as punctual and efficient as they were capable.

Death had taken her away from him after they had enjoyed what in retrospect he now told himself had been a marriage of modulated compatibility for thirty-eight years. During these four years without her, he had chosen to remain both ambitious and productive. Rarely did he find time for his Newport home. Most of the time, he was living in New York or in London, Paris, and the Orient. But he did not care to sell it, so much did he value the memory of the years he had spent there with Amanda and with their son Austin, who was thriving as a junior executive in the Marnham Steel Corporation, and with their daughter Rebecca and her husband, Kevin Farrell, who had died together in a plane crash en route to Pittsburgh.

For this reason most of all, his desire to keep alive his recollection of those happier days, he had regarded Robert

Finley as absolutely essential to the efficient management of his Newport estate, with its Tudor ambiance, water-front setting, and twenty-five acres. Trained as a civil engineer, Finley had not merely monitored the upkeep of the property. He had redefined both the natural and the man-made beauty of the land that carried forward the Marnhams' prestige as well as their history. But he, too, had died.

"He just wore out," Evelyn had explained, though no explanations were necessary. An autopsy had revealed a subtle heart malady that had eluded detection even from an eminent cardiologist. But he had appreciated Evelyn Finley's remark, nonetheless. She was a matter-of-fact woman who had loved her husband very much and who would not embarrass his memory with a show of maudlin pieties.

He knew that Finley's death could not be avoided or postponed. Nor had he imagined that anyone coming to the position that Finley had held for twenty-nine years would be as effective--at least, not in the first year. But this week had convinced him that Alain Aubray would—within the mere span of a year—gradually equal and then exceed Finley's successes. That Alain would accept only a year's appointment to the post dismayed him, at first. But his decision to move forward to other challenging assignments, once he completed his work of restoration and enhancement, was not surprising. There were many other formidable commissions that even now were beckoning him.

Strong-bodied and handsome, Alain wore his knowledge and his assurance with a nice understatement. If he was aware that his six foot stature and his rugged physicality gave him an advantage over those men who were not similarly favored by nature, his quiet authority gave no evidence of narcissistic self-reflection or of a careless displacement of the less impressive persons about him.

There was within his appearance something extraordinary and altogether promising. The well-honed muscularity and the even-tempered manner were, if the truth were to be told, auspicious elements of his personhood, as were his ruddy complexion, dark hair, brown eyes, and full, sensual lips. But his knowledge as a civil engineer and as a landscape architect, his brave service as a first lieutenant in the recent war, and his realistic view of the world were the elements that gave him a distinctive gravity.

In the years before the war, he completed his undergraduate studies in civil engineering at the *École Polytechnique* in Paris. He also completed a master's degree in landscape architecture and urban planning at the Harvard Graduate School of Design. Returning to France, he assisted major companies in the designs of roads, canals, and an apartment building, as well as in the planning of pipelines, water distribution systems, and drainage facilities which included bridges, dams, and levees. When the war came two years later, he fought in the French Sixth Army at the Second Battle of the Marne. There, at Dormans in the summer of 1918, he survived a grievous wound to his chest and wounds just as grievous to his left arm and leg.

Once the war ended, he married Charlotte Dussollier, whom he had met when she was a student at the Sorbonne. Two years younger than he, Charlotte was a light-skinned beauty with a full-bodied figure. She had titian hair, blue eyes, a turned-up nose, and lips that must have brought him a special pleasure when she smiled. Her genuine interest in the well-being of others made her, Gerald believed, as warm-hearted as she was quick-witted.

She, too, had served in the war. Determined to be of use during that hard time, she enrolled in an accelerated nursing program sponsored by the French Red Cross and by the French Army. Skillful and empathetic, she worked long hours attending the wounded whose bodies the war had left intact and the maimed whose bodies had been deprived of one or more limbs. She also took care of those soldiers who were dying. In the first days when she was assigned to their ward, her nurse's composure nearly failed her. All of these men were young, and their torn bodies and bruised minds still craved life.

The Aubrays had come to New York eighteen months after the war ended. Alain had spent most of those months convalescing in a Paris hospital. He and Charlotte were grateful that they had survived the war. But no longer did they believe that whatever worthwhile contributions they made to the world would change its speckled nature. Still, they were hoping to do their part. They were, in fact, looking to find a measure of contentment through careers that challenged and excited their aspirations.

"Let's bring something original into our work-lives," Alain told Charlotte on the day that they had embarked for an altogether new experience in the United States. "And let's explore our sensuality in new ways, too."

He was pleased at how readily she agreed.

"That might help us to make sense of things," she said.

Their path was made easier than it might have been because of Alain's Harvard connections and because of his friendship with Phillipe Darrieux, the curator of the fashionable Courtney Art Gallery in Manhattan. Within a short time, they settled in Greenwich Village and for the next three years made a modest success. Alain secured engineering commissions in New York City, and Charlotte took a teaching post at a private school for girls in Manhattan.

By chance, while he was attending the exhibit of canvases by Caillebotte, Pissarro, and Matisse at the Courtney, Gerald mentioned to Phillipe and to his wife Emmanuelle that he was in search of a governess for his granddaughter. Mrs. Darrieux had been a loyal friend of Amanda ever since their days at Bryn Mawr. Through the years she and Philippe had shared many festive occasions with the Marnham family. It was only natural that she should inquire how Eleanor, who was still grieving because of the death of her parents, was faring at her school in Connecticut. Though he did not explain the girl's troubled residence at the school, Gerald did remark that he had decided that his granddaughter would—-for the next year, at least—continue her studies privately, with an excellent teacher as her guide.

"Could you recommend a suitable young woman for the position?" he asked.

He was not surprised that Emmanuelle could recommend such a woman. Mrs. Darrieux knew everyone who mattered in New York, from the Mellons, Rockefellers, and Astors to the designers and builders of the city. She knew as well the significant hoteliers and chefs, the most notable jewelers, milliners and couturiers, and highly regarded painters, musicians, and playwrights. She also knew the Aubrays. Before the war, when she and Philippe spent part of their summers on the French Riviera, they traveled in the same circle as Alain's parents. Georges Aubray was a distinguished surgeon who had made a fortune for himself through his wise investments in New York and Paris real estate. When he and Bérénice retired to their home in South America, she and Philippe saw them less often. Then the war came, and—–except for an extended visit to their home in Buenos Aires—–they saw them not at all.

But during the three years just passed, Philippe and Emmanuelle had renewed their friendship here in New York with Alain. They had heard about his brave war service and about his plan to rely upon himself more than upon his father's wealth to make his way in the world. There was no enmity between him and his father. He counted himself among the fortunate, of course, that his father had insisted that he accept as an early portion of his inheritance a substantial portfolio of stocks and bonds and real estate holdings and an impressive bank account.

By launching himself on a path different from that of his father, he was actually carrying forward an Aubray tradition. Both his grandfather, who had made his mark as a general in the French Army and later as a prime minister of France, and his father had thrived in different careers. Already, Alain had proved himself as a brave soldier. Were he alive, his grandfather would have been very pleased by his conduct in the war. Now Alain was beginning to make a success as a civil engineer. His recent commissions had honed his excellence as an environmental designer and as a landscape architect.

His wife had also enjoyed a privileged upbringing. Her father was a senior officer in the French Diplomatic Corps. Currently, he represented France in Indo-China.

Charlotte had recently completed her third year of teaching at the excellent Newbury School in Manhattan. There, she had guided girls from privileged backgrounds not unlike her own through advanced studies in foreign languages, modern history, the sciences and mathematics. But, according to Emmanuelle, she had grown dismayed by the school's old-fashioned pedagogy, which she believed constrained her students' academic venturing and their originality. It was her plan now to seek a teaching post independent from the confines of Newbury or of any school that in subtle ways sponsored lock-step conformity. A formalist with a modern perspective who appreciated none the less the wisdom of tradition, she wanted to help a girl of thirteen or fourteen to become not merely knowledgeable, but also self-reliant and inventive. Properly educated in this regard, the girl—growing into her womanhood—would bring to the wider world a pragmatic realism, a discreet aptitude for self-testing, and a decorous *joie-de-vivre*.

Hearing all these good things about the Aubrays, Gerald began to think about inviting both Alain and Charlotte to join his Newport staff for a year—Charlotte as governess to his granddaughter and Alain as the manager of the estate, a worthy replacement for Finley. But he would move cautiously.

"I'll invite them to spend a week in Newport," he told Emmanuelle after she had offered a favorable biography of young Aubrey and his wife. "I'd like to find out whether they relate well to the place and to my granddaughter."

That they related supremely well to the Newport scene, their success with the other members of his staff, with the friends whom he invited to meet them at a week-end party, and with his granddaughter made very clear. What impressed him most of all, probably because his need of a timely replacement for Finley seemed far more crucial than his acquiring a governess for his granddaughter, was the genuine fervor which Alain brought to his comprehensive survey of the property. No sooner had he mentioned to the young man that he wanted to revise and expand both the landscape and the buildings that defined his Newport estate, than Alain set to work photographing with his Leica every portion of the property. Using these photographs as a frame of reference, he then composed a set of architectural design plans that meant to invoke changes as functional as they were beautiful.

Accompanying him on many of these photo sessions, Gerald became aware that Alain found his proper niche in the direct statement and precise rendering of a scene. He was a gifted landscape architect drawn to photography as an instrument for documenting designed space and exploring the many reciprocal facets of an environment. He studied all of space in terms of its natural forms and human alterations, its urban and rural extensions, and its multiple possibilities for current use or for future transformation.

Insightful as much as it was empirical, his camera-eye keenly apprehended within the twenty-five acre property the elegant interplay of glacial history, ocean expanse and human habitation. His photographs recorded the full character of the place. Their imagery showed the sumptuous in association with the stark, the vast with the intimate. Now the place must advance the good work that Finley had accomplished. Prudent revisions and additions must link the current with the timeless.

The plans that Alain designed would maintain the Federal-period stateliness of the house and, at the same time, introduce a modernism which carried itself with minimalist sweep and elongated lines.

Discreetly, the Marnham estate would assert that tremendous natural forces had yielded compatibly and handsomely to the presence of human beings. It was this authentic statement that would give to the property an extraordinary solidity fashioned from a shared design at once pragmatic and civil. Already, the main house claimed its own expressive individuality. It was located not at the water's edge, but farther back into the land, gaining thereby elevation and foreground and prospect. Yet a new configuration would neither neglect nor compromise Gerald's desire to be near the ocean. A swimming pool and pool house and pergola, emblematic of the human will activating its own propensities, would stand at the water's edge. These forms would be enhanced by and imbued with the luster of its ocean perch.

Compelling, too (so Alain's plan indicated) would be the indigenous fraternity of seventy-five native oaks. Translated from a meadow nearby, they would define in various locations on the property their admirable congruence with the pristine land and with the billowing ocean. Although they had been stunted by salt air and strong winds, several of these trees would find their places in the arrival area of the estate. Each of them would be pruned and replanted to emphasize their mottled bark and natural distortions and to claim this seaward habitation as their proper heritage.

Gerald was equally impressed with Alain's revision of the entry drive as one confronted it from a southerly direction. Idiosyncratic, his plan accentuated topography. It enabled the drive to traverse rolling dips and knolls and to skirt contours before arriving at the main house. Not far from the house he would build a new garage and several guest cottages, each of them stone-clad and hunkered into the earth. According to his plan, one must step down three feet in order to enter them. These buildings would catch and distill the undulating land into a singular plane, which would then descend from the north side toward the ocean. The banked expanse of lawn would address without challenging the restless sea's monumentality.

As a landscape architect and as a civil engineer, Alain translated the truth of his seeing through direct statements about the external environment. His was a precise apprehension of implicated structures and symbiotic relationships.

"It's all about connectedness," Alain explained after Gerald praised his ingenuity. "It's all about the ways that we relate to one another and to the natural and man-made forms which surround us."

"Well, I like your plans very much," Gerald told him on the Monday that the Aubreys were leaving for their brief visit to Nantucket. They would drive there in the reliable comforts of their Bentley.

He was happy to tell Alain so once again on the bright Thursday morning in the week following the Aubrays' first visit. They were conferring in his study, where he had just announced to him and to Charlotte their appointments to his staff. "I think both of you will be very good for this place."

Conferring with him in his study more than a week after she and Alain had first met him, Charlotte found herself ambivalently impressed by Gerald Marnham's command of a scene. He was a tall, stately assurance made austere and gaunt by time's unflinching ordinances. Yet to her eyes he was no less a resilient aptitude and a staid ballast withstanding the world's confusion and indecorousness. How supremely well ordered he was and perhaps always had been. The coherent accuracies that defined him were reflected in the very room where they were conversing.

In this specific moment of their meeting, just after he had invited Alain and her to join his staff, he was seated, implacable and straight-backed, at his desk. It was a nineteenth-century bow-fronted mahogany pedestal partnered handsomely with a green leather top. The round brass pulls on its drawers embellished a distinctive aesthetic. During a carefully modulated encounter, she recognized the balance and proportion and intricate clarity of this special room of Gerald's.

While maintaining the requirements of their own discreet equilibrium, she and Alain were seated within the comforts of Carlyle chairs. Their generously-padded, button-tufted backs and fixed seat cushions were an Edwardian abundance, as were the serene-rich hues in stripes of beige and gold and navy. Their maple legs on brass casters enhanced a correct and amplified solidity.

Quietly seated on Alain's right, she noticed how effectively the room became a metaphoric continuation of the exterior life unfolding around and upon his property. For there, on the high-ceilinged, pale-yellow wall behind and above the desk where Gerald sat, the vivid splendors of Monet's *Regattas at Argenteuil* complemented and intensified the summer day's grand propensities—all the excited imagery informing the expansive arched windows that opened to a garden and to the sea nearby.

That imagery offered to her glance as she faced Gerald, and faced as well the windows' sumptuous prospect beyond and to the right of him, colorful sailboats that rose upon her seeing like bright flares in the distance hurrying across cerulean, sun-mottled waters. Mastering its own ascension, inhabiting as it did the wall directly behind and above Gerald's desk in vaulted, cathedral space, the extraordinary *Regattas* with correspondent powers also vitalized the spacious circumference of a discriminating man's study. Surely, on this canvas Monet not only emulated Nature's implicated harmonies. He also taught the spectator visiting it how, more authentically, to see.

Subtly and deftly Monet teaches us to see. So in keen attentiveness she mused as she first entered the room and before she imparted her wish to be for Eleanor Farrell the auspicious influence the girl needed if she was to be rescued. Braced by new perceiving (she told herself), we accept the aggregate of blotches in the lower part of the picture as gestures of paint translating colored ripples on the water. Broad, italic strokes clarify the painter's act even as they reflect and guide us to the upper part of the canvas and the instantly discernible reality of amber-luminous sailboats, cobalt-green hedges and trees, and houses wearing emphatic red roofs beneath an understated azure sky.

Still the bright flares that were sailboats flourished within sight of Gerald's property and upon her scanning glance toward the arched windows of his study before which she sat. Still their kinetic, sailing rhythms went on hurrying across sun-mottled Newport waters in the cerulean distance.

There was, she felt, something happily artful about this juxtaposition of Monet's canvas on the wall behind and above Gerald's desk and of the Newport seascape quickening the prospect beyond the windows of his study. This melding of literal and metaphoric and of outside world and inner reflected the balance and coherence of the life that Gerald Marnham invited to unfold around him. It was this disciplined symmetry and its scrupulously designed perfection which (she imagined) he sought as the most meaningful pattern of life—his life in particular and the lives of his son and his granddaughter.

Yet, Monet's complicity with Nature located the spontaneous in energetic daring. His peerless seeing was an extemporary gesture, or seemed so. There was little of that art in Gerald's engagement with reality. In fact, there was very little of that liberality we call instinct or intuition and, sometimes, adventure. For Monet (and, yes, for Eleanor, too—she had the same spirit) all of life was an astonishing kaleidoscope. It was a veritable stereopticon inviting each of us to define our own arts through its many colors. But Gerald, though an immensely successful corporate leader, did not seek the full spectrum of life. It was not his way to experience the manifold colors of life or to test their vibrancies and hidden values. Instead, he worked from the subdued palette that hesitates to identify its proficiencies through unconstrained gesture or willful experiment or impulsive daring.

So Charlotte believed. From his casual remarks about his relations with the daughter who had died and with a son who strove to fulfill his father's will, she was aware that Gerald had become inflexible in his prescriptions for their well-being. Even while experiencing a subdued dismay at his paternal arbitrariness, though, she respected him for heeding the voice of his own conscience. Yet that respect and admiration would not keep her from quietly invoking a more realistic program concerning Eleanor's future.

Before she expressed herself once more as the teacherly advocate of Eleanor's happiness, Gerald reinforced his own opinion of his granddaughter's situation. At this time he moved away from his desk and took his place in the handsome Chelsea wing chair beside her. Its navy vintage linen was trimmed with antiqued brass nail-heads, which represented another clarified proportion upon her senses. Since they had been speaking about Eleanor, he directed his words now to her rather than to Alain, who observed them in tactful silence. While facing her with a courtliness that pleased her womanly self-regard even as it revealed his patrician reserve, Gerald mentioned once again that she was going to be the essential component in his rescuing plan for Eleanor.

"You must bring her back to life again," he said.

After the deaths of her parents, Gerald had explained in their first meeting, his granddaughter suffered a breakdown. But, when she read the reports of Eleanor's teachers and of the psychiatrist who had lately counseled her, Charlotte believed that the girl's emotional problems had begun long before her parents had died. Eleanor's fear that they had abandoned her began when she was a little girl of four or five. Then and later, her parents were often away, busy with their careers as corporate executives. Their responsibilities often required them to be not only in Pittsburgh, but also in New York, London, Paris, and Shanghai.

Her mother and her father had, nevertheless, carefully monitored her education in the earliest years when an aged governess was teaching her at home and after that, when she attended Miss Porter's, a private school in Farmington, Connecticut. They wanted their daughter to be as knowledgeable and as poised as she was lovely and successful. They had little empathy for her shy reticence. To win their favor, Eleanor had always excelled in her studies and in other learning activities, which included horse riding, swimming, and skiing. She had also become a fine painter and a gifted pianist. At school, she had willed herself to be a leader. She became the captain of the tennis and swimming teams and the president of her class.

Although she enjoyed her popularity and the feminine loveliness that she had inherited from her mother, her uneasiness about her relationship with her parents never left her. When they did find time to be with her, they wanted to hear not that she had missed them, but that she had made many new achievements at school. Only then, after she had shown them the favorable reports of her teachers, did they permit themselves to embrace her and to allow her to kiss them.

"But this success is only the beginning," her mother most often and sometimes her father would remind her. "There is a great deal more that you must accomplish if you want to take an important place in the world."

After they were killed en route in their private plane to the headquarters of the Marnham Steel Corporation in Pittsburgh, Eleanor became very ill. Not even the affection of her peers and the motherly counsel of her teachers could dispel her grief. Within the first week of her hospital stay, her physician decided to transfer her to a private sanitarium. There, after months of wise treatment from a psychiatrist who specialized in the care of children, she began to be well again. It had been only three weeks since her doctor had allowed her to make her new home with her grandfather.

"Eleanor needs a teacher who can also be a helpful friend," Gerald said. "She needs to believe that even without her parents she can make her way in the world very effectively."

"You want her to become self-reliant," she said. "I, too, believe that is the essential lesson which she must master."

With quiet intonations, she was reinforcing his point of view.

"After spending last week in her company, I am confident that with the proper guidance she will learn how to believe in herself."

"Ah, yes," he said. "*That* is what she has lost."

"I'll teach her how to meet the surprise of the world."

Already, she could see, he appreciated her solicitous regard of his granddaughter. So perceiving, with carefully measured timbres he offered new words to reinforce his approval of her plan for Eleanor.

"The timing could not be better. She's nearly fifteen, and, after this year of home study, she will be away again at Miss Porter's School. Even with teachers and friends around her, she will have to rely upon her own capacities if she's going to succeed at being an individual."

"She was learning to be very successful as a self-determining individual before she lost her parents. She can learn to be so again."

Once again he found matter-of-fact words meant to reaffirm the importance of Eleanor's new schedule.

"Her returning to Miss Porter's next year makes her association with you even more important, because it favors her with more time to rally from her grief and at the same time to advance in her studies."

"A year from now she will be strong again and well prepared," she answered him. The cool poise of her voice defined her conviction. "On her own, Eleanor is going to make you very proud of her."

She rose gracefully from her chair. Alain's glance upon her intimated that her subdued beauty was a proper ascension in that moment dominating the room, until he and Gerald rose to meet her. As Gerald brought to her the manly composure that was his ingrained authority, his formality was as harnessed as he cared to make it. He took her delicate hands, decorous now with white summer gloves, into his own and clasped them in a finely measured expression of his gratitude for her belief in Eleanor's value and in that troubled girl's ability to make a scrupulous grandfather proud.

"I must confess that I am looking forward to such a time," he said. "For then I'll be convinced that she has come to know herself better."

He watched as she turned to join Alain just before the three of them began making their way out of his study.

"You can be a part of this, too," he told Alain. "Eleanor might even come to see both of you as replacements for her parents."

His remark prompted them to pause momentarily.

"Oh, we will not be her parents," Alain said. His words were direct and clarifying. "At this point in her life, nobody could replace them. She has already built a history of loving and needing them. If she thought we were trying to be her parents, she would surely resent us."

"We will be her teachers and her advisors," Charlotte quickly added. It was, she knew, important for Gerald to understand the persons that they would be for his granddaughter.

Hearing her explanation, he permitted himself a broad smile. He was accompanying them through the long, shadow-tinctured hall out to a waiting car, their handsome Bentley, and to the extraordinary August day, itself another ascension flourishing around them.

"You will be wise counselors," he said. "You'll guide her to a realistic view of things. That is what she needs most of all."

As soon as she and Alain were seated in their car, which would bring them to their townhouse in Greenwich Village, she peered through the open window. With warmhearted intonations creating subtle intensities, she declared the very thought which had inspired their visit.

"I think we will teach her a newer way to see."

Then it was that she noticed, as the car began a modulated departure—as if cars wisely instructed could make even departures charming—how pleased Gerald was with them, while he stood regarding their leave-taking. Her extemporary remark had, she hoped, drawn his keen mind toward an even firmer trust of them.

When Charlotte and Alain first met her, Eleanor appeared to be a quiet, tentative girl trying to find her way toward a life both bracing and original. But they saw more than that, because in this first meeting with her they noticed in Eleanor's sweet-natured affability a muted sorrow not unlike their own after the war, when they too had struggled to find their way back to the happiness their earlier experiences had promised them. That they no longer believed in the importance or the permanence of those promises did not diminish their willingness to guide this troubled girl toward her own realistic negotiations with life.

They found her reading quietly by the blue-rimmed well which was sequestered within an enshadowed alcove of the late Mrs. Marnham's private rose garden. All in their seeing were harmonies of floribunda and hybrid teas, delicate rosemary and damask and blue moon surfaces. Gerald brought them to her after he had concluded his first meeting with them in his study. No sooner had he observed them exchanging with his granddaughter a few affirmative remarks about the summery activities that, they hoped, she would enjoy—most often with Charlotte and sometimes with Alain, as well—than he was called back to his study to attend to some New York business that had followed him to this Newport retreat.

Alone with them now, Eleanor began opening her heart to them.

"I'm glad that you are going to be my friends," she said. "You will keep me from grieving away the summer."

"Oh, we don't want you to grieve," Charlotte said as she gently took her hand as a close friend does when she is offering comfort and affection.

"Your grandfather wants you to be happy once again," Alain told her. Though he kept a respectful distance from her, his courtly manner and handsome assurance suggested that he had her well-being in mind. "Your mother and your father would want you to be happy, too."

While accepting still Charlotte's gentle hand, Eleanor held her own right hand out to him as she drew him to her side. For a moment, flanked by the both of them, she seemed eased and accepting of the moment unfolding around them. Then, just as suddenly, she broke free of them.

"I wish I could be strong like them...like Father and Mother," she said. Her words were at first reluctant, as well as soft and tremulous. "I wish I could face life as bravely as they did."

She was standing now as when they had found her, pensive and willowy by the blue-rimmed well. Her weary unhappiness was muted, yet a palpable thing nonetheless.

At the moment just before they approached her, however, she had believed herself concealed by the rigor of her solitude. But in subtle witness they had arrived to notice how forlorn she appeared. They knew that she had returned to that place to hide this new onset of sorrow from them. Despite their having just met her, they felt that they perceived correctly the "idea" of this girl. They saw her as a bright and sometimes trammeled spirit yearning not merely to attend the world's progress, but to participate in its ambivalent nuances and sometimes in its emphatic gestures. Perceiving her so, they had determined almost instantly to be her friends. But, though she had been cordial and for a moment had opened her heart to them, they sensed that she had not yet decided whether she should keep them at a distance. She leagued them, perhaps, with a generation too "grown-up" to understand the joys and sorrows and secrets of her adolescence.

They thought it was a good time, here in the seclusion of the Marnhams' rose garden, to tell her that they knew something about the anguish she was experiencing.

"We've lost our dearest friends in the war," Charlotte said. "And Alain lost a cousin who had always been like a brother to him."

"We've seen so much death and misery," Alain explained. "We've learned with our own eyes that life can be very unfair."

"Our losses can become a bond for us," Charlotte said.

"We'll keep each other from falling into useless self-pity," Alain said. "Already, Charlotte and I are learning how to love the world again. We can show you, as well."

That they would help her claim her rightful share of happiness instantly lifted Eleanor's spirits. Upon witnessing her fleet smile, as hopeful as it was bright, Alain remembered as the flickering imagery of previous years, how life-loving and exuberant Eleanor appeared in the album of photographs which Gerald had allowed Charlotte and him to see at the conclusion of their meeting with him in his study. In those years all of the Marnhams spent part of their summers in Newport as a family whole and integral. In each photograph, Eleanor's glowing presence was already compelling. Her sprightly charm as a healthy girl of nine or ten was winning and impressive.

To observe her in this first hour of his knowing her, however, was to receive her as somebody different, if not completely separate—a reflection of a vital girl he saw in a photo and accurately remembered. Although nature had altered and clarified her lineaments and features, the very face and body and carriage she inhabited, all those amenities certainly left her intact. The imagery of herself in full bloom now told his apprehension none the less who she used to be and taught his eyes to receive her as a distinctive counterpart to the sunny girl in the photo he had seen only a half hour earlier. To his present glance, the sorrow that she held within herself was an additional layer of her existence. It revised the meaning of the photos, emphasizing their tentativeness.

Now, standing before their cautious solicitude, his and Charlotte's, and attending gratefully their sympathetic observation, Eleanor petitioned them for their understanding. The momentary hush, cloistered alone somewhere apart from the wind-stirred afternoon air, seemed itself like any other sensate being that showed an aptitude for listening. Only then did she reveal the truth of her situation.

"I don't want to go on needing Mother and Father," she said. "I loved them while they were alive, and I love them now as a memory. But I've had enough of death and all these months of mourning. I want life."

She paused, as if waiting for them to answer or rebuff the rebellious spirit of her complaint. Yet whatever words they cared to say, they held inside their circumspection, not a little impressed by her sudden flare of anger. So she went forward, her questioning voice now more defensive than petitioning.

"Is it so wrong to want life?"

She was challenging them to gainsay the rightness of her inquiry. But, quickly noticing their courteous reticence, she hurried on to express the vibrant idea that gave to the timbre of her voice a harder edge and a tough-minded urgency.

"I want only life."

"And we'll be a part of it," Charlotte gently promised. Her enthusiasm rose discreetly at the prospect of rescuing this appealing, vulnerable girl. For she saw in that rescue a worthy calling for herself. A proper care could infuse her days with a profounder meaning that might sometimes surprise, if not altogether startle, her.

"We'll show you the way back to happiness," she reassured Eleanor, as though happiness were for herself and for Alain a recovered possibility—and a bit of wild luck and blessed chance.

"There will be days and days of happiness for you," Alain told her. His husky timbres ignited friendly capacities and whatever other guardian powers he possessed for dispelling a haunted girl's grief.

And so there were hours and days and weeks of happiness to revive at first and then enthrall her. Now they drew her into festive occasions that flashed with quick time's waves and ripples. They took care always to guide her to the wholesome peers her family had in previous summers allowed her to befriend—hardy, keen-minded youths nearly full-grown now and well-bred ethereal girls.

The two of them sailed with her across the light of the sun welling beneath the tinted sea. With her they swam with acrobatic glee, all swift and gleaming spume-flecked motion. With a spate of life-loving friends (her trustworthy chums, along with Gerald's proven-loyal circle), they entered the colored velocity of a county fair. As agreeable chaperones in that summer of surprises, they dared her with them to climb her way to a perilous ridge. Just beyond a spotted raven's nest and twisted knots of grass, she--with them ascending adroitly--saw and heard, as for the first time because so proximate and actual, the rapid wing-beat of a black-backed gull. There, on that same ridge, they also observed the iridescent curve of cloud-flame cresting the hill above them and for one astonishing moment understood as well the symmetry and slant of the floating sky.

Through all these bracing occasions they restored her capacities for claiming the extraordinary possibility that was her young life unfolding. Yet they could dispel only intermittently the quiet sorrow that glimmered tensely. As if in spite of an hour's chance happiness, her sorrow revealed itself steadfast and intrinsic, like a palpable substance that was slowly burning away her soul.

Still, there grew around her, around this lost, lovely girl who with their guardian powers assisting might after all be wonderfully rescued, hours and days and weeks that possessed the very spirit and pleasure by which she herself yearned to be possessed. Flourishing and supreme, here-and-now experience rose upon her senses and was so much more intensified than any mind-held happiness that from her hovering past could only be a remembered idea. Or so they at that time told themselves and told one another. For her joining with them in the full fervor of summer moments hurried her into a brave exhilaration. Then she knew a sweep of liberty whose startling rush and lift and emphasis were realistic measures of how much of her bright promise they were capable of saving.

That there was so much brightness to save, they perceived with casual-seeming attentiveness whenever Eleanor gave herself completely to the day's adventure. Observing her luminous form ascending a sun-glanced hill or riding the crest of wind-sheared waves or taming the curve of a billowing sail, they saw how fluently, given her will, her identity translated its differences. On those days she was for them and for others with a mind to notice as a lovely blossoming of nature, a flowering of crisp intention and act and emotion. The various meanings of herself became distilled through an array of nuances and emblems and increments that refused to be brought within the rule of arbitrary definition or any other narrowness.

Too often, though, there lingered, as if fastened about the tense capacities of her sorrow, a guilty reluctance to bring her own fervor to the festive weeks that they were providing. Each day now they regarded as a favorable sign of her wakening spirit every occasion when Eleanor, as if suddenly confident and self-governing, willed herself effortlessly to explore with them a day that made happiness seem, if not permanent, at least diverse and plausible. For that reason they were heartened whenever she offered herself to the day's unexpected flare of surprise and to the promise, as well, of wildness not unlike adventure. This willowy image of a nearly blithe Eleanor brought them a quiet pleasure. For she appeared in those moments to be recovering all the happiness that she felt had been taken from her.

As they came to know her, Charlotte and Alain found Eleanor's poised reserve not without its singular charm and inspiring gravity. Her wind-tanned oval face, chestnut-brown hair, and clipped, New England intonations enhanced a quiet confidence and crisp directness. Her unmarred beauty and quickened sense of the deepest truth in things granted her a superb individuality. They were pleased that they were creating a special rapport with her. Whenever, with a convincing simplicity, they recounted life-loving exploits from their student days in Europe and, at the same time, related their particular joys in being new and promising, they noticed how tenderly Eleanor would glance from time to time toward each of them. With genuine elation, she listened to the splendid coherence of their narratives that, even in the rhythms of understatement, discovered their passionate natures and courageous willfulness. They had noticed, too, how apt and imaginative were the comments or inquiries she offered them as they told of their bold alliances with experience. Her well-schooled sociability identified her as winsome and wholly creditable. So impressed were they by the modulations within her of harmonies and tensions, a proper union of earthbound and ethereal, that they received as satisfying and inevitable the news that she shared their affection for Shakespeare's poems.

They had admired her sensitive commentary, for it mirrored their own reading of the poems even while imparting her own insights, which were often profound and sometimes original. One evening they heard her tell of her special affection for the one hundred sixth sonnet. Reading again and again the lyrical richness of this sonnet she most admired, she'd thought it a witty surprise that Shakespeare—or, rather, the persona through whom he spoke—should reproach himself for not achieving the mellifluous song he'd meant to compose in honor of the one he loved. His words (he'd declared) were inadequate to extol a being that surpassed all ordinary praise. In truth he required, so he believed, the divining eyes and tongues of the poetic chroniclers. He required, that is, a God-spun gift granting him the power to see and hear and describe as they had—the troubadours and minnesingers and *trouvères* of long ago. Theirs was a melodious art as invaluable as it was essential for presenting so sterling a reality as one's chosen lover.

It was the analogy implicit within the poem that the ancient verse chroniclers, singing the Platonic absolutes of fairest and best as they imaged the beloved coming into one's life, were not unlike the Old Testament prophets who, before them, had also seen, divined, and sung. Those prophets told us that Melchisedec and Moses, Enoch and Elijah, and Isaac and Jonah were foreshadowing figures of a coming Messiah. It was this analogy, perceiving one's lover as a god come to earth, a mystic equation of human-divine, which fascinated Eleanor. For to her mind it gave to the beloved a power to eclipse whatever other divinity had promised to save her.

"That is, I think, what authentic love must always be," she remarked, her voice a warm, disarming grace. "It is a religion unto itself—with its own promises and rewards and tests of faith."

At the dinner table listening to her while they were alone there with her except for the butler and the maid attending them, Charlotte and Alain smiled. They were pleased at her words and found in her charming affirmation a very romantic young lady. They found her charming and romantic once more when with crisp inflections she recited Shakespeare's poem. Then they'd observed the oblique light gently express her. A softer radiance (as if rising from within) belonged to her alone.

After that, they heard her tell of experiencing the flamingos during the summer that, as a nine-year-old girl with her parents and her Grandmother Marnham, she was traveling through the southern coast of France. On that August afternoon they were visiting the exotic Camargue, a landscape of shimmering lakes and sand dunes and reed beds. The Camargue was, as well, a park-like reserve sumptuous with billowing birds and their symphonic dissonances along the Grand Rhône which forks just north of Arles and, flowing east, spills into the tangy-scented Mediterranean.

It was there that for the first time Eleanor saw the flamingos. With delicate hues they were wading through the solacing waters of the *étang de Vaccarès*, the largest of the lakes in the Rhône Delta. Their tall and slender emphases possessed in the moment the reflecting waters they themselves were possessed by. The pink flush and black tips of their downward curving bills and roseate legs and plumage tinged the breeze-cooled air and fertile waters with a summer glow her yielding senses effortlessly savored. Intrigued, she noticed how, graceful and dexterous, they placed their heads beneath the mirroring lake. They pumped water through their bills and scooped backwards to catch with large, fleshy tongues small invertebrates and smaller plant matter that satisfied need or habit or instinct.

More remarkable to her roused apprehension were they on that afternoon than all the other picturesque birds arriving before her awareness as though to please her. There, she hurried as if to meet them at the threshold of the place that they were then inhabiting. Sovereign and proprietary over teeming, mottled wetlands, the black-wingéd stilts were extraordinary with legs red and long and plumage blending white and charcoal. In a flash, a flurry of energy and swift, irrevocable rhythms, they picked incessantly at their prey, all the while consuming them. Far from her still, yet no less astonishing, tall and private and disdainful on a grassy islet, a sleek-blue, wily heron moved with solitary deliberation into waiting, restless waters. Masterfully, it held its outstretched neck forward and angled down stiffly the sharp accuracy of its bill, just before piercing through the silver sheen of an ample fish.

Closer now, after with her parents and her grandmother she passed through a sequestered alcove and wended her way toward glimmering marshes, she saw the crouching brightness of bitterns. They—all of them with buffy colors—were active hunters in those reedy locations. Closer yet, with her parents and her grandmother she passed now by a green, luminous field discovered only on the easterly path they, a moment earlier, had left behind them. Here, frisky egrets showed pale yellow bills and lacy plumes the color of snow. While they foraged, proficient and erect, they held their wiry necks tightly coiled before striking. When she and her parents and her grandmother reached a low, ferny embankment, she saw—quite suddenly, there in the ripples and sunspots of the lake—a green-wingéd teal. With dark rufous head, legs gray and agile, and small, delicate bill, it was dabbling at the swaying surfaces of water, the better to lift up tiny fish.

How clearly nature revealed to her eyes that day its casual betrayals. She recognized in its splendor a darker intimation about the danger within its beauty--an intimation that her keen mind and the early promptings of her intuition had already taught her. That beauty could so naturally destroy did not alter her acceptance of the scene or taint the pleasure that sang to her heart because the earth contained such flux and entanglement and profusion. It was the surprise and mystery of beauty that intrigued her. Always, beauty suggested that it was something other than its outward appearance at first declared. The mystery and its promise called her soul to all the places she cared to remember: to art and music and books and to those remarkable human beings, a few, who mattered more to her than any other promise.

Now it was that she saw again the enthralling flamingos. But this time they were navigating waves upon waves of sun-caressed clouds. The pink flame of their wings was a flush or flare upon the floating sky. Just then in their spiraling ascensions she saw them, momentarily, even as they disappeared before her approving witness inside wind-glanced circumferences of clouds. The heaping layers of low cumulus and vaporous trails of cirrus were all cerulean sky-tint and yellow ocher ambiance in alliance with cream whites and grays and the glow of alizarin. Exhilarated beyond decorum's permissible expression, its nuanced reserve the signifying quality of her class, she was running now as if she were a girl enchanted. Flinging herself free of all restriction, she ran toward the dazzle of flamingos and sky-hills and cloud-waves. Her intention was to follow so admirable a flight of birds until every one of them had vanished. All the while, she cried out the words declaring herself to them—to the peerless birds who knew the secrets of the sky and cloud and wind.

"I want to," she cried out. "I want to."

Her voice was an emphatic declaration as much as a tremulous lament.

She had felt a restraining hand, elegantly gloved and feminine, placing itself on her shoulder. Only then did she pause in her earth-held flight. With surprise she turned to observe her mother's cool serenity express itself in a loving smile and to hear quiet, accurate words guiding her back to her proper self.

"What is it that you want, Eleanor?" she gently asked while studying with pensive directness the complicated individuality of this beautiful daughter. "What are you running toward?"

She noticed all of them now. Her father and her grandmother were arriving just behind her mother to stand before her. Because they apparently enjoyed the charm of her secret yearning made suddenly palpable, they smiled through their own curious inquiry of this altogether unexpected Eleanor.

"Tell us. Do," her father advised. His deep resonant voice was frugal of emotion. "Tell us what you want."

She could not, in the first moments of her seeing them, locate within her disarranged attention the necessary words that would shape an adequate answer. The surprise of herself openly declared and of their quiet contemplation of her stranger manifestation inhibited whatever exuberance and spontaneity she had for once freely summoned while in their presence.

"I want to be like them...like the flamingos," after a moment's reflection she heard herself saying. "I want to be lost and then find my way back."

Her father, still watching her closely, allowed his smile to stay, though almost imperceptibly. He regarded her innocent openness as no small merit in her favor.

That time Grandmother Marnham, enhancing the propriety that had shaped her, glanced affectionately at her. With a grown-up's voice of counsel she spoke words that suggested her wise balance.

"Those birds are not lost," she said, trying to be helpful. "They know where they are going."

At her grandmother's attempt to revise her fanciful perceptions, she frowned.

"They may become lost sometimes," she replied. She did not care for her grandmother's words that to her mind seemed condescending and even imperious. "Everyone becomes lost, at least once in a while."

"Well, don't *you* try to become lost," her mother said, regarding her daughter's startling wish with new unease. "Not in the clouds or anywhere else, my dear."

She took her hand now, as though she meant to remind her of the emerging bond between them, where nobody should ever become lost. Then, guiding her return to the path the four of them had been traversing, she imparted with carefully modulated finality the words that would hurry them away from an unhappy subject.

"When you become lost," she said, "you may never find your way back."

Hearing Eleanor, five years later, tell of her exhilaration before the splendid flight of the flamingos, Charlotte and Alain perceived in her that evening a charming ingenuousness. Her disposition was poetic and idealistic. In their eyes, she appeared to be a bright girl capable of declaring her own spirited challenge to the world. Perhaps, when she called out to the flamingos her wish to follow their journey, she meant to subvert whatever hesitancy or reticence within herself made her vulnerable and might defeat her. It was this willingness to share graciously the truths of herself that endeared her to both of them. By interpreting a sonnet and describing a sky become radiant with colorful birds, she had revealed who she was and what she believed and how, with attractive and intricate subtexts, she embraced romantic ideals.

"She's very romantic," Alain said after he and Charlotte had retired to their suite of rooms in the Marnham home. "That can be a good thing, if she learns to use it well."

"She'll need more than that," Charlotte said. "She has to see the world for what it really is."

Then, because Eleanor's untouched loveliness had ignited the memory of his earliest passion for his wife, he cast his heated glance upon Charlotte. With wily intimation, she met that glance as if she were looking upon a new and satisfying lover. For Eleanor's romantic exuberance had also stirred her appetite. Roused with a fervor they had not known since before the war, she and Alain would influence this night to become one of life's happier occasions.

During the weeks and months that followed, this complicated matter of recovering her authentic presence in the world gave Eleanor a special pleasure. For, just before she entered this period of self-recovery, she had disengaged herself from the singular identity she had been cultivating with the assistance of her parents, her teachers, and her own will. Not only had she lost the often radiant and sometimes too-delicately pensive girl her mirror's imagery had allowed her to peruse—the unique and hopeful person whose identity she had been creating all through the earlier years of her life. But she had also lost the more recent imagery of an emerging young woman as well. That person had been herself no less, though a familiar stranger still who dwelled most often as in secret within her impassioned thought. Lately, she had been an imaginative and sometimes ingenious girl who was learning to negotiate effectively with the world even when she had to endure long separations from her parents. When they died, she appeared at first to turn away from this promising, strong-minded young woman whom she was learning to be. Disarranged by her grief, she had neglected the upbuilding of her character. Yet, after the first months of this journey with Charlotte, she found herself accepting the disciplines of a new, authentic life. The person she was becoming was as contemporary as she was studious and altruistic.

At the close of her hospital stay, she had returned with her grandfather to the coherent splendors of his Federal-Revival home along Ocean Drive. That home was a stately amplitude of twenty-five acres that each year taught her, with nuances subtly different from any she had before experienced, the bracing freedoms of the sea's crisper breezes and of full-flowering fields and congregant majestic trees. All in the comfort of her seeing was married to a green world nurtured and enhanced by the inspired design of her Grandmother Marnham and by that formidable woman's efficient cadre of landscape architects and gardeners. When her doctors advised her that it would be better for her to continue her studies at her grandfather's home in Newport, she had not protested, even though she knew that she would miss the friends and the teachers of whom she had grown very fond during the years she had spent at Miss Porter's.

Possibly, her reluctance to return there derived from her intuitive awareness that acceding to her grandfather's plan for her would fortify whatever harmony she could compose in her relations with him. Or an uneasy insight persuaded her that, by remaining at home, she would elude another fall into despair. Away from the solacing environment that her grandfather's home had always been for her and away from the stewards and keepers of his household whose familial presence she had come to cherish, she would surely fall into despair. Possibly, it was that apprehension which influenced her to continue her studies at home. Or, more likely, it was her understanding that, because of her losing her parents, she could no longer return to the girlhood innocence of her peers. In every other respect, those young ladies were like her, a well-born blend of straitlaced and spirited.

Or, most probable of all, she recognized that in this year of home study, she would more freely navigate experience—its prismatic diversity and pleasing capaciousness. Even while under the watchful guidance of Charlotte and Alain and while in their company, she would frequently visit art galleries and scientific exhibits and attend theatre and opera, chamber concerts and symphonies. She would also attend university lectures pertaining to philosophy and mathematics and offer her charitable services to the needy.

Whether each of these possibilities influenced her acceptance of a schedule which would keep her away from Miss Porter's School, an environment which had enabled her to thrive, or one of them more than any of the others, she could not, even in those moments when she paused long enough in her busy schedule to consider the rewards and liabilities of so choosing, tell herself with assurance that she knew. So tenuous was her certainty of all that the life unfolding about her signified—its ellipses and ambiguities testing nonetheless her steadfastness and her courage.

That her grandfather had asked Charlotte Aubray, a specialist in modern languages, to be her instructor was all to the good—the good, that is, of her continuing evolution as a fourteen-year-old girl becoming both educated and aesthetic. For Charlotte would help her to hone her knowledge of French and German as well as Italian and Spanish. She would also share with her the memory of having lived in Europe for many of her early years. Just as important, she would show her how to make her way in the rugged world.

Even in the first weeks of their relationship as teacher and pupil, Charlotte taught her how to make her life useful.

She influenced her to respect the earth she inhabited and to be, through positive actions and lifelong learning, its prudent benefactor. In these first weeks, she persuaded her to translate herself through the good works that accurately represented her strong-minded personhood. Exuberantly, with Charlotte as a knowing guide, she pursued new involvement in ecological programs (including the protection of the forests in southeastern Rhode Island and the preservation of the islands and wildlife of Narragansett Bay). She was involved as well in social services (on behalf of handicapped children, the elderly poor and the homeless, and the unemployed who needed retraining in marketable skills). She continued to read biographies of leaderly activists such as Julia Ward Howe, Jane Addams, and Florence Nightingale. In this season that she regarded as her convalescence from grief, she renewed her affinity for worthwhile occupation. She sensed that her life was once more becoming an expression of using time well.

She was aware that Charlotte was guiding her away from her uneasy, problematic self and into a formidable home-schooling that would prepare her for her college days. That Charlotte had taught young ladies at the exclusive Newbury School was all to the good—the good, that is, of her grandfather's pragmatic aims. He wanted her, now that she had left behind Miss Porter's School for a year, to make a friend of Charlotte. With this gifted teacher as her mentor, her grandfather had reminded her before he embarked on a series of business trips that would take him out of the country, she would learn to choose and to appreciate the gifts that the world kept offering her. She would also learn to fulfill all the obligations her acceptance of those gifts, in good conscience and with fair-minded reciprocity, entailed.

It brought her a special pleasure to communicate the whole day long with this remarkable teacher exclusively in French or Italian, German or Danish or Spanish. She was conscious that each day not only intensified her disciplined aptitudes, but also prepared her for a life in the wider world. That experience (she imagined) would be even more adventurous and creative than the everyday reality that now spun its ambivalence around her. It was always challenging and sometimes surprising to collaborate with remarkable Charlotte. With infinite variety, this astute teacher accompanied her to the further discovery of her immense and untested possibilities. In ways even more effective than those her previous schooling had allowed her, she was learning how to be the maker of herself and the shaper of her destiny. Out of her best capacities and with nearly spontaneous symmetry, she was fashioning the unique being who was her evolving self.

So it was, in the full consciousness of her evolution, that for the next year she learned from each day's challenging studies and altruistic endeavors the virtues of maintaining an intellectual rigor toward herself, especially in tense or formidable circumstances. She also learned the virtues of helping those who are poor or sick or abandoned in old age to a lonely dying. Though it was not Charlotte alone who challenged and guided her to enlarge her capacities for achieving her worthiest aspirations, the influence of this woman worked, nevertheless, its affirmative powers upon her. Within a few weeks of their meeting as teacher and pupil, they quickly achieved a natural rapport. Charlotte became for her a gentle advisor, a discreet confidante, and a superb mentor. Not only did she draw from her a flawless performance as a multi-lingual student of the world's varied cultures. But she also accompanied her with quick-witted and ingrained precision through advanced programs in philosophy, biology, and calculus.

More than that, in this year with Charlotte as her guide, there occurred during the many Samaritan visits they paid to the sick or poor, as well as to the aged or injured, the clearest evidence of her progress away from the sometimes impulsive and often self-absorbed girl her privileged background had influenced her to be. True it was that, within the first few months of becoming reacquainted with the less inward and more altruistic facets of her character, she had drawn always upon her capacities to help those far less fortunate than she. And true again that, while on beneficent visits to the needy and in the presence of Charlotte's authentic empathy toward the suffering and the needy, she had acquitted herself effectively. With the quietude of a humble nurse, she had administered the corporal works of mercy that had brought her to the working class suburbs which stood, unobtrusive and ordinary, beyond the visible rims of Newport. But she had never completely entered the experience of sharing her humanness with these struggling members of her species who often, despite their hardships, maintained a proud and undaunted resilience.

Now, during the later Samaritan visits of this first season of her recovery, she discovered within herself a profound sympathy for the anguished and afflicted and abandoned. There grew in her a genuine desire to do all that she could to help them. In this period she often brought her solacing presence to a dying girl of twenty whose stoic resignation intensified an ethereal loveliness. On other days she encouraged new self-determination in an embittered war veteran who—at twenty-four—was learning to walk again, assisted as he was by a prosthetic leg. Quietly moved by his plight, she persuaded her uncle to finance his enrollment into law school. When this young hero earned his law degree, there would be a place for him within the legal department of the Marnham Steel Corporation. In a more recent month, she worked for many hours helping to paint and to furnish three large brownstones, so that the children and the widows of firefighters and policemen killed in the line of duty could make comfortable homes in attractive, modern apartments. To these afflicted human beings and to others like them, she also offered with her enlightened teacher the sustenance of food and clothing and empathetic words.

There were, at this time, many other frail or fallible persons whose spirits revived because of her presence. As if each time were a revelation meant for her alone, there came upon her awareness the truth that each of these suffering and broken and needy belonged to herself. They belonged, that is, to the human family she represented. Her heart's new knowledge and the clarity of accurate recognition taught her to receive them, in the very hour she was assisting them, as upright and worthy relations.

In that spring, both Charlotte and Alain were surprised and very pleased by her spontaneous expressions of sympathy and by the efficacy of her Samaritan deeds. They began to believe that this rigorous period (in truth, nearly a year) of displacing her grief was making Eleanor a most capable human being.

Nor were they alone in noticing Eleanor's admirable influence upon a scene of tattered hopes or painful illness, irrevocable loss or careworn frailty. Gerald, having returned briefly from his latest business trip abroad, also observed the favorable signs of his granddaughter's new-found maturity. He had, on two occasions, assisted Charlotte and Eleanor in their visits to the sick and the needy and never failed, in the diplomatic stillness of his accurate perceptions, to appreciate the girl's hard-edged and unhesitant confrontation with the dark blight of existence from which her own life's safe amenities had shielded her. How startling it was, at first, to witness so radical a change, even in her appearance. Gone was the grieving, introverted girl with the auburn glow upon the curly ringlets of her child-like, flowing hair and a trouble-haunted intensity within her blue eyes. Gone too was the dissatisfied girl with a hint of hauteur in her perfect profile and the hint of bitterness within her genteel smile and the sometimes rigid tension in her feminine gait. In their stead was a young woman with auburn hair pulled back to form a sensible coil at the nape of her neck. With steady, encouraging eyes and determined profile...pursed lips and assertive gait, she hurried to meet the sober and problematic world.

"She is becoming a very promising young woman," Gerald remarked to Charlotte, one afternoon in early May.

They were quickening their pace along the winding flagstone path which guided them in their brisk afternoon walk past terraced banks rising one behind another and an artfully graded lawn that sloped into a meadow of mild spring's flowers. All in their seeing were orange butterfly weed and red-violet musk mallows...gold and white oxeye daisies and sapphire blue Douglas irises. The path brought them past long, precise hedgerows and the granite wall that directed the eye agreeably toward a wind-stirred sea. It brought them, as well, down the bluestone steps hugging the rugged bluff and onto the tawny sands of the beach.

Before arriving to meet those steps, they'd smoothly descended from the hilltop perch which held the Marnhams' ample and pristine Newport home seven hundred feet from the shore.

That Gerald, during his bracing walk with Charlotte, would remark upon Eleanor's progress seemed, at the moment, appropriate and pertinent. For as they accelerated their pace, the better to attain the clearest expression of their keen vitality, they chanced to glimpse Eleanor seated supple and erect on a splendid bay-colored Arabian horse. She was cantering in the palpable distance to their left, along undulating verdant land that scanned amidst a wide array of hills a grove of early-blooming lilac trees. Their tints of rose pink and azure and amethyst were swaying, graceful and submissive, before the will of the wind. Swaying, too, were cream-white flowering cherries and the flourishing golden rain trees. How poised and adept she appeared to their seeing. With the assistance of a professional horse trainer, she was guiding a limber girl of ten and her eight-year-old brother—a wiry, athletic lad—to ride with the buoyant confidence they'd gained in many, careful weeks of instruction. (They two, lad and sister, were mounted favorably on short and hardy chestnut-brown Caspian ponies.)

"She has become, if not altogether new, then surely someone whose differences make her capable of surprising you," Charlotte remarked.

At this time, she persuaded Gerald to pause with her momentarily. From afar, they observed Eleanor bring patience and empathy to the lessons which she and the retired, yet still agile, jockey were offering to these strong-hearted children. Their parents, who were slowly convalescing in a Boston hospital, had suffered grievous burns in a fire that had injured sixty other persons and had consumed the textile factory in nearby Middletown. There, they had worked long and arduous hours.

"How right you are," Gerald said.

He was pleased that his granddaughter continued to thrive and pleased, also, that she had opened her heart so generously to those two sturdy children who were learning not only how to ride a Caspian pony, but how to prevail in spite of misfortune and disappointment. (Each of us must learn that lesson and keep on learning it—even a girl as privileged as Eleanor. So he remarked to Charlotte, whose gentle smile suggested that she agreed with this conventional wisdom that his understatement kept from sounding too prosaic. Still smiling, she went on watching the four riders hurry into the nebulous, waiting distance.)

"That is one young woman who will never lose her mystery," she declared after a momentary reflection upon Eleanor's poise. "I need not remind you, I know, that a tremendous thing has been happening to her these many months. She's discovering some of her best capacities and some of her obligations, too."

"Ah, yes, *there's* the adventure, and she's testing herself in it."

So remarking, Gerald—with resilient Charlotte keeping effective pace—hurried forward to the sun-dappled sands of the beach. Standing in closer proximity to the restless and shimmering sea, they were conscious of the serenities of floating clouds (cumulus and feathery), an azure-bright sky, and the gold-flecked horizon. Now they heard even more clearly the crash of spumy, viridian waves upon the whiteness of glistening rocks and felt breeze-tossed mist upon their skin. In the same moment, they saw a host of gray-brown gulls, accurate and wily and steadfast. Each of these birds—with a broad ring of black color within its bill—was scooping plump mackerel from prodigal, indifferent waters.

That Eleanor's adventure should involve not only her Samaritan efforts, but also her cultivation of the privileged society into which she was born, Charlotte was certain. But on that day she did not mention her plan to enhance the education by which she and Alain were assisting Eleanor in her self-willed transformation. There would be time, she knew, for her to do the thing that she believed must be done if Eleanor was to make her way in the wider world. That Eleanor was cultivating a genuine selflessness as well as a disciplined scholarship was all to the good. Her conduct, with its assured decorum and genteel reserve, would please even the most austere dowagers of her class. But one day, before she returned to the protective atmosphere of Miss Porter's School, both she and Alain planned to introduce her to the discreet intricacies of her sensuality. Only then would she make her way effectively in an ambivalent world.

Alain planned all of it, this *ménage à trois* that would draw them into a labyrinth of his and Charlotte's own devising. With hushed elation and restless need, Eleanor consented to whatever ingenuities they might impose upon its wayward design. That, in these several months, they had come to know each other well was all to the good—the good, that is, of their liberated purposes. How bracing it was to be, as if at the very same moment, roused by desire newly wakened and with solacing ease confronted. On those occasions when with them she was enjoying some free time away from her studies and her community service, they were careful to bring her to a group of her peers. Always, she was aware that they were discreetly watching her from a distance while allowing her and seven or eight of her peers a latitude for navigating a responsible individuality. Because she was so often enclosed within this group of her peers, she could experience a promising intimacy with Alain and Charlotte only by an indirection that searches out the unobtrusive path or quiet alcove or private arbor.

At first she had to content herself with their presence obliquely, as if she were attracted primarily to the group and not to them especially. All during those splendid days when extemporaneous circumstance or summer occasions carefully planned by others availed them, they held themselves toward her as casual allies neither predominant nor ancillary to her engagement with the hardy, callow youths and lissome, adolescent girls from backgrounds similar to her own. No matter that they were for these gregarious occasions in the company of her friends' parents. Affable and upright with them, they appeared to enjoy their roles as chaperones both gentle and careful. While they were there, permitting themselves at times to join with the parents the mingling of keen-eyed youths and understated girls who had been her friends for several years, Alain and Charlotte were for her a charismatic influence. Their quick-witted repartee within the group and their good-natured fellowship eased her excited senses. She was conscious of being on the brink of experience altogether different and momentous.

Her being with the two of them alone brought her an even larger measure of happiness. During these extraordinary days, she knew the heartbeat hum of excitement. As if spellbound, she experienced the joy of being prodigiously alive, because for her they were spirit-driven earth-mates...full-bodied sensualities. How wonderful it was to be with each of them even obliquely, while they—as if they were her exuberant friends rather than her dutiful chaperones—went cantering along the meandering sands of a private beach on Arabian horses, bay or black or chestnut. The wind-raveling spray of afternoon breakers was a cool, luxuriant touch to warm skin and pulsing motion. Wonderful as well it was to enter the colored velocity of a county fair and on a visit to a picturesque farm to ride on a wagonload of sweet-scented hay. With frolicsome ease in sight of a sun-tinted sea, they also picnicked at the foot of rugged gray cliffs in Falmouth. The steadfast verticality of those cliffs scaled cloud-dwelling altitudes for miles upward.

Then there came those times when she was alone with Alain. The sublime chance of their unanticipated encounter was a sign or harbinger of happiness that would be theirs to claim in sequestered awareness.

One time, the very first time that was different from all those times when she consented to the group's priorities so that she might be near this man who cast his spell upon her, he found her alone, pensive and ethereal at the entrance of a sumptuous grove on the ample grounds of her grandfather's home. There, he met her with a smooth courtesy and asked whether he might join her. After she agreed, he sauntered with her into the light-reflected shadows that lent mystery to the grove. Together, they entered breeze-stirred and fragrant symmetries of lilac trees white, lavender and crimson; orange-red rowans and translucent green aspens; and comely mimosas with feathery leaves and powdery gold flowers. As in a dream, she soon arrived with him inside the blueness of a gazebo where, sitting next to each other, they spoke of many things—music and art, poetry and aspirations and freedom. On the rim of a sudden stillness between them and in the heat of his passion, his body grew taut and his breathing became tighter. Momentarily, he cupped her lovely face with his rugged hands. Then with gentle proficiency he drew her willowy grace to the lithe muscularity that was himself and planted upon her lips a tender kiss. With shy reticence she drew away as quickly as she could. But the stillness that came to watch with him her graceful movement told her that her warm blue eyes and warm, delicate flesh left none the less their spell upon him.

He would not on that afternoon take her, though the intensity of his gaze and the warm touch of his hands suggested his need for her. Here, within a sheltered July grove on the Marnhams' ample property, he would not yet allow his body the invigorating privilege of taking her. He meant first of all to befriend her. Because she was a demure and well-born young lady, he would have to waken gradually her sexual need of him.

Several days later, while they were held still to the Marnhams' seaside home, they happily met, this time by a careful design of their making. Her excited senses were roused by him more easily now in the sumptuous harmonies of a rose garden, all else in their seeing gold and cream-velvet textures and profusions of floribunda and hybrid teas. Even then he would not take her. Instead, he permitted himself only the muted pleasure of intimating how much he enjoyed being with her. As she paused at a blue-rimmed well, she received with easy elation his quiet words. In her eyes he appeared more handsome than ever before. Now she told him that her need of him was growing more essential.

"I'm glad you like me," she said. Her confession was as direct as it was extemporaneous and therefore more natural than his remark. "It makes my liking you so much grander."

Nor (she perceived) would he take her on a later afternoon when he'd found her alone in the shimmering meadow of silver grasses that hurried toward a yellow ocher horizon, verdurous as well and luminescent. The delicate grays and violets of low stratus clouds were floating in the sun-washed sky. She was seated poised and accurate at her artist's easel in a blue-mist summer frock and broad-brimmed white linen hat. There, in that solacing privacy a quarter of a mile from the Marnhams' main house, though on her grandfather's property nonetheless, sweet-scented grasses and flowering trees were softly swaying around her. That day, she was surprised from her pastime by his being suddenly and marvelously there for her. So pleased was she by his having come freely to her, that she caressed his sun-bronzed face with the fair coolness of her hand.

Even then he would not take her. Now, though, he could see that her desire was as a fuse disarranging in an altogether new way her uneasy heart.

As if he wanted to excite through his absence her need of him, he withdrew from her company for a week. On each of these days she saw him from a far distance, as she often had seen him in the months that had too swiftly passed. He was working with teams of architects, masonry and landscape contractors, and tree movers to re-create her grandfather's large estate. So it was that in his absence Charlotte brought her once more into a confederacy of energetic and life-loving peers. These bright young people (all of them fourteen or fifteen) shared with her and Charlotte as well as with their parents days and days of swimming and sailing and water-skiing. But not even her friends' exuberance or their parents' smooth hosting of each occasion or Charlotte's charming anecdotes could allay her longing for Alain.

One evening during this cycle of days and nights when Alain was hard at work and not available to either of them, Charlotte allowed her to sleep with her. Alain was downstairs in the study, busy with the revisions of architectural plans and engineering charts. It was not the first time that they had spent the night together, as though they were sisters bringing comfort to each other during the tentative fury of a lightning storm or the uneasy aftermath of a disappointing day. Tonight, though, while they enjoyed their solacing nearness, Charlotte drew from her the words that revealed her more-than-ordinary feelings for Alain as well as for her.

"You love Alain the way a woman loves a man she wants to sleep with."

Charlotte caressed her as she spoke the words. She was obviously pleased. More than that, her smile suggested that the thought of a schoolgirl's loving Alain roused her.

"I love him so much," Eleanor confessed. "I want him to love me, as well."

"Ah, my dear," Charlotte said. "You must say what you mean. You want Alain to make love to you."

"Yes, I do. Very much. But I think I also love you in that way."

"Then he will be very pleased," Charlotte said. "He has a large appetite and needs the both of us."

Now, because their words had not only resolved her unease, but had also promised them new pleasures, they spent the hour before they fell into sleep speaking with sisterly briskness of the new fashions in hats and dresses, of the extensive travel they were planning, and of their plans to pilot a plane. Although neither Charlotte nor she mentioned Alain again that night, she perceived very clearly that this French woman whom she found altogether intriguing was as excited as she that the three of them would soon share the same bed and their sensuality.

"I can't bear to be separated from you," Eleanor told Alain when he was free to enjoy a day with her. With unresolved contentment she accepted now his fevered embrace of her while she whispered her plaintive words. They were standing in the lush privacy of the Marnhams' rose garden that had become for them a favorite meeting place. "There is no happiness for me in any place where you are not."

She had hurried to him after Charlotte told her that they three would be spending the weekend in the home of their Nantucket friends. Those cosmopolitan persons were visiting their relatives on the West Coast. Soon Alain, Charlotte, and she would be joining the festive lightheartedness that was theirs to possess while they swam in prismatic July waters or sunned on colorful fabrics in the exuberant light of the pleasing afternoon. At last languorous and temporarily blissful, they would loll in the comfort of canvas-backed chairs. The coil and curve of beach-sand would be a warm intimacy against their leaning, outstretched hand gathering it to the soothed touch.

So Charlotte promised her.

Without revealing to Charlotte her veiled purpose, she hurried away on the pretext that she had promised to help Mrs. Appleton, their primary housekeeper, select flowers from one of her grandfather's splendid gardens. Together, they would arrange them in delicate vases for the dinner table as well as for the rooms where four guests from

New York would be staying overnight. She hurried away with a rapturous heart, though not at first. Instead, she lingered on the beach with Charlotte and a few of the Aubrays' poised, summery friends who were passing through on their way to Bar Harbor in Maine. She waited until Alain arrived. Within the liveliness of that affable circle, he looked tawny and lithe and accurate. The stylized confidence of Charlotte, standing near him while they conversed with two dark-haired women, was to her eyes an attractive counterpoint enhancing Alain's quicksilver singularity.

When he turned to greet her, though, she received him casually. The modulations of her joy, made cautious so that others might not witness her wakened need of him, were stays against confusion. With correspondent and still mute elation, she noticed his surreptitious glance a half hour afterward summoning her to the garden behind the main house. Patiently, she waited there until he arrived, comforting herself with the thought that twice before the garden had served well their desire to be alone, together.

There, at that clandestine meeting in a fragrant garden, she saw most clearly, with an unexpected awe rousing her appetite, the intensity of her love for him. So essential on that afternoon did he appear to her and so urgent was her love for him, that she paused. She felt a momentary compunction before the prospect of freely enjoying the pleasure of his love during all the summer days that were left to them. Her need of him, she had to admit, exceeded her affection for Charlotte. But the thought that she might have Charlotte's love as well as Alain's recalled her to herself, to the already hardened part of her nature that resisted hesitancy and convention and the sentimental.

"We're going to have a first-rate time together," he said. Once more he drew her willowy radiance into his embrace while he eased her disquiet at their having been separated for the long week just passed. "We're just beginning."

Her happiness, now under his spell, brightened at so auspicious a thought. Yet she consented nonetheless to a decorous protest.

"But I want to be with you all the time."

Appreciating the absolute charm of her, he gently laughed. "Nobody is together all the time," he said. "The world's a very busy place and occasionally needs us for other purposes."

Now it was she who kissed him, the light pressing of her lips upon his own a delicate sensuality...an exciting subtlety.

"I don't care about the world," she declared a moment later. Happily she lost herself in the enclosure that was his embrace of her. He was the longed-for sanctuary.

He beamed, while with courtly assurance guiding her toward the privacy of a flowering gazebo.

"Well, then, be happy, for Heaven's sake. Right now," he said. His voice was smoky with his roused pleasure at her touch. "Because we are together and because we have days and days of summertime before us."

He did not take her even on that afternoon, harnessing through self-command the raw intensity of his passion for her. He was, at the same time, aware that Mrs. Appleton or their New York friends or a crew of diligent gardeners or butlers might by chance come there and discover them. Besides, he had already devised the episode by which, with Charlotte as an ardent partner, they could freely—and in a setting as secure as it was romantic—consummate their love. The three of them were, he told her, in mind and spirit already married to each other.

Through this idea, a convincing belief asserting their bond with each other, he came to persuade her of the rightness of his plan. At a picturesque home within the secluded seaport of Nantucket, they would—in fragrant privacies and without the Church's approving seal or any other legal document permitting them—celebrate the marriage of their bodies to one another. On that night they would activate their own personal laws. That they, by so doing, would at the same time subvert narrow convention and protect themselves from the public's accusing eyes would serve well to enhance their mutual pleasure.

"How clever you are," she said just before kissing him once more, exhilarated and breathless.

"There are many ways to have an adventure," he told her. His full, sensual lips caressed now the exquisite lobe of her right ear. "We've found the proper day for this one to begin."

In Nantucket, Eleanor shared with Alain and Charlotte the quickened pleasures of sailing on the sun-mottled waters of Vineyard Haven and swimming with a smooth swiftness at Tisbury Town Beach. Assertive and reliable, they also paddled on the sinuous propulsion of the Deerfield River in nearby Zoar.

One afternoon she walked with them in the tawny glow of the beach, musing about the capable lives they were then inhabiting. They mused as well about their plans for the future. Still they knew the tangy scent of the sea. Still the splash and ripple of massive waters broke upon the shore. Still the slant light of the sun shone upon the beach like flame or phosphorescence.

"I want to help the world even in some small way," she told the two who were, with her, in a reflective mood as they sauntered barefoot along the soft, coiling textures of cool, silvery sand. Their white shirts and slacks billowed in the breeze and granted them a temporary emphasis upon the afternoon. "I want to study medicine so that I can make life better for the poor people in our country."

Charlotte, hearing her words, imbued as they were by pragmatic altruism, studied her with special interest.

This was the first time that Eleanor declared so openly her belief that she had come into the world to make it a better place.

"You're aiming very high and very nobly, too," Charlotte observed.

Her favorable response was altogether genuine, though carefully muted by all that her wartime experience had taught her about human nature.

"Do your part to make the world better, without believing that you are performing miracles."

"Oh, I won't be a miracle worker," Eleanor said. Lighthearted that day, she laughed at the thought. "But I plan to be helpful."

"Being helpful can be a good thing," Alain said, "if you can make your goodness wily and resourceful as well."

"Does goodness have to be wily?"

"Yes," he answered her. "We live in a rugged world."

As the three of them sauntered along the beach, she noticed all the while, though merely scanning the looming distance to the right of her, the roar and rush of spume-flecked waves leaping and echoing with sonorous powers. She noticed, too, that her optimistic words had brought to Alain as well as to Charlotte a momentary stillness and a subtle frown. But it was Alain who now advised her that neither her goodness nor her helpfulness would alter the world's marauding instincts.

"Don't imagine that you will cure the world of its bad habits," he said. "It will take plenty of courage simply to offer your good deeds to a world that is so problematic and dangerous."

Now, with a clipped intensity harnessing his bitterness, he spoke of the casual depredation roiling across the globe.

In Germany Adolf Hitler had begun, through a political uprising in Munich, his insidious forays against democracy. In Italy Benito Mussolini was governing through a Fascist-controlled Parliament. By means of that Fascist organization, he arranged the kidnapping and the assassination of his primary opponents, including the Socialist leader Giacomo Matteotti. In Asia Minor Turks and Greeks had recently clashed in decimating warfare. In China there raged a relentless war between the forces of General Wu Pei-fu in Peking and Chang Tsu-Lin's Manchurian Army. Within a few hours their brute combat claimed seven thousand lives.

In America the lynching of innocent black men in Chicago led to six days and nights of rioting. Because of its fear and hatred of foreigners, the United States denied its freedom to immigrants from Russia, Poland, and Italy. In America's southern states the Ku Klux Klan carried forward its murderous policies against African-Americans, Jews, and Catholics. The Presidential Administration of the recently deceased Warren Harding had tarnished itself with the scandal of Harding's cronies, including the Secretary of the Interior and millionaire business men, misappropriating three huge oil reserves on government land in Teapot Dome, Wyoming, that had been set aside for the use of the Navy. Even more grievous in America, poverty blighted the lives of hardworking farmers; and Indians, African-Americans, and Mexican-Americans lived marginal existences as the nation's disinherited.

"The most affirmative philosopher confronting all these harms might well wonder how any of us could find a way to redress even a small portion of the wrongdoing."

"I know what is in the world," Eleanor said. "Both of you have helped me to understand it in a new way."

She paused. She was searching for words that would redefine her perspective without denying Alain's review of the world's troubles.

"All that you have said is true enough," she told them after her pensive moment. "But it won't stop me from trying to change things. I will not allow the world to make me cynical."

"There's nothing wrong with being cynical, if it keeps you grounded to the realistic level."

"When you live on the realistic level," Charlotte said, quietly complementing her husband's point of view, "you may very well change things for the better—at least, once in a while. But don't imagine that the world was made to conform to your will. It doesn't play fair, and it isn't about to change its habits so that you can always win the game."

"Complicity with the unexpected is an essential requirement for anyone who wants to meet the world on its own terms," Alain said. "That is the only time when the world will tolerate the bit of wild courage that is in all of us and the romance."

"In spite of the worst of things, there *is* romance," Charlotte said. "There is beauty, too, and favorable adventure, if you know how to see things for what they are."

"That is a lesson I keep learning every day," she said, while she held out her hands and drew them closer to her.

The warm touch of their hands around hers roused the love she felt for them. Apart from that complicated love, she felt a pity, too. Its newness startled her, because her adulation had always received them as perfect and beyond her power to interpret the subtleties of their characters. But with an awakened clarity, she understood now that the war had destroyed something important within them.

Later that day, when dark clouds and an uneasy wind promised a stormy evening, they decided against sailing across the already restless waters in a sturdy yawl which belonged to Alain's friend. Instead, after they returned to the spacious house where they were staying, they gave themselves wholeheartedly to preparing and cooking a fine dinner. Charlotte's fresh herb omelet, Alain's sirloin steaks served with green peppercorns and sautéed potatoes, and Eleanor's choux pastry fritters accompanied by apricot sauce made their meal especially festive. A magnum of *Veuve Clicquot* enhanced their pleasure at the table.

So, too, did their conversation, which was as lively as it was varied. They spoke of the achievements of women aviators, including France's Raymonde de Laroche, Germany's Melli Beese, and America's Lilian Gatlin. They remarked upon Paavo Nurmi's victories in the Summer Olympics, which had been recently held in Paris. An extraordinary athlete from Finland, Nurmi had won four gold medals for his swift performance in the fifteen-hundred-meter race and, only hours later, in the five-thousand- meter event. Two days afterward, he made as strong a showing in the team cross-country competition and, on the following day, in the three-thousand-meter race. They admired his spending hours upon hours in grueling practice for the games and living on black bread and raw fish.

They also discussed Paul Cézanne's *Monte Sainte Victoire (1904-1906)*. Alain respected its mosaic-like pattern that integrated the land and the sky. The canvas was a monumentality of square brush strokes and sharp edges or planes of color, including cerulean and cobalt blue, viridian green and emerald, cadmium yellow and ochre, and—in the foreground—umber and black. As interpreted by Cézanne, Monte Sainte Victoire was an unconsoling yet majestic solidity. The silhouette of the mountain itself was both a defiant beak and an aggressive prow.

With quiet feeling, Charlotte then spoke of the six songs that Beethoven composed for his sorrow-laden *To the Distant Beloved*. How subtly, Charlotte said, and within a simple, strophic melody, Beethoven conveys throughout the cycle the implicated order that is our memory. Its vivid impress upon our senses calls forth the past within the present, even as it imbues what-once-was with a loss and regret melded with what-is-now and what-will-be-forever. Each of the songs is a landscape that separates. But it is the very first song that invokes the pain of distance. The singer of that melody is a lonely being sitting upon a hill and gazing into a nebulous mist. He is cut off not only from the far-off pastures where in years gone by he had found his beloved, but also from that whole cycle of years that had brought him his best happiness.

As if this talk of Beethoven and the loss of one's best happiness were their inspiration, Alain and Charlotte then spoke of a kayaking adventure which, a few years before the war, they had experienced within the southwestern islands of the Åland Archipelago in Finland. There, on summer recess from their university studies, they paddled along Bronze Age trade routes that connected what is now Russia to Sweden and Northern Germany.

In those days, Alain explained, they rode on the impetus of their bolder venturing. The favor of the world seemed theirs to possess as long as they connected their daring to well-honed skill. It was a tremendous thing to journey with Charlotte five hundred kilometers from a southerly cluster of islands to the southwest coast of the mainland and then east to Helsinki, the capital of Finland. More than a few times, they pitted their determination against abrasive winds and rocky shoals. As they island-hopped among the islets, they kept the crossings short and always looked for shelter.

It felt exotic, Charlotte said, to camp with Alain next to a seal-hunter's hut on Enklinge Island. They also camped in a deserted light tower on Kökar Island and next to a sauna and a church within the harbor of Aspö Village. One time, caught as they were, on the rim and momentum of lashing winds, they and their two guides hauled their boats onto flat rocks, bows pointed in the whirling atmosphere.

"It was positively aboriginal," Charlotte said, "to nestle—there among the jagged rocks—within a rugged crevice which was lined with moss, dried branches, and driftwood."

On those more-than-ordinary days, Alain reminisced, taking up once more the narrative of their adventures in Finland, it was splendid to pass gray and red granite cliffs— bedrock rounded by ice glaciers—in the sheer openness of hastening motion. At the edge of the expanding Baltic Sea, they witnessed white-tailed eagles and wily gray herons flying around low, rocky shores that were backed by alder and moss, by stunted pines and dwarfed birch, and by shallow, reed-filled ponds. They passed as fleetly well-worn farm buildings painted with red ochre, and deserted, gray-ancient huts that had once housed fishers and eider hunters.

Splendid as well it felt, whenever they found themselves in the luminous folds of dawn, to tread cautiously across slippery rocks covered with a thin layer of deep-green algae. At noon they read in the clouds the power of the southwest wind, and at night they covered their eyes with scarves and were lulled into peaceful sleep. The brief Nordic nights, filled with light and more light, were themselves a prophecy of the morning sun peering from high above the horizon and a prophecy, too, of warm, comforting air filled with mellifluous bird-song.

In Finland, Charlotte said, they knew together the thrill of confronting effectively the gray-green shoulder-height waves that slapped against their faces as their kayaks, fully loaded, cut heavily through the foaming density of the crests and through roiling gusts of wind. All the while, they soared on motion's swifter hurl. They were pleased then that raw, potent nature had withheld its more fearful dangers and, with no special regard of them, had shared with the elusive moment a show of playful fury.

"One of our guides told us that danger was our friend," Alain said, musing quietly now upon that thought. "Maybe it was."

"Well, danger was definitely playing with us," Charlotte said. "You and I had a good time during that vacation."

"In those years," Alain remarked, with the trace of a wistful smile, "we believed we could make the whole world our friend."

For just an instant, the bright glow of happiness covered their faces. It was a happiness that no other memory had summoned—at least, not while she was with them. Eleanor had listened with special interest to their recollections of summer days that had occurred nearly a decade earlier. The kinetic imagery of their telling reminded her how much she missed kayaking with her school's team. But their looking back to their happiest time reminded her, too, that they carried with them always an unresolved burden of sorrow. She felt such love for them and such pity. Without their quite understanding why she did so, yet cordially accepting her gesture, she rose from her chair and hurried to caress them. Because she was so moved by their muted sadness, she gave each of them a kiss. Her kisses, planted softly upon their lips, brought her a new and thrilling pleasure. Their eyes, misted by the wine they had consumed and by the narratives they had shared with her, gleamed at her touch. The intensity of their glances told her that her kisses had also brought them a new pleasure.

At the close of the evening, Alain and Charlotte persuaded her to recite three poems of which she was especially fond: Elizabeth Barrett Browning's "If thou must love me, let it be for nought / Except for love's sake only"; Emily Dickinson's "I live with him, I see his face"; and Edna St. Vincent Millay's "If in the years to come you should recall."

"I feel very good," Charlotte said, a half-hour later, after they had completed the tasks that returned the dining room and the kitchen to their pristine appearance. "We've brought romance back into our world tonight."

"Let's keep romance for a few hours more, at least," Alain said. He had gathered them to himself and was accompanying them to the master bedroom.

Then, in the next hours when they heard the waves break against the rocks and when the summer rain kept lashing against the French doors that looked upon the balcony and the sea beyond, Eleanor accepted completely this first night of love with them. The light of the lamps upon the tables that flanked the ample bed in which they lay so pleasurably close to each other illuminated Alain's rugged body as he enfolded her within his nakedness, which to her eyes was vivid and persuasive. The light revealed, too, the sensual touch of their fingers and hands as they explored every inch of each other's body. That night she accepted Charlotte's tongue upon her tongue that united them in a long kiss. She also accepted the fragrant kisses with which she touched her forehead and eyes and nose and mouth. But it was Alain's touch that roused her especially. Even when he smoothly mounted her and she noticed Charlotte caressing his arched and rugged back, she was pleased that the three of them were there together. Charlotte had placed her body close to her husband's, so that whatever pleasure he took from his new partner would also belong to her. Soon, though, she forgot that Charlotte was there. The moment that Alain entered her, she collaborated with him alone. For desire was firing their bodies to some adroit and thrilling symmetry.

A MORE THAN ORDINARY LIFE

After she retired from Bryn Mawr in 1920, Amelia Winthrop sometimes thought about the past. She remembered having lived in Europe for much of her early life. With her parents and her two brothers in that era, she had maintained a special affection for the people and the customs of an often turbulent continent. Her mother, born in the Vosges, a splendid region of rivers and lakes and forests in northeastern France, had studied in Heidelberg, Seville, and Rome and had earned a doctorate at the Sorbonne. Her father, New England-bred, had, after his years of study at Brown, Harvard, and the University of Strasbourg, as well as in Padua and Barcelona, taught at the University of Paris. Later marrying, he had spent several years with his equally proficient wife teaching in Spain, Italy, and Germany. With her, he had translated into French the novels of Nathaniel Hawthorne and George Eliot and into German the essays of Ralph Waldo Emerson.

It was during those European years that Amelia and her brothers, older than she by five and seven years respectively, had learned how ambivalent and enthralling was the earth, which in their clear-sighted perception—hers and her brothers'—kept expanding and redefining its circumferences. Their young experiences also reinforced for them a truth that their parents had, through humanitarian engagement with diverse societies, so well expressed: the boundaries that separate people are artificial. They are often imposed by the mean-spirited inclination to regard the foreigner as the alien Other—the indoctrinated adversary.

From personal experience, she well understood the cost to the soul of being regarded as the Other, as an awkward presence different and insufficient. For she had, from the time of her birth and for eighteen years thereafter, suffered from scoliosis, a malady defining the slight curvature of her spine which kept her from claiming, with agile motion and easy gait, her rightful share of childhood happiness. By the time she was eight years old, she had endured two unsuccessful surgeries and months upon months of being held bound by wretched braces that merely succeeded in hampering whatever freedom her natural movements had allowed her. Only then did her parents come to believe that she must focus not upon what nature had neglected to give her, but upon all the gifts that would enable her to succeed in spite of the obstacles placed on her path.

Yet it was wearying to her spirit to watch the effervescent solidarity of her schoolmates, as though she were peering at ballet grace and perfect angularity from outside a brightly lit window. Well-bred girls, they had been taught to conceal dismay or pity at her misfortune and to include her in their society, she being one of their class, whenever occasion made inclusion plausible or palatable or unobtrusive, though not while their group was swimming or playing tennis or attending Miss Lawlor's dance classes. How painful it was, in an altogether different way to the ungainly frame that held with so spare a frailty her beating heart and yearning soul, to lack the steady rhythms of healthy breathing and to endure, regardless of the season, the recurring infections tainting her lungs and to writhe within the night-wail of sleepless anguish, because of her sorely oppressed back.

But even then, during these harsh years of her trial, the earth often sang to her senses. Hearing, she would allow her brothers, big-boned and athletic, to coach her, as gently as burly youths could whose usual way was a courtesy cobbled from casual roughness, in outdoor activities which required an accuracy primarily from one's eyes and hands and arms: skeet-shooting in October's sun-dappled fields behind their house, fishing on the banks of a freshwater pond in April, and rowing a gleaming-white coracle across a summer lake. It was in these hours especially that, vibrant and quick of aptitude and energized by the novitiate that her brothers in temporary league with her need were providing, she suggested before their beaming approval and to her tough-fibered will the extraordinary capacities that so often lay dormant within the prison of her body.

Her brothers, with their blunt affability, respected her coolheaded disdain of pity, her own or that of others, concerning her affliction. Sometimes, while at home on recess from school, with its masculine obligations and competitive allies, and before hurrying away to summer camp or to mountain climbing or, with their father and uncle, to deep-sea fishing or, in winter, to ski resorts and ice hockey, they would notice her solitariness. It was as natural and upright in its self-reliance as if her experience of things had never acquainted her with malady or need or muted aspiration. So noticing, these two vigorous brothers had, one time in the soft and cleansing rain of Lancashire, England, climbed with her up a summer-green hill to drink of the crisp water leaping off itself, all the while hurrying white over the rocks. There, the moss-covered root of an ornamental maple (with coral-red branches and shoots and leaves brightly viridian) cupped the flow as if to accommodate the thirst of a pair of strapping youths laughing through a sudden shower as they ventured toward the copious tree with their frail, eight-year-old sister. Her measured gait and quicker breathing made her a less conventional visitor, as did the lovely sheen of her chestnut-brown hair and the careworn pallor of her plain, oval face with its blue-curious eyes and upturned nose, its dimpled cheeks and determined mouth.

On these excursions with her brothers, which were extemporaneous and more enjoyable for being so, she one time inside the autumn woods within the Vosges, not far from their comfortable chateau in Gérardmer, sighted a young deer's tracks in the moist path. Its agility had sprung from the very spot and lightly left its imprint. She was even more stirred by the profuse beauty of France during the following summer when she'd turned eleven and explored with her brothers the Livradois-Forez region of eastern Auvergne. Then, she beheld far off at the end of a gravel road, just before it receded beyond her witness, the shaded ambiguity of the forest which—while teasing her awareness as if it were an after-image...a forest apparition configured from her earlier seeing—flowered anew within intermittent sunglow and just as quickly faded. A year later, once more accompanied by her brothers during their Christmas recess from Cambridge, she spent the holidays with the family in the Bisenzio Valley north of Prato in Italy, with its Alpine hills and rugged terrain and swirling, thunderous river. Now she knew, as if for the first time because it was so proximate and emphatic, the russet textures of a confident fox leaping across new-fallen snow, a fleet-footed sufficiency upon an eider-soft earth.

That summer following, on the warm days of mid-June having just begun their retreat from Rome, where she had for a year gone to school while their parents taught university students and researched their book about Hawthorne's experience of Italy, she and her Cambridge brothers—and in those weeks her parents as well—vacationed in Amalfi. They swam in the cold clarity of restless Mediterranean waters that hurried about the pale, towering cliffs rising, arrogant and reliable, toward the terraced villa where for that month they were staying. The villa was poised at the top of a serpentine array of steps that each morning brought them down to the white sands of the beach and to the cobalt blueness of the sea. Flame-tinted and flourishing, the waters accepted the adequacy of her swimming form, the odd curve of her back on those buoyant days forgotten.

It was bracing to experience the vivid earth with her affable brothers on those spontaneous occasions when they offered her their guardian camaraderie...and with her dutiful parents during a rare holiday from their scholarly pursuits and obligations...or in seasons made extraordinary and festive by their meticulous presence together with that of her sanguine brothers. And not only with them, parents and brothers, was it a tremendous thing to experience the vivid earth—though their interest in her, their protectiveness toward her, and their careful fostering of her self-dependence were at all times exciting influences upon her. But she also enjoyed being with those uncommon schoolmates whose individuality startled others. Their idiosyncratic natures rendered them to ordinary witness as odd or overly imaginative or even radical. Yet always their authentic perceptions, empathizing with her difference, accepted her as one like themselves. Receivers and creators both, their active minds interpreted and embraced the earth's infinite variety.

She remembered often now, a half-century and more later and with a special affection in this her retiring cycle, the pristine joy of living in Büsingen. As a quick-witted girl of fourteen, she learned to speak Swiss German that year when her parents, on sabbatical from university teaching, were preparing their translation of Emerson. So marvelous it was, especially on a school day at the threshold of autumn while with eight of her schoolmates and two of her teachers cruising in nearby Neuhausen on a roomy cutter along the upper Rhine River, to approach with a child's grateful and tremulous awe the spumy and echoing heft of the majestic Rheinfall. To her eyes, the rock spire rising from its center was a fathomless and cascading omnipotence.

Much later in that school year, during a different field trip with a dozen of her classmates and three of her teachers, she roamed carefree and exuberant along the circuitous paths winding within Büsingen vineyards and farmlands and forests which were waking the fertility of May. In early June, on an extraordinary afternoon with six other girls and with two favorite teachers as well, she peered at a hot-air balloon. Astonished and elated, she was standing on a hill outside the town not far from the ancient holiness of St. Michael's Church and in the company of songbirds and wildflowers and fragrance breezes. Rainbow-tinted and prevailing, the balloon drifted across a blue-radiant sky.

So, in these ways, she contented her sometime-troubled spirit by responding to the various calls to her of the earth and sea and sky. Because these visits to the earth's natural splendors and, sometimes, to its man-made wonders never failed to rouse more fervently her joy of life, she came to value them as much as she valued her study of languages and art, mathematics and science, and poetry, history, and music. The beauty of the world and of the mind's best capacities fortified her spirit and fortified also her plan to pursue, even as each of her parents was now so effectively doing, the life of a dedicated scholar. Yet, as she in these ways eased her spirit, she could not break free of the thought, which she translated with pitiless accuracy as a language for the most secret part of her soul, that her malady—the very body that represented her being—made of her a frail and hapless prisoner.

Because she was, even as a hampered and vulnerable girl, both resourceful and gifted, she kept on resisting the limitations that her malformed body imposed upon her. If she could not be an exemplary specimen who, with charismatic individuality, enhanced the very space her body navigated, she must make, even as she was, a proper journey. Hers must be a worthy life's adventure undeterred by a timorous capacity that confuses its fear with prudence and abides therefore in tranquilizing isolation or self-defeating circumspection. Nor would she, like the false steward from Saint Matthew's epistle, hoard or stifle or conceal whatever gifts the God who made her human had granted her. So, with the clarified seeing that derives its perceptions from suffering and disappointment, she came very early in her adolescence to believe.

Now especially, after the failed surgeries, she willed herself to savor her long hours of study and the self-sufficing powers earned in her solitude. For through them she meant to claim her right to be in the world, leaderly and proficient. Sometimes together with a solid union of classmates and more often, with unobtrusive assurance, alone, she won prestigious awards for her school in various competitions that drew upon her studies of languages and literature, science and mathematics, and music. She won as well the trust and friendship of her peers who, in her junior year, had elected her the vice-president of their class and relied upon her influence as they worked with their teachers to change the school's course of studies and to expand its foreign exchange program. What happiness then to live in a world offering her palpable access not only to nature's tremendous beauty, but also to the mind's superior knowledge. And what a lift—a validation of her spirit and ingenuity and compensation for the flaw she carried upon her back—to compose from the inscrutable workmanship that was herself a harmony between her odd, sometimes disconcerting presence and the world's stern judgments. This modulated reciprocity was not unlike the fluent music she, with nimble fingers and flawless timing, called forth from her piano in the solitude and rain-gloom of a November afternoon.

That in these adolescent years and in the evolving ones of her young womanhood she was making a place for herself in genteel and scholastic circles encouraged her parents to imagine that she might one day be married, and happily so. Now it was that they drew her to Sunday afternoon teas at their home as well as at the homes of her schoolmates and to the afternoon socials her school sometimes sponsored. They wanted her to meet boys her own age who were being taught to cultivate, with civil manner and reasonable vitality, a reliable association with emerging young ladies who belonged to their class. At first she was reluctant to participate because of her sometimes-unhappy experience of a handful of peers and a few adults and because of a collateral knowledge that these boys, potentially as arrogant or cynical as their gender permitted them to be, might not regard her with the brisk and likable nature of her brothers. She was pleased, nonetheless, to find herself accepting, with confidence and affirmation, the gentle push by her two best friends and by her parents and her agreeable teachers towards the occasional shy youth whose temperate speech and quiet sensitivity appealed to her admiration for the poetic. They pushed her as well toward the rugged youths—a few—who were in their well-honed masculine ways as creative and idiosyncratic as she was.

It was altogether bracing to the belief in herself that she was carefully building to win the attention of a good-looking athletic boy as tall as he was brawny or to converse with a lanky, bespectacled lad who, while anchoring their meeting to conviction and enjoyment, met and even challenged the intricacies of her intellect. Yet each time, though there were very few times, she allowed her heart to respond with more than ordinary affection to these chaperoned encounters which excited all her senses, she noticed, bonded as it was to the boys' modulated affability, the nearly imperceptible withholding of themselves and of the unconditional approval they brought instead to their easier friendships with other girls in her class who, though often less imaginative than she and less interesting, wore their prettiness with graceful and straight-backed composure. So perceiving the lie of things—the tangle of fictive arrangements coiling themselves at the surface of benign courtesies—she willed herself to move through these social occasions with equanimity and matter-of-factness. She received them as tests of her ability to connect, with careful ease and if need be with a bit of wit, to young men who might collaborate with her to create the momentary warmth of a respectful fellowship, but who would never with her reveal the romantic aspect of their nature or offer, even, a passing infatuation. It was in this period that there grew in her heart a hard, secret place which sealed off her capacity to feel deeply about the young men she met, for fear that by so feeling she would render herself vulnerable before their dismissive judgments.

About the time that she turned eighteen, her parents, having never abandoned their hope of finding a solution for the problem of her physical malady, brought her to a new and effective team of Swiss surgeons. After several tests and consultations, these men successfully performed the surgery and bone grafting which fused her curving spinal vertebrae so that her back could attain the beauty and proportion of a straight line. For nearly a year afterward, she was constrained by a steel rod and its emphatic hooks. Unable all the while to move, she never once complained or thought bitterly upon her confinement. Instead, with a spirit as practical as it was logical, she dictated from her sick bed to the compassionate nun who was her nurse a detailed journal that organized and advanced her plans for the year succeeding. At that future time, she would apply the first rewards of her freedom to new travel and to the worthwhile life she envisioned as a college student and, later, as a scholarly teacher.

Her sense of who she was in the world recomposed, as if her earlier form were but a chrysalis working all the while its metamorphosis, she in that summer of new-found freedom reveled in the gleaming waters of Positano on the Amalfi coast. There, multicolored houses and myriad shops (sequestered within narrow, winding streets) and the Church of Saint Mary of the Assumption, with its magnificent Byzantine dome, and the Fornillo guard tower, stalwart and resilient, poised themselves upon green, abundant hills cascading seaward. In the exuberance of a June afternoon, she rose out of the blue flare of glistening waters with her swimming partner. He was an engineer (her older brother's colleague) who, upon meeting her that day, had responded with an attractive courtliness. With him ambling across the warm, tawny sands of the beach to rejoin her brother and his wife, she possessed (for the first time in that teeming location which through so many years of her childhood had noticed her with her parents) a lithe and nubile symmetry.

So essential was that summer to her hard-won serenity and so fundamental were its occasions to the positive valuations by which others assessed her, that for all her life afterward she cherished the memory of it. In that season not only swimming in Positano both excited and solaced her, assuaging if not quite dispelling the quietly insistent bitterness that had, for so many years, tormented her soul. Not only or even predominantly was it Positano which verified for the world and for herself especially the sheer health and wholeness of her newborn physicality.

Rather, two other experiences later that summer challenged her quick wit and stamina even more compellingly. In mid-July she dared herself to go beyond others' safe expectations of her and beyond even the rigorous standards her parents always applied to her development. First of all, she canoed with a young, masterly guide and his equally athletic wife in northern Scotland, while hurrying across swifter space through the sinuous River Tay into the churn and roar and rough crescendo of the Grandtully Rapid. Then, in August, she rode the nobly formed muscularity of a Portuguese Lusitano horse in Poughkeepsie, New York. On a team with three other girls who, like her, were to begin their college life at Vassar that autumn, she competed in a chasing competition when they raced across the hilly expanse of an emerald-green countryside.

How well trained and adept she felt, folding forward from the hip with her seat out of the saddle. Her lower legs all the while held a vertical position on the girth as she pushed her weight down into her heels to maintain a straight line from her elbows through her hands to the horse's mouth. It was wonderful to remain in synchronous balance with her horse because her spine, supple and relaxed, enabled her hips and back to influence and absorb, with an easy affinity and unimpaired confidence her earlier riding had not known, the Lusitano's superb impulsion and elevated paces and agile intelligence. It was these risk-taking experiences which sealed as a reward for her proficiency the resolute belief, which she had espoused long before the success of her surgery, that she would be an active influence in the wider world, its ambivalent sureties and unforgiving randomness notwithstanding.

So it was that, self-determining and ambitious, she went forward to make her presence in the world as helpful as it was meaningful. She earned first her degrees at Vassar, Heidelberg, and Grenoble. After teaching in France and England for a decade and after the publication of her exemplary books about Proust and Balzac, she accepted the invitation in 1887, when she was forty, to teach at Bryn Mawr. There, she went on helping bright young ladies (primarily from privileged American backgrounds) to begin their adult lives in the world as capable and self-reliant. Through her teaching, not only did her students amplify their knowledge of languages and literature, philosophy and history and science. But they also cultivated an unflinching courage and versatile aptitudes by which to redress the hardships and suffering of the many deprived families that inhabited the coal-mining towns located at some distance from Bryn Mawr, though in Pennsylvania nonetheless. She guided them into this American program of helping others with the firm centeredness and steadfast conviction she had inspired her European students to emulate when they carried forward similar missions in the slums of London and in the impoverished villages of France.

How useful they could be to the world, it was her habit to tell them during all the years of her tenure at Bryn Mawr. They must become essential not merely at some future time through the success they would create for themselves as wives and mothers or as self-reliant careerists, but here and now through their effective involvement as college students in the welfare of others. Nor by helping others would they annul their bond with the worthy vocations for which they were preparing and which identified to themselves and to others the special talents that they must in good faith activate. Instead, they would learn to meld, with their unique talents and training and with their hopes and aspirations and promising evolution, a willingness to relieve the heavy burden of those persons far less fortunate. Indeed, they did learn. Within the last decade of the nineteenth century, they with her, even while fulfilling academic obligations, found time to raise corporate money so that better housing and new schools and gymnasiums were built in three coal-mining towns. They found, too, a strategy for influencing local, if not Federal, government to mandate a factory inspection system that insured the safety of workers.

Visionary as well as pragmatic, she and her students also worked year after year to support the American Civil Liberties Union and, as advocates of a cause which in their time would be only in part resolved, to promote the equality of women at all levels of industry and at the designated places where they should have the right to vote for the leaders of their choosing. Later, in the first years of the twentieth century, her Bryn Mawr young ladies, sometimes through the prestige they carried from their families, persuaded governors and senators to inaugurate a juvenile justice system which rehabilitated through careful technical training errant youths who had lost their way or had never, because of poverty or displacement from their foreign homeland or because of the world's inveterate racism or their own acquired hatreds, been given a chance to grow and thrive in an atmosphere that fostered a healthy self-sufficiency.

Later still, in 1916, when Europe tore itself apart with war, she and her students marched to Washington. They urged members of Congress to vote against America's pitching itself into the conflagration and urged them as well, through a diplomacy far more life-enhancing, to work with our allies to effect a judicious peace. During this same period, hearing of the brutal treatment of black people in the South (the hanging of innocent men in barren fields amidst a wilderness of trees and the rape of helpless women at their workplace or in their own modest shelters and the Jim Crow laws subverting a whole people's natural and inviolable rights), she and her students, while assisting the brave and tireless staff of the National Association for the Advancement of Colored People, initiated scholarships for black women at Bryn Mawr and for black men and women, both, at Pennsylvania State College and at the University of Pennsylvania.

There was, she often felt, in every one of these fruitful, exciting years during which her students through word and deed quickened the stalwart nature of their characters, a tremendousness abiding within their souls. With her, they directed their passions toward generous aspirations and toward the surprise of enduring things. As they did, so also did she identify herself through many passions apart from her social activism—her love of the mellifluous sounds of Spanish and Italian, for example, and her love of the elusive tints of autumn. There was the influence upon her spirit of Schubert's *Piano Sonata in B-flat Major*. For the young, dying composer achieved the emotional distance—the compassionate detachment—one earns legitimately only through one's own suffering. There was also the astonishing poetry by which Homer and Dante and Milton communed not only with her soul, but also with all of her senses. And there was the vigor and freedom she discovered while horse-riding across the dales of Yorkshire in early June and swimming at dawn in Tuscany within the emerging July radiance of a cerulean sea and climbing the green hill behind her chateau in Lausanne to peer upon solitary cliffs and cloud-tangled horizons and the majesty of mountains ascending toward a cobalt blue sky. All of vaulting space kept spinning still its rapid flow while on that hill she lifted her laughing demeanor toward the far-away heavens. Her arms were outstretched and swaying and her body circled in exhilaration even as sun and cliffs and clouds and snow-covered precipices were wheeling with visible motion about her.

Yet, while with all these passions she expressed a heart that grandly yearned and a mind that encompassed the nearly prodigious, she was in a fundamental way unlike her students (she supposed, never having through all her years of teaching conversed with them about so private a matter), because she had not, even once, given herself to a man.

But, when she was thirty and teaching in England, she had fallen in love with Brian Grainger. With whatever mysterious spirit informs one's affection for another, he returned her love, though without the carnal desire which would rouse his erotic need of her. Disappointed, she learned through his own telling during a visit to his capacious homestead in the Yorkshire Dales that he loved someone else. In that northern area, he and his partner, Peter Darnell, admirably served as veterinarians many seasoned farmers and cattlemen, in addition to raising their own horses and sheep and cattle. It was on the first day of her visit that he told her he preferred his own gender sexually. He shared an honest and profound love with Peter, as well as his bed. Always, she came afterwards to perceive, he would be for her a strong, platonic friend, though her own physical need of him must go unrequited. Yet, even against her conscious will, as if it were a wilderness or perversity of desire, she went on loving him. His lanky grace was an emblem of rugged assurance. His sculpted, wind-tanned features were empowered by blue eyes brightened from within the quiet of their knowing and by an aquiline nose and hint of a smile and the solidity of square-jawed resilience.

They had met first in London, when mutual friends, Neal and Carolyn Brewster (a colleague from the University of London and his equally cosmopolitan wife) invited her to their cozy home in South Kensington. They wanted her to join them and Brian for a dinner meant to celebrate the valued friendship the affable couple shared with each of them. Neal, not much older than she and already a notable scholar of John Donne's *Holy Sonnets*, had gone to Eton with Brian during the years when their fathers enjoyed a highly successful association as textile manufacturers in Manchester and in London. Later, while the experiences of young adulthood drew them toward different universities and vocations, they'd managed to keep their friendship alive. They would see one another from time to time, especially when Brian traveled by train from his homestead in North Yorkshire to address a congress of other veterinarians in London or to secure from a wholesale pharmaceutical outlet essential supplies for his and Peter's busy practice or to arrange through a reputable dealer the purchase of several horses. He might buy a light gray Tersk from the northern Caucasus, perhaps, with its fine head and well-sloped shoulders and its strong body and deep chest. Or a Dutch Warmblood, just as splendid with its sheen of brown enhancing a sturdy back and sinewy hindquarters and an alert expression.

For the first time, she experienced his reliable masculinity, tempered as it was by an easy courtesy and an understated strength. All the swift life which he represented hurried toward her as if, because so unexpected, he had been sent there by auspicious chance or by the Brewsters' well-meaning calculation to introduce and clarify, even, a more intricate possibility for Brian's and her existence than any they had yet tested.

She saw in the very first hour of their being together how compatible they were. In that favorable company, they were spontaneous and natural while exchanging anecdotes with each other and with the Brewsters about their various sojourns alone or with relatives or friends in the Swiss Alps or the Scottish Isles or the Upper Loire Valley. They spoke as spontaneously about their ongoing study of botany and ecology and music and about their love of the speed and unforgiving accuracy of rugby. (Brian and Neal, a beaming Carolyn remarked, had been first-rate players at Eton.) Later, casual and assured, they mentioned their having traveled, though in different years, from London to Paris in a hydrogen balloon. The thrill and tension of journeying skyward in so irrevocable a venture satisfied, for that time at least, their resolve to maintain a cheerful equanimity before the face of risk.

Yet, in spite of their compatible fervency on the occasion of their first meeting, he rarely called on her in the months ensuing. Nor was her pride consoled when the Brewsters carefully explained that Brian's crowded schedule seldom allowed him the freedom for recreation in London. Still, she kept remembering the authentic chemistry between them and the sometimes-tensile reserve of the man even on that special evening while, listening to her articulate words, he scanned in sober reflection the blush that visited discreetly her wholesome demeanor. His earnest apprehension to her eyes intimated the awe or respect or quiet pleasure that sires a lasting love.

But when weeks went by without her hearing from him, she began to interpret his prolonged absence as, after all, a lack of interest in her or in the prospect of compromising his autonomy by wooing a genteel woman whom convention would require him eventually to marry. She had read in a recently published journal of sociological studies that not a few strong-minded men preferred to stay single. They eased their carnal needs by seeking out, from time to time, the company of loose women. Not caring to dwell upon the reason for his reluctance to create with her a promising association, she immersed herself even more rigorously within the formidable obligations of her teaching and research and social activism and tried to forget him.

So, she found herself surprised, as well as elated, when—through a courteous, if laconic, note—Brian drew her once more into their friendship. She, in turn and without hesitation, accepted this new, affirming overture, shortly thereafter journeying with the Brewsters to his hundred-acre homestead in Littondale. He and Peter had invited the three of them to spend the weekend there within the bucolic aptitudes of that long-ago July of 1877, when they would be passing through the undulating greenness of Yorkshire. For Brian meant, she came to understand during that visit, to clarify the modest friendship he had with her over the course of a year advanced whenever, on five or six occasions, he'd had to be in London for business concerning the farm or his and Peter's veterinary practice. At those times alone with him, and once with him and the Brewsters, she had enjoyed dinner at elegant Claridge's near Hyde Park or attended a performance of Shakespeare's *Twelfth Night* at Covent Garden or a concert of Bach and Beethoven and Mozart at Albert Hall.

She and the Brewsters, having arrived in mid-afternoon, had sampled the Norwegian housekeeper's excellent muffins and cakes and tea and had met that good woman's husband, a wiry six-footer who was the judicious foreman of that extensive property. With his wife's coaxing and the humble pleasure of a diligent craftsman, he showed them his fine woodcarvings of stallions and their riders.

Afterward, Brian and Peter had guided her and the Brewsters, mounted as they were on strong-limbed black ponies from the Upper Dales, to scan an impressive group of well-groomed horses and cattle which in that hour were grazing in an enclosed southerly field near the stables. On that day, they also observed a dozen prize-winning sheep as well as more Herefords and Holsteins grazing within a skillfully drained field at the foot of fertile, curving hills that peered upon a further range and in an easterly direction. Then they had cantered to a flowing expanse of lime-loving grasses and herbs a quarter of a mile from the home-field, there to pause in momentary contentment amidst the aromatic imagery of rock rose and birdsfoot trefoil and wild thyme.

Once they had resumed their progress, they noticed dry-laid stonewalls separating the farm's many fields. A river, stained by brown peat (albeit unpolluted), meandered through sloping verdant pastures. Hurrying then on to higher ground, they discovered within a broad swath of heather moorland plump blueberries and raspberries (with their vivid orange fruit) and glanced (a fleet awareness) upon the swiftness of a small, dark falcon (a merlin, Peter said), so kinetic and italic with flare of striped brown-red breast and wings short and pointed. In the full clarity of surprise and pleasure, they witnessed a roe deer with dancing leap and flash of tawny-hued agility hastening to the dense concealment of the stalwart oak woods that were lining like sentries the sides of the Dale.

After that, they sighted a rugged, red-haired field hand and three adolescent youths, hardy and limber and freckled (his sons, she'd thought) working amidst the gold blaze of a hay meadow.

Then they had made their way back to the home field and to the handsome guest cottage where she and the Brewsters would be staying. It was one of two cottages that flanked even as they complemented the large, two-storied main house, which was all blue-gray stucco and wide, eight-pane windows. The three sturdy buildings rose in congruent fellowship with the land and with its vegetation.

Exactly then he had told her why he could never be her lover or, for that matter, the lover of any other woman.

How ironic to hear his words in the very hour that gave him back to her. His confidence and affable spirit intensified her happiness at being with him. How ironic, too, that only a day earlier, just before journeying to him in Littondale, she had convinced herself that she was traveling not merely to see him, though she meant, of course, to acknowledge respectfully his hospitable beckoning. Rather, she told herself, she was traveling, like the Brewsters, primarily to survey some of the many Dales that lay astride the Pennine Chain of hills in the counties of North Yorkshire and Cumbria. In truth, she did, all through the three weeks of that bracing excursion and during the special days she and the Brewsters were visiting Brian and Peter, find herself thoroughly fascinated when on her cantering horse to experience the quicksilver montage of natural forms astride the hills hurrying before and behind and around her.

Keenly she sensed the roundness of the valleys and the rough verticality of crags and cliffs and the startlement of a far-distant waterfall. She saw as well the monumental, fissured rocks that had been part of the tenacious earth for millions of years. Marvelous, too, it was to see with her own eyes how, vulnerable and yet tremendous, our own human kind had with the earth negotiated through a hundred centuries an effective collaboration. Human beings had cleared woodlands and constructed villages and roads. They had cultivated crops and built barns and walls.

So there was, after all, a legitimacy in her telling herself that she had come to see the Dales, the arc and dip and billowing span of glorious valleys there in the north of England, even as she was in solid friendship being reunited with Brian. But she was unwilling to compromise an honest appraisal of her motives. By the time she and the Brewsters had, from their first afternoon's survey of the wide compass of Brian's and Peter's property, returned to the home-field, Peter had, with casual tactfulness, efficiently guided the Brewsters into the guest cottage. He had left Brian to converse with her alone after they'd dismounted from their first-rate ponies and led them to graze within a verdant paddock nearby. By that special time which to her senses galvanized her every movement next to him, she had cast away any thought that would disguise her primary reason for being there. She was in love with Brian and wanted him to be in love with her.

Then it was that he told her he could not love her—love her, that is, in a way that would satisfy her desire.

"But we are so good together," she'd declared, upon hearing the full truth of himself. Her statement was as much a levelheaded interpretation as evidence of her prickly dismay. "And you're not giving us a chance."

His earnest eyes held her firmly now, yielding neither to her flash of anger, nor to her subtle petition.

Accepting his influence still upon her apprehension, she hurried nonetheless to say the words she deemed forthright and necessary.

"You're being unfair to yourself."

"I could not live otherwise and still be myself," he'd said. His husky voice with its own matter-of-fact openness even then quickened her awe of his certainty and her love of him.

Nor did her comprehending his disposition annul that awe or tell her heart that she should refrain from loving him. Instead, she went on loving him. Sometimes they were alone and often with Peter, whom she learned to love as she loved her brothers. She learned to find joy in the sheer tremendousness of being with them, whether they were riding upon the lush and fragrant hills of Littondale or meeting in London for a lavish lunch or dinner or vacationing at a spa in Switzerland or kayaking in Finland. So empathetic were they three together, that they permitted themselves, during those halcyon days at least, to imagine that their more than ordinary friendship was strong enough to elude the world's brute accidents and casual betrayals. Their happiness together made them feel magical, conjoined as they were one spring holiday in their rented garret in Montmartre, where they were under the spell of having recently discussed the teachings of Plato and Lao Tzu and Jesus. Newly conscious of the infinite character of their essential capacities, they inhabited that one room in the purity of a love that transcended carnal egoism. For those three weeks, Brian and Peter chose to live with her as beings spiritualized and celibate.

But in spite of their transforming their friendship to some higher and ideal sphere, during those Montmartre weeks and in all the succeeding years that were given them, the world's brute accident and casual betrayal eventually confronted them. Five years after her first visit to the Dales, on one of those ambivalent days of March carrying within its less chilling wind and milder austerities the vague traces of spring, Brian bravely met his fate. While he was leaving Clive Andrews's farm in neighboring Arncliffe, where he had applied his skills as a veterinarian to an ailing Holstein, he happened upon a frantic Mrs. Andrews, who was trying to save her seven-year-old girl from drowning. The energetic child had fallen through a thin circle of ice while skating not far from the edge of the pond that adjoined her family's farm.

Momentarily, the young and plucky mother, seeing all from her kitchen window minutes earlier and hastening forth to the ominous scene, did rescue her daughter. But, in panic flailing about, the little girl quickly dragged that good woman, encumbered as she was by the weight of her wet clothes, down into the rippling water. Its jagged ice floated casually around her and around her fearful child.

Brian, too, saw all just as he was leaving the place. Disregarding any peril to himself, he'd spurred his horse on down the snowy hill to the icy bank of the pond. There, as if impervious to the cold, he threw off his boots and most of his clothes and jumped into the nearly freezing water. With the strong arms and hands that had served him well when tending his hard duties as a farmer and a veterinarian, he pulled the exhausted mother and her frightened child out of the circle of wind-tossed water to safety.

All seemed immediately thereafter to go well. Brian, having risen from out of the pond with Mrs. Andrews and her daughter, struggled to the icy bank. Shivering yet stalwart, he helped them to mount his waiting horse before taking his place behind them in the saddle. Then, once more that day he spurred his fine, brown Dartmoor, this time on to the warmth of the farmhouse at the top of the hill and to the gratitude of Clive Andrews. Unaware of the fearful trouble, Clive had kept a vigil in the barn over their ailing Holstein that, thanks to Brian, would recover. Perhaps, Brian should have remained with the Andrews family for the night, as they'd urged him to do. But, after drying himself before the bracing heat of the stove in their spacious kitchen and accepting the loan of warm, insulated clothing as well as a delicious, hot supper and a bit of brandy, he'd gone out again into the brisk wind and into late winter's ambiguity to assist the sick ewe of another farmer. As a consequence, he came down with pneumonia.

Called to their home two or three days later by a disheartened Peter, Amelia brought with her from London an eminent physician who, she compelled herself to believe, could save Brian.

But the physician, upon examining his patient, would not promise a favorable outcome. For Brian's lungs and throat and chest were sorely afflicted. With his nurse and with Peter and her assisting, the doctor labored many hours to ease the suffering Brian. Now she bethought herself to leave Brian with those exemplary caregivers and travel to Essex, about fifteen miles from London. Efficient and determined, she sought out the parents who, as disapproving as they were harsh and judgmental, had turned away from the oldest of their three sons ten years earlier, once he had explained to them why he could never love a woman.

"He has not been my son for a very long time," Mr. Grainger declared to her. He and his wife had received her into their imposing Georgian house because they knew of her scholarly parents, whom the Queen herself had invited to tea on more than one occasion. They also respected her own achievements as a university scholar and teacher.

They had listened to her gentle explanation of why she was there, and they had permitted themselves to listen as well to all the words that she had summoned in praise of Brian's skills as a veterinarian and as a farmer. She also spoke of his beneficent regard of others, including the honest workmen and their families with whom he and Peter shared the profits earned from their farm. That the Graingers—in forlorn stillness and with the hint upon their brows of unstated anguish—heard politely all that she'd had to tell them convinced her that, in spite of their proud willfulness, they still cared about what was happening to their son.

So she pressed forward now the urgency of her being there.

"You must go to him," she—with her own steely determination—finally insisted. "As much for your own sake as for his. He may die. And, if he does, you will never have another chance to tell him that you still love him."

Mrs. Grainger, ordinarily subservient to her husband's hardened will, was the first to waver. For her repudiation of Brian's unorthodox relations with Peter harbored disappointment more than enmity. All the while conscious of betraying her motherly intuition, she had acceded with faint-hearted reluctance to the covenant she had made with her church's codes and society's laws and her husband's cautious sovereignty.

"I shall go," she said. Her steady, hazel eyes and nearly tremulous lips and taut carriage prepared themselves to withstand whatever protest might come forth from Mr. Grainger. His subtle tyranny, roused in the names of marital fidelity and filial obedience, had for those ten long years denied her and their two younger sons the freedom to communicate with Brian.

But to her surprise and to Amelia's as well, Mr. Grainger also consented.

"We both shall go," he said, as though his decisive words were father to so crucial a thought.

How suddenly vulnerable his gaunt and ascetic demeanor appeared then to the two women regarding him within the suppressed unease of their own tensions. In this moment they noticed, too, how difficult it was for him to intimate, even, the unquiet sorrow he had from pride and ingrained narrowness so furtively concealed. Perhaps it was the presence of steadfast Amelia standing without hesitation before him while defending the merit of his son that first gave him pause. Or possibly it was that harrowing vertigo which overtakes our mind and heart and very soul before the unalterable news of a loved one's imminent dying...that fiercest reeling of the senses that throws away whole territories of our knowing, all the landmarks and milestones and safer imagery of our experiences, and leaves us standing alone, helpless and unavailing, at the dark edge of an abyss.

Possibly it was that which gave the formidable Mr. Grainger pause. Or, more likely, it was his belated willingness to admit the folly, the imprisoning casuistry, of accepting society's proscriptions against those strong-hearted men and women who fall into love with a person of their own gender. Or, just as likely, a native intelligence—summoning at last and in this life-altering visit from Miss Winthrop the more discriminating powers of his reason—suggested to Mr. Grainger the shallowness of defining an individual primarily or even at all through his or her sexual orientation, as if the microcosm that was oneself, a world within the larger world one came forth from the womb to inhabit, was after all and before all else a merely carnal enterprise. True (for most of his adult life he'd clearly perceived), many men and women choose to be so, abasing the divine potential within themselves through mindless gratification of their biological appetites. But that was a separate issue. For one could choose to live as a beast whether one was engaged in carnal intercourse with the beloved of one's opposite gender or with a loved one whose gender was the same as one's own. The essential question for humankind ought not to ask whether one is heterosexual or homosexual, but whether one transcends one's bestial instincts—whether one in the daily and rigorous practice of living validates and elevates one's being human.

Whatever the influences that disturbed the usual habits of his entrenched certainties, Mr. Grainger during Amelia's visit allowed himself to be aware, as in a sudden flash of recollection or an unobtrusive revelation, of his too-easy abdication of a well-placed belief in his son Brian. How foolish he had been to define him by referring to narrow, cultural interdictions and to the public's insidious hatred of the different, rather than to his own heart's intuition. For there, in the most profound recesses of his heart, he had never denied that Brian was an extraordinary young man. This remarkable first-born of his offspring had always validated his goodness through reliable word and deed, through finely honed ability and unfailing generosity, and through iron-willed courage.

"Perhaps he won't die," Mrs. Grainger kept saying an hour later, after boarding the hastening train that would carry them to Littondale.

Silent, Amelia patted the weeping mother's cold, veinous hands. The comforting warmth of her own hands was her only reply.

Later, in the uncertain hours after their arriving that evening at the capacious farm, Brian woke from his crisis, aware that both his mother and his father were standing by him. Now he lived at ease with himself, supremely elated by this longed-for return of his parents. For his mother, rueful and affectionate, shyly kissed him, and his father, without betraying the regimented powers that held emotion taut, clasped his hand vigorously. With manner idiosyncratic and sincere, they assured him that, in spite of their withdrawal from his life, they had always loved him.

"I've missed you so much," he (their uncommon son with raspy inflection and a rugged grimace that could not keep back his tears) declared.

Then, for fear that so heartfelt a scene would tax his patient's waning strength, the physician asked Mr. and Mrs. Grainger and Amelia to withdraw for a while from the sick room.

When they three, who only an hour earlier had arrived from Essex, approached the door and were beyond Brian's hearing, Mr. Grainger, forlorn and ashen, turned to Amelia. As if the words that had tormented his mind for so long needed confessing, he uttered before her immense sympathy their specific remorse.

"I was always too harsh with him," he said. "I'd never, for such a long time before tonight, told him how important he is to my own happiness. I don't think he ever knew how much I love him."

"He knows now," Amelia said, "because tonight you and Mrs. Grainger have clearly shown him how you feel."

They, at the door still, smiled gratefully before her encouragement. But so anguished was the firm control they struggled to master, that she found herself hurrying to comfort them further.

"Tonight, you've had your son again."

Her words, understated and compassionate, intensified nonetheless their new understanding of all that they'd lost by forfeiting for so many years a healthy bond with their first-born son.

"But an hour isn't enough, you see. It isn't enough," the disconsolate father said. He was harnessing yet the furious energy of his grief as he trudged wearily from the room.

Mrs. Grainger, meaning to complete her husband's explanation even while struggling against her own show of sorrow, was the one to clasp Amelia's hands now while speaking.

"We want so much more of him," she said. "So much more."

Her lips trembling again and her composure nearly disarranged, she patted Amelia's hand as though they'd been friends for many years and then hurried to her husband.

Amelia, about to follow and close the door behind her, stopped in surprise when she heard Brian call out to her. So, turning back once more—with approving nods from the doctor and the nurse, who in the clarity of a knowing diligence were tending their patient, and with an inquiring glance from Peter, who kept his guardian place in a chair by the window—she moved slowly toward her truest friend and listened to the thought he wanted to tell her.

"Thank you for bringing them back to me" were all the words he could manage to whisper, because his breathing had become so rough and hollow.

Then all that night and all the day after, while maintaining a careful vigil, they—his parents and Peter and Amelia, as well as his doctor and nurse—worried that Brian within those hours would die. But by early morning of the third day of their being there with him, a new spark of vitality illumined his eyes and face and momentary, gleaming smile, as he told the nurse that he was hungry.

"Well, you will have the best hot breakfast we can cook," his mother exclaimed. She was happy now to interrupt her vigil and hurry to the kitchen to join his housekeeper in preparing the meal that the physician allowed: orange juice and thin oatmeal, as well as soft-boiled eggs and buttered toast and large, steaming cups of tea.

So, because they at that time were granted the hoped-for miracle, Brian did not die.

Days later, when his convalescence was proceeding very well, the commendable physician, reviewing his case, wondered whether his own medical capacities had saved Brian. He wondered too whether the bracing rescue might have derived from the young man's love of his faithful Peter or from his parents' unqualified acceptance of all that he represented. Possibly, his rescue came from the knowledge that his dear friend Amelia cared so deeply for his well-being that she would risk rejection or humiliation or an angry scene, so long as she might effect a reconciliation between his parents and himself. Whether it was any of these things or some more than others which saved him—or Brian's own strong will to go on living, stalwart and altruistic—the physician never, even to himself, declared. Through his life's experiences, he understood well how complicated are the influences negotiating our responses.

That time they had been blessed (Amelia through all the years succeeding told herself gratefully) because Brian had afterward so completely recovered. With Peter even now, thirty-eight years later, he was bringing well-wrought skills and authentic generosity to so many others. He'd been blessed also because he had gone forward to achieve with his parents, for the additional three decades which time allowed their seniority, a renovated affiliation. His relationship with them had enlarged their capacities to love and to respect each other's worthwhile individuality. She had been blessed as well because with him and with Peter she had through all those years shared and continued to share the purity of a wise friendship. The platonic subtexts of their association kept enhancing their mysterious need of so uncommon a solidarity.

But it was in this present period, just after retiring from her academic obligations at Bryn Mawr, that Amelia (her belated searching glance no longer giving to her earlier responses the tincture of the inevitable) questioned with probing objectivity why, in spite of her unrequited ardency for Brian, she herself had not gone forward to marry a man who could love her in the erotic way that most men love women.

Now her inquiring regard of the life that she had always with venturing diligence bravely embraced suggested to her keener insight that a subtle inwardness had kept her from marrying. From her frail and hampered years, she had learned too early to value and rely upon her solitariness. Held as a prisoner for such a long time by her own physical liabilities, she could not, when finally freed of them, allow herself to be held prisoner once more, this time by the conventions of marriage, or allow, even, a man for whom she might feel romantic desire to invade the privacy of her body, which so often had tolerated the bruising penetration of a surgeon's scalpel.

During those years while she was young, she could not, even in her mind's approximation of the reality that might unfold before her should she so consent to marriage, be the dutiful wife her own mother had been. Her awareness of that bright woman's quietly deferring to the will of her demanding husband cast its pall upon whatever plan she, her nubile daughter, might momentarily invoke to bring herself on to the path of upright and eligible men her own age. Not even her brothers' spirited likability, harnessed as it was to their big-boned and quick-witted authority, could convince her that she and any of the fine men she came to admire in her professional life might become compatible.

Nor could she consent to take a lover, though more than one professorial gentleman had with casual aplomb intimated the possibility of attaining with them so fleet and secret a happiness. No, she would not consent, because she did not care to reduce herself to the role of a "kept" woman, not for a year or a month or even one night.

For all these reasons, then, one prevailing upon her conscience more than another in various seasons, she had deemed it best for the independent life she had created never to marry.

Yet now, looking back (pensive before the austere past that illumined her celibacy), she willingly admitted the truth that with her romantic yearnings and with her latent fear she had suppressed. In this one mysterious aspect of her life, she had not been brave.

A SUBLIMATION OF DESIRE

In his uneasy youth, when urgent sensuality had first caressed him, Everett Marsden knew the torment of renunciation toward which his father quietly guided him. Then he understood the lacerations of the heart. By denying himself the love of Kirsten Hallstrom, he cut away the deepest roots of his being. With stoic discipline he learned to live as someone who, at least in the beginning, was no longer himself.

Even now, nearly three decades later, he wanted to believe that his father had been right. He and Kirsten *were* too young to make their way, alone or even together, at the edge of a wayward and callous world. Nor should he at sixteen, his father asked him to perceive, allow himself the wild liberty of violating codes of responsible behavior which had been, these seven hundred years and some, the Marsdens' preeminent legacy—more valuable than any other wealth they had achieved. If he could not hold in mind the well-being of the family name, he could for the girl's sake keep before him the plan of life she had been advancing without him. Kirsten was a most promising girl whose scholastic training under the wise tutelage of her parents ensured her a brilliant future in medicine. (They were eminent research scientists attached to one of his father's corporations.) Since he harbored genuine feelings for her, he would not (his father knew) keep her from becoming so much more than a conventional woman who gave herself too completely to this makeshift religion of carnal love.

Those, of course, had been his father's words, not his own. It was a dignified plea recited, he was made to feel, on behalf of the girl's interests rather than in favor of (or, at least, before) the fatherly investment which bound him to monitor the continuing activity of a son not yet full-fledged. On him, despite his being second-born, his father had conferred his own name, Everett Marsden, with the Roman numeral VI appended to specify his place in the vigorous line that possessed the name while defining and redefining its meanings and dimensions. That he must do his unimpeachable part to maintain and enhance the honor of the name should be (as it had always been) the primary reason of his existence.

What could matter more than his honor or Kirsten's honor, which was also imperiled?

Fortunate, indeed, it was that his careful mother and he as a dutiful father had noticed—on more than one occasion during these weeks that the girl and her parents were spending bright, summery days as their guests here in Newport—how subtly he was drawing her away from the disciplined life which, in association with her teachers and her parents, she had been cultivating. Fortunate, as well, it was that he and no one else had discovered them naked and rebellious in the act of love within the flower-rimmed and sequestered gazebo which stood, splendid and comforting, on the southerly portion of their property.

Upon apprehending them, he was willing to concede (he told him in private conference later) that there was something healthy and nearly inevitable about this first experience of romantic love which the two of them had been exploring, so inquiry revealed, for several weeks now. He was even willing to cheer inwardly that he, Everett, the second of his promising sons, might in the distant future very well achieve a happy marriage of body and soul with a young lady who would come into his life at the appropriate time. But mindful of paternal obligations, he must now take steps to protect not only his son's interests, but also the well-being of this exceptional girl.

His being sent to an Episcopal seminary school in Clairmont, New Jersey, for two years before Princeton would help him to find again the stoic and virtuous selfhood he had too casually abandoned. Away from this girl and the habit of their intemperate sensuality, he might become once more a reliable Marsden. A Spartan regimen under the influence of priestly teachers would reacquaint him with the trustworthy behavior that, until this dangerous episode, he had always and authentically represented.

If, in the socially oppressive summer of 1886, he were to continue his romance with this extraordinary girl whom he so precipitately declared he loved, she could not retrieve the virtuous name she would have already squandered. Nor could she call back the moment before this betrayal of her best interests. The world in those days watched women with jealous and peremptory eyes. It granted them obscure homage as shapers of homes and children, but it would not publicly recognize their self-reliant identities or their tremendous possibilities as worthy leaders in the world. It was, then, positively fine and forward-looking that Kirsten's parents should influence her to become a disciple in their field. With them and with other colleagues, she would surely discover new ways to interpret the world's equivocating secrets.

"You must not hold her back," his father said, as if he were petitioning more than advising him. "If your love for her is worth anything—-your love not only for the body, but for the whole mind and idea of her—you must let her go. Only then can she make herself the exemplary woman she has the power to be."

Because he did not care to deprive her of the possibilities that might be better than his love, he willed himself to let Kirsten go. As from a far-off corner inside uneasy dream, he fulfilled the pledge he had made more to himself than to his father that he would not indulge his need of her and thereby appropriate the splendid life that, with her parents, she had been coherently shaping.

Nor would he allow her to imagine that in future time they would once more be united. Believing so, she would never free herself of whatever spell his love had wrought within her. He would, if she went on anticipating his return, always be arriving. He would be a prevailing apparition that bound her to invalid promises and all the while condemned her to a castaway life that seeks in vain the rescuing ship or hoped-for messenger. Better to imagine him, if at all, as one who had died, for in so severe a conviction would lie her strength. Since final absence, the vanishment that annuls communication, is death, then let his disappearance from her life be as if it were his earthly dying. Let it be not only his earthly dying, but his eternal as well, since he could not persuade himself that heaven would conjoin their sundered fates.

Yet his willing her to go so irretrievably gave him even then bitter pause and caused him later to wonder whether he had loved her bravely enough. Perhaps his parting words were—as she called them—only a ventriloquial recitation. Perhaps they *were* a puppet's echoing that mimed his father's thoughts for his own, the better to appease his father's dismay and prove to himself his capacity for grave sacrifice. For a long time such doubts assailed him. They rendered nearly insupportable the anguished burden he carried always. Only gradually did he come to accept his heart's first and most profound confession—that he had let her go because he loved her.

Through all the years that followed him afterward, the thought that he had abandoned their love goaded his mute dismay. Only the knowledge that he had not held her back from a better destiny could from time to time console him. Yet even now his memory of their having loved each other so passionately taught him in new, painful ways that his sacrifice had defeated him. By freeing Kirsten from the tangle of his own emerging biography, he had given away forever his heart's happiness. In these hours of accurate self-reflection, he admitted that without her he had not lived completely. This bitter awareness followed him through every rigorous success he went on to win, despite his ingrown sorrow.

Nor could he forget her.

Even when he was on summer leave from his seminary experience at Saint Michael's, the memory of those days with her stayed with him. But he did not go to her. He did not go that first summer after their parting, while with extraordinary peers who could rightly call themselves her equal she continued to study in New York. Nor did he make further inquiry about her once he understood, the year following, that her mother and father had sent her to Switzerland. Living with her erudite grandparents, she was enrolled at the same time in an estimable university where so many scientific Hallstroms had given favorable accounts of themselves.

Neither did he go to her at the close of his own university days at Princeton. On a winter's recess with his rowing team, he had skied in Lausanne and with no inconvenience might have stopped in Basel to find the picturesque chateau inside which, he'd known for some time, she stayed with her relatives, unless she were away attending learned sessions in Paris, Berlin, or Vienna.

"You make too much of her," his best friend, Michael Courtney, told him with a casual ease that muted his good-natured bluntness. At Princeton, they were roommates and fellow athletes. There, when they were completing their junior year, Michael had found himself pleased that he had shared with him and no one else the story of his romance with Kirsten. But here in Lausanne a year later, he had grown impatient with this brooding memory of Kirsten.

"She looks perfect to you," he said, "because she's the one that got away."

"She *was* perfect," he answered him.

"Then look her up. Having a romance doesn't mean the two of you have to marry each other."

They were in their hotel room, grooming themselves for a night's celebration. With genuine camaraderie and as a sign of his good will, Michael patted him on the shoulder.

"It's your move, buddy."

"I wouldn't be good for her," he told him. "With me, she couldn't have the life she wants."

As he began adjusting his tie, Michael glanced at him pensively and then allowed himself a knowing smile.

"I think you like your suffering," he said. "You like telling yourself that you've made a sacrifice in the name of love."

He knew that, with his light-hearted remark, Michael meant to dispel his brooding. But this talk of Kirsten made his heart too heavy to meet his friend's casual words with an equally light-hearted rejoinder. Instead, an ingrained sadness informed his reply.

"I can't forget her."

Quickly Michael pulled him back to the evening that was waiting for them.

"At any rate, you're bound to forget her tonight," he said. "From what I hear, this Denise What's-her-name that you're meeting at the party will make you forget every other girl you've slept with."

He and Michael had shared that conversation a quarter of a century ago. Though they remained close friends even now, never again did they converse about his love for Kirsten.

The memory of Michael's words reminded him that he *had* enjoyed all the women that he'd slept with through the years. To himself and to nobody else he was willing to admit that. But, except for Isabel, he had not been in love with any of them. Nor did he love Isabel (before or after they were married) with the desire and the passion that his love for Kirsten had roused in him. How, then, could he forget her?

Even through the periods of dominion when he made his way inside corporate towers and the world seemed his to borrow—an exotic plant he had learned to cultivate—he remembered those days with Kirsten. From time to time he experienced—and always as if it were to be a suffering different from any he had yet endured—a near-failure of nerve or an absence of discipline or a loss of confidence in his ability to tolerate yet another fevered night when his body and spirit literally ached for Kirsten and he believed that he must go to her or go on slowly dying.

But he did not go to her.

He did not go then or later when, at the threshold of a liberating awareness of his true powers and a reliable flourishing of his own career, he had longed to see face to face the vision of the unattainable ideal that in his romantic yearnings she had become. To his private seeing, her image was now as ethereal as it was flesh-tinted.

He did not go to her even when, a decade later, she had returned to America. By then she was a tough-spirited physician whose pioneer therapies brought her with missionary zeal to migrant workers afflicted by disease and malnutrition in California. Her work brought her as well to the impoverished sick in New York and Chicago.

She was married most happily, he'd been told, to Hans Schlossberg, the renowned surgeon from Zurich who had formed the bold medical team of which she was a prominent member. Their team ventured into turbulent ghetto districts and dying, forgotten towns to create for an abandoned people life-sustaining dispensaries, nurturing shelters, and new, empowering hope. Dr. Schlossberg was, perhaps because he was a true aristocrat, an unassuming man. He was many years older than she and yet a sensual husband apparently, for together they had brought into being four healthy children. He himself, long since a validated Marsden, had composed a lasting pact with loyal Isabel, whose quiet love often guided him toward a steadying contentment and twice favored him with daughters bright and obedient.

No, not once in all those uneasy years did he go to her. He was determined to honor his pledge to himself as well as to his father and, though she would never know the measure of his sacrifice, his pledge to her most of all. When in the same season that Washington bestowed upon her and her husband a well-deserved Presidential award for their field work in medicine, he saw her fair, no longer delicate face partnered with the cragged profile of her eminent husband there on the cover of a first-rate news magazine. Then he knew he had done the right thing. He had saved her for more than her fulfilling marriage and for more even than those angelic children. He had saved her, with all her prodigious gifts intact, for the good of the world.

Yet it happened, with not the slightest contrivance or preparation on his part, that one mild November afternoon in 1912, several years after the lift to his spirit of that magazine cover, she came to *him*. The prestige of her name and the credibility of her petition brought her quickly past his corporation's junior officers into more private and subtly palatial chambers. There, he and his senior administrators often conferred with high-ranking visitors about matters of the weightiest import. That who she was and why she was there most clearly qualified her for his immediate attention, the junior staff had rightly determined. More than a few times, in what he had regarded as off-hand yet always judicious remarks at a company dinner or a business seminar or an especially festive gathering at his home that included some of his firm's most astute people, he had lauded the Schlossbergs for all they were doing to rescue the city's downtrodden and, by extension, the city itself. Everything about their restorative enterprise within a progressive hospital and innovative clinics bespoke the rarest altruism and a masterly application of their team's medical gifts.

"Schlossberg thinks like a general well-trained in logistics," he told the governor at a convocation of business leaders which meant to recognize New York's solid achievements in business and the arts, in technology and medicine and higher education. "His organization is hard-pressed for funds, but you'd never know it, because he has a knack for deploying equipment and personnel in just the right locations."

From so peripheral a comment grew their inspiration—his and the governor's—to do something for Schlossberg's crusade. They would be if not magnificent, at least helpful. With careful and patient effort that made discreet overture a respected ally, they drew a quiet philanthropy from corporate donors who found in unobtrusive giving a most authentic honor. That Marsden industries had excelled all others, even those that in their own right always enlarged the meaning of munificence, gave him a staid pleasure that tightly harnessed itself to a convincing objectivity. He and his colleagues had chosen the Schlossberg team as the principal recipient of corporate generosity for no other reason than the merit of its mission and the efficient launching of a bold social experiment.

Because he did not plan to reveal who he was to her or to imagine that his generous endowment allowed him the right to link hereafter his life with hers, the natural act of his giving gained for him a quiet purity.

Then suddenly, on the second Tuesday of that splendid November, she came to him, completely palpable and just as miraculous as in his most solacing dream of her. But no longer was there about her appearance or her carriage the radiance that had made her seem heaven-sent. Now beauty hovered by her without embracing, a polite relative acknowledging their association with neither exuberance nor emphasis. Still, beauty had not left her and, from time to time, within the vitality of her luminous smile and the gentle sheen of her honest gaze, they—she and beauty—gave quiet proof of the ease with which they had redefined one another.

After informing him of her arrival, a company vice-president ushered her into the comforting plush of his conference room and stayed just long enough to declare new praise of her and guide the two of them along the beginnings of the path on which they would briefly make their way. At first he noticed the full-bodied health of her assertive motion. Every gesture casually imparted her self-assurance. He also noticed the clouded amber of her hair, mist-laden like the after-image of sunlight. He noticed as well, as it shaded the bright flesh of her face, the muted tint of weariness--what he accepted as a natural hue of mature character. Her strong, adept hands were, he knew, among the chief instruments of her powers as a physician.

Once they were left alone, he escorted her to the soft embrace of an upholstered leather armchair and placed himself with a gentleman's practice inside a similar softness opposite her. Now he found himself experiencing for the first time since they had gone their separate ways the warm blueness of her regard.

Yet how different was his response to her within the burnished luxury of his executive rooms twenty-six years afterward. How subdued and tenderly melancholic it was to see that this autumn woman seated serenely before him was not, after all, the girl he had known well and had always loved. Her being somebody else without being anyone except herself (the lineaments of her original splendor hidden now beneath time's revised intention) gave him noticeable pause. His momentary silence gave him time to make peace with startlement. She was the first to speak, because after they had been left alone together, he did not immediately say the words that would suggest he knew who they had been for each other. She may have imagined that the complete surprise of her had annulled, for him, all casual speech or that, in spite of the person she had been for him, she had left behind no clarifying memory.

"Perhaps you have forgotten me," said she in a mellow, confident voice that to his ears sounded like the voice of a stranger until he recognized the Swedish accent firmly anchoring itself to wistfulness. "The years take away so much. If there ever was a reason for you to remember me, I think they would have taken that long ago."

He had wanted, at the start of this fleeting encounter, to tell her that it wasn't what the years had taken which estranged him from the certainty of who she was. All that he'd had of her he had kept entire. Rather, it was what the years had withheld which, even in that instant while he looked with courtesy's undisclosed sorrow upon her, showed him in the belated summary of herself before him how much of her he had not had, nor ever would. Time had already dissolved the imagery of who she had been in the years that had separated them.

Instead of telling her so, he heard himself reciting the safer words that, he believed, would be for their situation more appropriate. His words were as formal as the protocol he felt he must maintain if he were to stay on the correct path.

"I remember you as a tremendous promise for the world," he said. "I'd been told you were going to make a very special life for yourself."

He saw that she understood at once his ceremonial manner. She offered him now her own skillful formality. She discovered within it a resonating ease and a natural provenance for replying to his praise of her life as a very special one.

"It *has* been very special," she said with agreeable enthusiasm, "and it goes on being very special, because it has brought me to you once again, this time to speak not only for my husband and myself, but for our colleagues as well. We shall always be grateful for everything you have done to help our mission."

In this courteous explanation of why she was there, he recognized the efficient textures of diplomacy. It was a strategy perhaps for modulating with cordiality her meeting, after an interval that compassed so much of his life, the more complete reality that he had become—this Everett Marsden whom she had for a brief while known so ardently. He was now for her as she was for him someone else—if not a stranger totally, most certainly a variation. Each was a different version requiring new insights and interpretations. No longer did she see in him the brown-haired youth who defined with well-honed brawn the persuasions of self-regarding independence and free-spirited passion. What she saw on that November afternoon (she would tell him with matter-of-fact words at the close of their remarkable encounter and he, afterward, record her words in his memory) was a leaner, more ascetic muscularity which, with his tall frame and silver hair, provided a commanding authenticity for his captaincy in a capricious world that often compromised both conscience and truth.

Because they were not now what once they had been to each other, there was between them already, he sensed in their first new moments together, a thoughtful attention to the persons they had become. Theirs was an intelligent *rapprochement* expressing cool-headed engagement through amicable rhetoric. It was only after they had taken their final leave of one another and he was allowing the imagery of their meeting to revolve over and over inside his reflection when he realized, not without bittersweet surprise, that they had accommodated themselves so casually to the vanishment of the persons they had once been for each other.

While they were there face to face together, the bleached afternoon light of November enclosed them inside a privacy of illuminated shadows, as though a portion of his ample chambers had become for that hour at least a refuge or retreat or haven. These rooms stood then as a sanctuary for holding in repose his sorrowing unease and his anguished awareness of having looked too closely upon the face of lost time and forfeited his most precious memory. While she was there with him, he saw that her well-worn loveliness would now and always replace his idea of her young self unchanged. But only for a moment would he allow dismay to hover about him. Instead, he took pleasure in receiving her as the stalwart woman she had become. Once again he knew the solace of having saved her for the extraordinary life still in her making.

Offering at last the honest words that recognized this revelation of themselves together, he went forward to meet her in these new moments unfolding and answered her comment in kind.

"I'm the one who needs to be grateful, Mrs. Schlossberg," he said, "because you and your colleagues have given me so much."

Her quick mind perceived at once his chivalrous reversal of their identities as benefactor and recipient. Gently, she consented to the trace of a smile lingering on her lips. But she did not speak. After so long an absence from him, she was still attuned to the rhythms of his intention and aware, because of his nearly imperceptible pause, that he was even now too carefully weighing the consequences of revealing his heart. She sensed that he meant to say more and waited for hesitation to leave him. When he did speak, yielding after some moments to the thought compelling him, his voice carried a husky cadence. Just for a moment, he allowed his long-checked emotions to show themselves as taut and impassioned.

"All of you have allowed me to be a part of something magnificent."

By including her colleagues in this open expression of feeling, he could better clarify, as much for her as for himself, the meaning of their unexpected reunion. Perhaps by contemplating her at work with eminent physicians like herself, he could more reliably define the boundaries of his new association with her. No longer struggling against it, he deferred to the hold of the past upon him. With a touch of philosophy he now accepted the momentous pull of their being there together.

Perhaps addressing his need and in the same instant confirming her own certainty of how they must proceed, offered a proper sign of her friendship in the simple

For more than an hour, they sat in comforting proximity and spoke discreetly of many things: of schooling and marriage and children; of the disappointments (a few) that put them in mind of their fallibility; and of the joys (more than occasional) that almost convinced them they belonged among the blessed. Most of all they spoke of the adventurous experiments each of them, without one another, had made from their lives. This new experience of her pushed him, in the moment they rose to take their leave of one another, to say the very words his mind had taught his heart never to say.

"Think of the marvelous lives you and I might have had together."

His remark was like a palpable motion of the soul taking hold of the moment. He reached out to touch her hands once more with the manly grace that gave him possession of himself first of all, even as it claimed a sovereign influence over her. She did not resist. Instead, she drew her finely wrought hands to meet the warm tips of his fingers. Then, after pausing upon them as though she meant to postpone her manifest purpose, she consented wholeheartedly to this outward sign of there still being a pact between them. In her mind, the meeting of their hands was a farewell gesture that compromised no current priorities and acknowledged only what in good conscience they could allow themselves to sanction—a respectable solidarity. On this wave of sensitive awareness, she met his heartfelt declaration with warmth both embracing and earnest.

"It was too early for us," she said with straightforward conviction. "We hadn't yet learned how to collaborate with chance or with the impossible or the unknown."

Responding in kind to her healthy matter-of-factness, which reflected his own aptitude for truth, he found himself telling the thought that had sometimes provoked a new, more insistent yearning for her.

"The wonder," he said, "is that we never tried to get ourselves back."

As was her habit, she studied him with musing consideration before replying. Then, a courteous inflection touching all her words, she proceeded to the idea that, specially in his nights and days of urgent longing, had guided him always to the self he had chosen to create.

"Oh, that was our particular strength," she said, "...our never trying to get ourselves back."

Her hands, he noticed, were warm with the heat of her blood and still firmly clasping his own. It was as if this show of unity were granting to her the right to comment on the long-ago time from which they had willingly separated themselves and just as willingly hastened away.

"That," she said, with crisp modulation so nearly like emphasis, "was the thing which made who we are now possible and even probable."

She perceived after all, from the fathomless distance separating them, the pristine quality of his sacrifice. She understood the fury of his wound and guessed at the throb of memory whose life had never abandoned him. They were the heart of her sacrifice, as well. The two of them, alone and yet together, shared the sacrifice and anguish and memory as the unobtrusive office of selfless love.

If, just before she entered the threshold of his here-and-now seeing, she had allowed herself to doubt for the first time that after twenty-six years he would remember her, this reunion had dispelled all her temporary apprehensions. Their meeting had been a spontaneous notice confirming the pledge of faith that long ago they had made to one another.

Yet there was this hour, too, she had assured him.

With the gallant, protective spirit that expressed an essential part of his response to women, he was then accompanying her to his ample limousine. The waiting driver would bring her across town to the teeming city's hospital. There, with her inspired husband and their extraordinary colleagues, she would go on serving humankind.

There was, she warmly reminded him, this exhilarating hour they had just now shared inside the plush abundance of his office. It had been an hour altogether new and different. For them, it had been not a return, but an arrival that would be, she was certain, a threshold of lasting friendship.

(They did meet on several occasions, five or six, in the years left to him afterward. But they were always in the company of others, including—before she fell ill—his dutiful Isabel as well as Hans Schlossberg. Never again would they meet in the shadowy intimations of enduring love which in that November reunion they had so judiciously expressed.)

He smiled with courtly acquiescence at her promise of abiding friendship. And then, just before she entered the soft-textured privacy of his car—just at that moment when she turned back to observe him once more because, he believed, she meant to impress on her senses his parting glance—he caught sight of her young blithe face. It was a flash of an apparition somewhere within or behind the admirably mature face he was there beholding.

Then suddenly she was gone from him. The whole form and breathing reality of her, enclosed within the swiftness of his limousine, vanished inside the traffic. In this muted drama of their leave-taking, he found himself able with new certainty and with empowering finality to accept their hard-made choice—his and Kirsten's. Though they had never journeyed long into the uneasy narrows of each other's consciousness, he was convinced that she saw as he did the rightness of their having gone their separate ways.

Yes, they might have made a brilliant marriage. But to belong to the Marsden circle, she could not—as a young wife at the end of the nineteenth century or even now in 1912—be so public a servant as a physician. Nor with good conscience could he betray his allegiance to the reliable centuries of his family's traditions. Yet, deprived of her power to save, she would have become a disarranged self, and he, as her gentle oppressor, a lesser being as well. Perhaps it was their authentic love for each other that made them understand as early as their young time a truth that often eluded the more experienced and philosophical. Some lovers who become so much together might, if reality were granted its possibilities, become so much more apart.

ABOUT THE AUTHOR

David Orsini is a Phi Beta Kappa graduate of Brown University. He has taught literature and composition in secondary schools and colleges within Rhode Island. In addition to *Bitterness / Seven Stories*, he is the author of *The Woman Who Loved Too Well, The Ghost Lovers, The Weaver of Plots, Vanishing by Degrees, The Subtleties of Seduction*, and *Schemes, Disguises, & Traps*.